DATE DUE

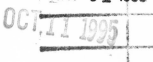

Man of Blood

Also by Margaret Duffy:

Rook-Shoot
Who Killed Cock Robin
Brass Eagle
Death of a Raven
A Murder of Crows

Man of Blood

Margaret Duffy

St. Martin's Press
New York

Library of Congress Cataloging-in-Publication Data

Duffy, Margaret.
    Man of blood / Margaret Duffy.
        p.   cm.
    ISBN 0-312-08261-4
    I. Title.
PR6054.U397M36   1992
823'.914—dc20   92-24916
                                                                         CIP

First published in Great Britain by Judy Piatkus (Publishers) Ltd.

First U.S. Edition: October 1992
10 9 8 7 6 5 4 3 2 1

The knight is a man of blood and iron, a man familiar with the sight of smashed faces and the ragged stumps of lopped off limbs; he is also a demure, almost maidenlike guest in hall, a gentle, modest, unobtrusive man. He is not a compromise or happy mean between ferocity and meakness; he is fierce to the nth and meek to the nth . . .

'Notes on the Way', C. S. Lewis,
Time and Tide (17th August, 1940)

Man of Blood

Firstly

Take us the foxes, the little foxes,
that spoil the vines.
Song of Solomon (2:15)

No one was quite sure why the operatives of the Metropolitan Police department F.9 were referred to as Foxes. When they were referred to at all, that is. Not many people, not even in the Met, knew they existed. Some said that the reasoning behind the terminology was obvious; their radio call-sign was Foxtrot Nine and the nickname had followed.

Head of Operations, Commander David Rolt, did not mind that his department was thus labelled, in fact it amused him. He himself used the expression and had gone so far as to call the back-up team – a more conventional unit, comprised of far more conventional personnel – the Hounds. These two small bodies of men and women, consisting at present of some twenty-four officers, made up F.9.

Headquarters, outwardly a perfectly ordinary-looking detached house near Woodford Green in Essex, was situated right on the edge of Epping Forest. A large noticeboard on the wall near the gate announced that it was the head office of an export company. The cars that went in and out were, to all intents and purposes, private ones; two-way radios not being particularly noticeable. When F.9 required official vehicles – the kind that boasted flashing blue lights and sirens – arrangements were made for them to be provided by the police transport compound at nearby Romford. F.9 had priority in nearly all such matters.

On a grey February morning Rolt sat in his office on the ground floor – the first floor of the house being given up almost entirely to accommodation for those who sometimes worked on the premises for a week, himself for instance, this undertaken in the large underground complex that none of the neighbouring residents knew existed – feeling unusually restless. Which is not to say that anyone observing him at that moment would have noticed anything different for he was not a man to display his emotions for the world to see. Asked to describe him, a new member of the department would say that he was aged between forty-five and fifty, a little over six feet in height, with blue eyes and black hair. They might add that he had a pleasant, deceptively quiet voice with no discernible accent, that could change instantly to something that made strong men yearn instead for the cat o' nine tails. The more observant might enlarge on the description by stating that Rolt was always smartly dressed – no one had ever seen him in slacks, never mind jeans – and his only weakness appeared to be listening to the music of Dvorak or tapes of working steam engines, one or other of which was usually *fortissimo* in his office.

Those who knew Rolt better – the undercover Foxes, for example – regarded him as their Rock of Ages. Rolt was in charge and, in a real departure from the police norm, no other officers came between him and them. He issued orders and when they made contact, usually by telephone, with information or asking for help, they did not have to explain everything to a duty sergeant and then possibly to an inspector, they got *Rolt*. This was necessary, for some of the Foxes worked so deeply undercover, penetrating criminal gangs for months, even for years, and usually in conditions of extreme personal danger, they wanted to speak to the man with his fingers on the pulse of the criminal underworld. Rolt had an assistant, Ellis, for the times when he was off-duty. But when a big job was on, Rolt stayed put.

The Commander's present restlessness was not caused by worries brought on by any particular assignment. Right now things were comparatively quiet. There was to be a raid that night on a Soho amusement arcade that a Fox had reported as being a staging post for drugs. Rolt was keen to discover

2

which narcotics gang was using the premises, but it did not promise to be anything really important.

He glanced at his watch. In half an hour's time he had to attend a meeting at New Scotland Yard. Present would be the deputy commissioner from the Met, Berkley, to whom he was directly responsible, several other senior officers who were familiar with the workings of F.9, and the Chief Constables of Strathclyde, North Yorkshire and West Midlands, the latter three on a fact-finding mission. Rolt had already seen Berkley that morning, a weekly up-to-the-minute report session in Rolt's office developing into what amounted to a carpeting. Berkley, for some reason, was not happy with results. There had been complaints that suspects had been treated in heavy-handed fashion. This would have to stop, Berkley had insisted with his customary imaginative selection of adjectives. F.9, he had reminded Rolt, was an experiment. And just because other forces were interested in the idea this did not mean that he, Rolt, had *carte blanche*.

"Some of them go to prison with criminals but that doesn't mean they have to behave like yobs," Berkley had said, expletives deleted.

Rolt had not reminded him that successfully behaving like criminals was the only thing that kept some of his team from early graves. In a way he understood Berkley's concern, for F.9 had been his idea and he was terrified – Rolt felt that this was not too strong a word – of failure. If we fail, Rolt mused, as he pressed a button on the intercom on his desk and ordered a car, it won't be from lack of endeavour but for lack of support from highest authority.

He met the deputy commissioner again in the lift taking them to the third floor of New Scotland Yard. Berkley appeared to have mellowed slightly since the early morning meeting.

"The Len Dorney case . . ." he murmured.

"Well on course," Rolt told him. "Seven of his gang were grabbed at that warehouse job we'd found out about. I'm confident we'll get the boss himself soon."

"You've still got a man inside?"

"Inside inside," Rolt replied. "He volunteered to do time with them. He's as keen to put Dorney out of business as we

3

are. And they'll want him back. He was practically Dorney's right-hand man."

"Who is it?"

"Code-named Homage. I'm sure you know who I mean."

"Of course." Berkley shrugged. "It mystifies me really. When I suggested that undercover people be sent down with real rogues so they could report back with their future plans, and also any intelligence concerning break-outs and so forth, I thought we'd have the Devil's own job in getting them to volunteer. But you obviously have no trouble in that direction."

"There's extra money."

"Homage doesn't need extra money though, does he? His father's one of the landed gentry."

"His old man's cut him off without a penny."

"What, because he's in prison?"

"Yes, and because of the security angle, he can't explain why he's there."

"Most F.9 personnel just tell their families that they're in advertising."

"Homage's problem is that his father's always closely checked what he's up to."

"When's he due out?"

"Soon."

Berkley chuckled. "It's just as well we have the ear of the judiciary on such matters."

The meeting went well, the Chief Constable of Strathclyde ecstatic at the thought of police officers raiding clubs and other premises under suspicion in the guise of gangland heavies.

"Only sometimes," Rolt explained, "if I think protection rackets are involved. You learn an awful lot in the first few seconds. Crooks shout different things at those they regard as trespassers on their manor than they do at the law." Too right they did!

"And then the back-up team, the Hounds, raid the place ostensibly acting on a tip-off and arrest the lot?"

"That's right. After a while, though. When the Foxes have been through the contents of the safe and leaned a little on the resident mobsters. When they're picked up it preserves their

4

cover, of course. Even though they wear masks. Voices can sometimes be recognised."

"F.9 gets to the parts that Special Branch can't reach,' Berkley said with an unusual lapse into humour.

Chapter One

It was raining the day Piers Ashley was released from prison. The fact is worth mentioning solely because it was the only thing he noticed about the morning, his mind otherwise a complete blank. No one was there to meet him – not that he expected anyone – and he preferred it that way. So he turned up the collar of his thin summer anorak against the February north-easter and walked until he came to a taxi-stand.

He stood, shivering gently, and forced himself to think in constructive fashion. He had been told that release would be a shock and it would be a couple of days before mental stability returned. But he had not expected this inner deadness, a numbness of spirit that could not even be shocked away by the thought that he could always go and chuck himself in the Thames.

"Far too good a swimmer," he muttered at the leaden sky, the icy rain drops pattering on to his face. Oddly, the clean coldness, a stark contrast to the past six months of his life, restored a little of his normal *élan* and he went over to a nearby phonebox.

No, his orders were that he should lose himself for a week.

As he turned away a red Range-Rover came to an abrupt halt only yards from where he was standing.

"Piers!"

Looking at the girl who was driving was a little like seeing himself in a mirror, the fair hair longer than his and softly framing what was usually a serious oval face. But now she had found him she was no longer serious, instead smiling broadly.

6

"Piers! I was coming to meet you but got held up in the traffic."

"Hello, Thea," he said warily.

"Well? Get in, silly. I can't stop here."

He shook his head. Go away, he inwardly pleaded. Right now I haven't the reserves to play charades.

The drivers of several cars were leaning on their horns to let his sister know that she was causing an obstruction.

"Get in, you great dunderhead!" Thea shouted in her famous carrying voice. She had that stubborn look on her face, the look he remembered from their childhood when he had failed to respond to her equally famous commonsense.

"Look, Mummy's taken him to Italy so you can come home for a while. She's got you a job. Oh, Piers, if you stand there much longer looking mulish, I'll come and get you myself."

"She would too," Piers said to an old lady who was grinning at the pair of them, his feet taking him in the direction of the vehicle of their own accord.

"You *look* quite well," Thea said when he was sitting beside her and she had pecked his cheek with a sisterly kiss. A few hundred yards down the road she spun them into a side street – it had always amazed him how she could make heavy four-wheel drive vehicles dance on a sixpence – and parked.

"I'm fine," Ashley said, smiling into the piercing scrutiny.

"I've brought some of your clothes from home to my flat. You can get changed and then I'll take you out to lunch and – "

"Thea . . ."

"Piers, you mustn't spoil it. I know you think I'm bossing you but – "

"Thea . . ."

She sighed, surveying him sadly. "You're not coming home, are you?"

"No."

"Don't you even want to hear about the job?"

"No."

"She'll be very hurt – you know that, don't you?"

"I don't need a job."

"Fine," she countered sarcastically.

7

"I'm sorry," he said softly.

"At least have lunch with me."

"I'd like that very much."

Thea's Kensington flat was situated just round the corner from where she ran her nanny agency. There was no real need for her to work for her living, their father being quite prepared to give her a generous allowance to stay at home and help him run the estate. This was fairly large – several thousand acres of Sussex – and comprised the main house, Ashleigh Hall, the village, Ashleigh Coombe, and several farms. No one was quite sure why the spelling of the family name had been changed, the present head of it, Mycroft Ashley, asserting it to be nothing more than the result of an error by an eighteenth-century clerk engaged in drawing up a title deed for one of the farms. For some reason the new spelling had stayed.

"This is civilised," Piers said, sinking into a vast blue leather sofa.

"Like it? I had the whole place re-decorated while you were . . ." Thea stopped speaking in confusion and went a little pink.

"*Inside*," Piers said. "Say the word. It doesn't bother me at all."

She went into the kitchen and re-emerged with two glasses of white wine. "I know it's a bit early in the day for this," she said, handing him one, "but I feel like celebrating. It's lovely to have you back."

"To a sister without parallel," Piers said, holding up his glass and meaning every word. How easy it was to slip back into a luxurious lifestyle. The perfect fluted wine glass in his hand, for example, the outside misted with drops of condensation that caught the glittering light from the lamps. The watercolours on the walls of the room; Thea's expensive perfume; his clothes in a neat pile on a chair – cashmere sweaters, crisp cotton shirts, silk ties.

"You're a witch," he said, smiling.

She came to sit by his side. "Please, please, don't go back to that dreadful bunch of crooks you got in with."

Ashley took a large mouthful of wine. This was the penalty coming. Living the lie. But he couldn't tell her, not yet. He

8

said, "I must go back, just for a short while. Then, I promise you I'll – "

"But you don't have to go back at all!"

"Yes. I said I would."

"But you'll get caught again."

He shook his head. "No, not this time."

There were tears in her eyes. "You're so *pig-headed*! Of course you'll be caught. The police aren't stupid. They'll be watching you closely from now on."

Ashley set down the glass and stood up.

"Where are you going?"

"I'm not staying here if you're going to lecture me," he said, hating himself.

There was a short, tense silence.

"I'm sorry," Thea said stiffly.

"I don't want you to apologise," he said, sitting down again. "And you have my word that from now on I'll do nothing that'll result in my being put behind bars, ever." It was the best he could do.

Something strange happened to him then and he had to get up again and go to the window where he gazed out, unseeing, having to dash away the tears that threatened to run down his cheeks.

Thea, all too aware of what was happening, and appalled, said, "Mummy says you can have the lodge."

Ashley cleared his throat. "Have the Jacksons moved out then?"

"No, not that one. The old lodge – the one at the western entrance where we used to play."

"It's a bit of a shambles."

"You'd have to fix it."

"But – "

"And as the job means you'll be near home, it would be ideal. I can't see Daddy objecting to your being there if you're in steady work."

"So what is this job?" Piers asked, intrigued.

"Selling earth moving machinery for a firm based in the Midlands. Your area will be Sussex and West Kent."

"I've always fancied driving a digger," he said, mostly to himself.

9

"We knew that," Thea said regally.

"So how's mother arranged all this?"

"An old flame of hers organised it for you."

He stared at her. "An old flame . . ." He closed his mouth when he realized it was open.

"There's a company car, a small salary and lots of commission if you're successful. Oh, please come and see the lodge. It really does have possibilities. It would make you a super little home."

Ashley knew that it would make her really miserable if he told her he already had a home, a studio flat in Shepherd's Bush, and a car securely locked away in a rented garage. It would look as though he was cruelly parading his ill-gotten gains. But the idea of a country cottage that he could do up himself was highly appealing and would be useful for the day when his father forgave him. That is, *if* he forgave him. The problem was that F.9 personnel did not go through the police college at Hendon. No passing out parades and so forth. So what do you tell a man who has always kept a close watch on you to the extent of hiring a private detective to check on your friends?

"I'll come and see the lodge," Piers said.

In her impetuous way she ran across and hugged him. "I can give you a hand when I'm at home with painting and so forth, and I know there are things like spare curtains and rugs just shoved into drawers." She giggled. "But Heaven knows, you could walk around starkers all day down there and no one would see you. It's right off the beaten track."

"But I don't want the job."

"Why not?"

"I'd rather work in London."

"As you wish," she sighed. "It's your life." She took up her drink again. "To the Ashleys – the bloody stubborn Ashleys." The glass halfway to her mouth, she said, "There's Giles, though. He's at home. He didn't go back to Oxford after Christmas because he's had glandular fever."

Giles was their younger brother.

"I can handle *him*," Piers said grimly.

His sister gazed at him severely. "No, leave Giles to me. If the two of you get together and start arguing it'll only cause more trouble. He'll be going back to university any day now."

When the bottle of Sauvignon was almost empty, Thea said, "Why do you do it, Piers? You could have had anything you wanted at home."

"At a price," Ashley replied, answering a different question. "At the price of being watched all the time because I'm the eldest son. To be shoved into the Ashley mould."

"Please tell me one thing," Thea said quietly. "Tell me you've never done anything really horrible."

He solemnly clinked glasses with her, and then, slightly tipsy, kissed her forehead. "The *only* horrible thing I've ever done was to beat up a couple of mobsters who were out to get me first. Oh, and I once drove the wrong way up a one-way street."

"You're quite impossible," she said, laughing. She always knew when he was telling the truth. Which set her thinking.

It was doubtful whether the distaff side of the Ashley family had realized the exact state of affairs so far as the West Lodge was concerned. In a word, it was uninhabitable. The roof was leaking, some of the ceilings on the verge of falling down piecemeal. There was woodworm, dry rot, wet rot, rising damp . . . in fact just about everything that could go wrong with a human habitation. Piers came to this conclusion, gloomily, as he wandered around the lodge that same afternoon.

Its charm – and it was likely that his mother and sister had not looked beyond this – depended heavily on two tall chimney pots that looked like the old-fashioned twisted sort of barley sugar. And the ladies had probably last seen the cottage in summer when yellow and pink rambler roses hung in fragrant swathes from the walls. Now, in the middle of winter, with most of the roses having apparently been torn down in a gale and one of the chimney pots lying on the flattened and rotting long grass of the front lawn, it little resembled the picture-postcard cottage of childhood memories.

The front door was the only thing that appeared sound; two and a half inches of solid English oak furnished with large black iron hinges and a massive knocker in the shape of a lion's head. The door opened directly into a large front room with an open fireplace. At one time there had been a range beneath the wide chimney but now this was gone, the grate housing a pair of rusting fire-dogs, a lot of soot, and what looked like the remains of a jackdaw's nest that had fallen down the chimney. Two small leaded windows overlooked the wilderness that was the front garden and there was another window at the side completely covered on the outside by Virginia creeper. To the right of the fireplace a doorway led into the other front room, this slightly smaller and again with a fireplace and three windows, two at the front and one at the side. To the rear of both of these rooms was a tiny scullery, a storeroom and a long, narrow room that reminded Ashley of a skittle alley. There was evidence of rats.

Upstairs – and Piers was extremely careful where he put his feet on the disintegrating floorboards – there were two bedrooms at the front, a boxroom and bathroom at the rear. He turned on one of the taps over the basin in the bathroom and after a short pause two earwigs fell out followed by a torrent of rusty-coloured water. The towering toilet cistern looked as though it was knitted to the ceiling with cobwebs. He decided to postpone testing pulling the chain.

Thea, who had gone to the Hall to change into old clothes, was coming down the narrow path that led through the orchard to the lodge. From the bathroom window, which was broken, Piers watched her approach. They could easily be mistaken for twins, he thought, Thea didn't look four years older.

"It's a real mess," he called down the stairs as she came in.

"*That* bad?" she asked disbelievingly.

"That bad," he confirmed. "The place'll have to be completely gutted. New ceilings and floors. The wiring's probably lethal and the plumbing looks as though it was installed during the Wars of the Roses."

"But surely you can live in it?"

"Yeah. I'll buy a hammock and sling it between the front door posts. It's about the only thing that doesn't have woodworm. Which leads me to another point . . ."

"Woodworm?" Thea enquired, coming gingerly up the stairs.

12

"Mind that loose board – it's rotten. No, buying things. It'll cost thousands to put right. More money than I have."

"Oh, *that*," she said as though it was of little importance.

"Thea, why has this house been allowed to fall down? It could have been restored and sold."

"Probably because honourable father's spent a small fortune on the Hall itself. There was dry rot gobbling up the attics. And the central heating boiler went bang one night and had to be replaced. Surely you remember? I wrote and told you. He's been trying to replant the park after hundreds of trees were blown down in the gale. It all takes a lot of money."

Piers pensively kicked the wall near where he was standing and a lot of wet-looking plaster fell down to reveal the stone beneath.

Sadly, Thea said, "You'll just have to choose the best downstairs room and live in that."

"I can do it gradually. I could get a secondhand caravan and live in that while the work's done."

"That's if . . ."

"Yes. That's if Dad doesn't chuck me out."

"I'll work on him," she promised with a smile.

The Hall at Ashleigh Coombe, near Arundel, always surprises visitors – it is open to the public in the summer months – who expect to find a mansion, for strictly speaking it is a castle. At one time, at the commencement of the building of the second dwelling on the site, it was referred to as Ashleigh Castle, probably on account of the fact that the only surviving relic of earlier days was the Barbican or outer gatehouse. This is an almost exact copy of the one at Lewes Castle some thirty-five miles to the east which dates from the fourteenth century. It is a roofed building of three storeys with twin circular towers linked at the top by a parapet with openings. Decorative flintwork faces the stone walls.

Ashleigh Hall as it stands today has the earlier Barbican in its centre with living accommodation in two wings on either side. Included in the right hand wing is a replica of the great galleried room that was destroyed by fire, together with most of the original building, in 1672. Fortunately many family treasures were saved from the flames; standards, paintings, weapons, armour, so some of these adorn the rooms today.

"The cedar!" Piers exclaimed as they approached the Hall. "It's gone!"

The Atlantic cedar had been growing for at least a hundred and fifty years.

"Blown down in that damn gale," Thea said. "If you go really close you'll see its successor – a little twig of a thing about two feet high. Mummy reckons it'll be as twice as tall as she is when she dies."

He suddenly felt that he had been away for years.

"There's just us and Giles," she said, hunting for a key in her bag. "The staff are on holiday too."

By staff she meant Mrs Jackson, the housekeeper, her husband Tom who had been Mycroft Ashley's batman in his army days and who was now a fairly indispensable all-rounder whose duties ranged from occasional butler to handyman, Madge, the cook, and David, her nephew who made himself generally useful. David was slightly mentally handicapped. These were the full-time staff. A few local ladies were also employed as "dailies".

"How did you know I was being released today?" Piers asked as they went in.

"I rang up a few weeks ago. Someone said you were getting remission for good behaviour." Thea flashed him a smile and went ahead, switching on lights.

Giles did not seem to be at home, or at least, he did not respond when Thea called him.

Piers left Thea unpacking shopping in the small kitchen that the family used just off the enormous one that visitors saw with its gleaming copper and roasting spits, and wandered back into the entrance hall, the ground floor of the gatehouse. Only the ticking of a grandfather clock broke the silence as he stood, motionless, with his back to the huge door they had just entered by. Ahead of him a wide staircase ascended and then divided, curving left and right. On the panelled wall of the landing where it split and directly facing him was the portrait of Sir Richard Ashleigh, knighted by Elizabeth I. Sir Richard's eyes always seemed to stare accusingly at you, wherever you were standing. Knighthood or no, Piers had always thought he looked a bit of a wimp.

He went up the stairs, giving his illustrious ancestor a two-finger salute as he passed.

The long gallery of the right wing was exactly as he remembered it. Nothing had changed, not the smallest detail. One side, to the right, was open to the great room below that took up the entire height of this part of the building. It was like a church, only without pews, nothing marring the perfection of the highly polished wooden floor. The lower part of the walls was covered with linenfold panelling, the upper bare plaster painted white, the starkness alleviated by swords, pikes and other weapons arranged in patterns. A few other swords, Sir Richard's among them, hung over a carved stone fireplace in the centre of the long wall facing him. There was very little furniture in the room; a few chests with arrangements of flowers in copper bowls on them, a couple of oak chairs, a Chinese screen at one end. Three suits of fine Flemish armour stood at this farthest end. Piers could remember Giles getting into trouble for popping a ferret in through the open visor of one of them and then being unable to persuade it to come out. Tom Jackson had been fetched to remove an armoured "foot" and had lured the animal out. Tom seemed to have a way with everything.

Piers continued with his wanderings. After prison his present surroundings were totally unbelievable. His feet sank into the deep pile of the red carpet. All sound was hushed by rich hangings to match and tapestries depicting medieval hunting parties, the horses not treading on one bright flower beneath their hooves.

Reality came as a ghastly shock: a bucket of water balanced on top of his bedroom door.

Thea heard the crash and his shout and raced up to find a lot of water soaking into a Wilton carpet and her brother stunned. She ascertained that no lasting damage had been done to the latter and ran for cloths with which to clear up the mess.

"He might have used a plastic bucket," Piers groaned. Momentarily, he had been knocked cold. "And the bloody little coward ran off before we arrived." He went out to stand in the galleried corridor, discovering that he was gripping the balustrade tightly with both hands, dizzy and shivering.

"You're absolutely *dripping*," said Thea from behind him.

15

"Have a hot shower and then I'll get us something to eat."

He turned. "I don't really know why you're bothering."

"With you?" she asked, not looking up from her mopping. "Yes."

"Wasn't it always me who fixed your grazed knees?"

In his slightly lightheaded state Piers could picture himself as he stood thinking about what she had said: broad-shouldered, blond, possibly a little bovine. Yes, perhaps some people, usually women, were put into the world to fix the grazed knees of younger, oxlike brothers and take the thorns from dogs' paws and so forth. Ministering people. Angels probably.

"Thea, will you get married one day?"

She lifted her head to stare at him. "Eventually, I suppose." She added, with enormous sarcasm, "When I have the *time*."

He realized that he had a huge, inane grin on his face.

"Go and have a shower."

He went, still grinning.

Chapter Two

With orders to lose himself for a week Piers decided to start work on the lodge. After months cooped up he relished the thought of being in the open air. The weather had turned bright and cold, so cold that hard physical labour was necessary in order to keep warm in his new "home". The real surprise was that he had an aptitude for it. He was, of course, required to keep himself to a high standard of fitness and had tried not to lose this in prison. But tools that he had never handled before came easily into his grasp and felt at home there. His whole body rejoiced in the swinging of the axe with which he felled the dead elm tree that stood right in front of the house, blocking out a lot of light. He chopped and sawed for the whole of the first day for he wanted to put the wood into store for the days when fires would burn once again in the open fireplaces.

Only a matter of yards from the lodge was a track that had at one time – in the days of horse-drawn mail coaches – been an important turnpike road. The main entrance to the grounds of the Hall had in fact been at this spot. But frequent landslips in the vicinity of a quarry had made the road too expensive to maintain and, after a new one had been constructed to serve the village, the old way had fallen into disuse. It was still passable by vehicles if care was exercised but only a few estate Land-Rovers used it now, taking a short cut to the timber yard. The only sign of life or movement that Piers saw that first day were rabbits, birds and a roebuck.

Thea, it seemed, had decided to commute to London for a few days in order to look after him. Piers had not asked her to.

He could fend for himself. She might, he thought, be worried that he and Giles would have a row if their younger brother returned home. But there was no sign of him, much to Piers' relief. They had never got on.

It was getting dark when he stowed the last of the wood he had sawed into the small lean-to store at the rear of the lodge. He was still left with the main trunk of the tree and several large branches, too large to tackle with hand tools. He had brought a couple of sandwiches and an apple with him for lunch plus a thermos flask of coffee but by now was utterly famished. In the dusk he walked to the big house, a thin crescent moon guiding him through the orchard and up a broad ride, once the old carriage drive. This swept round to the front of the Hall in a wide curve but those on foot could take a short cut across the grass into the kitchen garden at the rear and from there through a back door.

As he left the gravelled ride he saw the lights of a car at the front of the house. He stopped, knowing it was too early for Thea to get home, and then took a few steps in the direction of it. But the vehicle was moving off, the headlights swinging towards him. For a reason that he could not afterwards explain he stepped quickly behind a large rhododendron bush, the beams glinting momentarily on the glossy leaves and then away. He heard the car crunch down the drive and then accelerate into the main road.

The family's private accommodation, mostly on the first floor of both wings, comprised some ten bedrooms and four bathrooms, two of these *en suite*, and two shower rooms. It was a tradition that children of the family had rooms in the right hand wing, known as the Red Wing, parents in the other. This dated back to the days of nannies, nurseries and so forth when children were seen and not heard, and preferably not glimpsed all that often. Piers, as the eldest son, had always had the largest bedroom in the Red Wing, as had his father before him. This rigidity of attitude was one of the many things that had angered him – why he had opted out – and he could remember yearning to be permitted to have another room right at the end of the house that had its own small and intriguing tower with three stairs that led up to a tiny window. He walked along to it and went in. There was no bed or other bedroom furniture in it now, just a locked glass-fronted cabinet containing three shotguns and a .22 rifle. Fishing rods were stacked in a corner. Almost certainly, they belonged to Giles.

He showered, found some clean clothes and went back downstairs. Smiling to himself, although he might not have realized it, he took a key from a hook on a dresser in the kitchen, unlocked a door and descended into his father's wine cellar. Walking past the racks of champagne, port and claret, still smiling, he selected a bottle of Chablis that he knew to be well worth drinking, returned to the kitchen and put it to chill.

"D'you think we ought to?" Thea said later, scanning the label. "This is one of his favourites."

"How much would he have to pay a man to do up the lodge?" Piers asked, picking up a corkscrew.

"While the cat's away . . ."

"Right. The mice do play." He opened the wine and carefully poured some into two glasses. "Your health."

"To woodworm and dry rot," she chortled. "May they forever flourish."

"Now tell a chap why the two ladies of this family want the black sheep at home."

Thea registered shock.

"Philanthropic and Fairy Godmother stuff apart," he added.

"It's just that – "

"Thea, you're on *edge*. I've never known you to be on edge. And it's nothing to do with my being nabbed for driving a stolen van used in a robbery and going to prison for six months."

There was a silence broken by Thea saying, "You always were highly perceptive." She took two dinner plates down from the dresser and polished them thoughtfully on a tea towel. Then she said, "Something strange is going on, but I don't know what it is."

"What kind of thing?"

She gave him a very straight look. "You know when Granny died last year, how badly Mummy took it?"

"Yes."

"She still hasn't got over it. But I've a feeling that what's happening now, although it's connected, is different."

"What does Dad say? Have you spoken to him about it?"

"Yes, but you know what he's like. If a horse or dog's ill he's a genius at knowing what's wrong. He says she'll get over it and it's her time of life and so on. It was how I persuaded him to go to Italy with her, saying that the break would do her good. You know how he hates foreign holidays."

"Have you tackled Mum about it?"

"In a gentle sort of way. She just says she'll be all right and goes to her room where I know she cries."

"I can't see that it's worse than some kind of depression."

"Men!" she snapped. "Perhaps you're not so perceptive after all. Mummy's never depressed. She's always said to me that you should never bottle anything up but sort it out. Get to the bottom of problems. So it has to be something serious, doesn't it?"

"And how does my presence help?"

"Well, as far as I'm concerned, I'd appreciate your advice. As to Mummy . . ."

"Go on," he prompted.

"Her underlying mood is that when you come home, everything will be all right again."

"But *why?*"

"I know I'm not imagining this, Piers. It's because you're big and strong and tough."

"To protect her?" he whispered.

"Yes, to protect her."

"But from what?"

"I simply have no idea."

"I'll talk to her when they get back." Meanwhile, he thought, suddenly remembering the car he had seen, he would keep his eyes open.

On the second morning Piers had not been at the lodge long when a Land-Rover came bouncing down the old turnpike road. He recognised the man who got out, having an idea that his name was Kevin. Kevin was carrying a chain saw.

"Thought you might like to borrow this," Kevin said after the two men had shaken hands. He added, misinterpreting the hesitation, "It's mine – not one of the boss's."

"I've never used one," Ashley admitted, assuming that by "boss" his visitor meant the estate manager, Charles Morgan.

"No sweat," said Kevin, starting the saw and taking a couple of slices from the trunk of the felled elm as a demonstration. He had also brought a safety helmet, goggles, a can of petrol and a bottle of chain oil. He stayed until Piers felt fully confident with the saw and then drove off, brushing aside any thanks.

By lunchtime, the whole of the tree had been reduced either to logs or large rounds that would have to be split at a later date. Piers wolfed down bread and cheese, stacked the wood out of the way under cover and then spent the entire afternoon knocking down ceilings. Filthy and literally reeling from tiredness he returned to the Hall, taking the chain saw with him, had a much needed bath and then fell sound asleep on a sofa. He did not even wake when Thea came in and was only roused, finally, by the smell of steak grilling.

On the third day he finished taking out all the rotten timbers. Having learned from Thea that the estate had a permanent contract with a local haulier for the supply of builders' skips he had arranged to have one delivered, and when it arrived – the driver quite beside himself over the condition of the road – started to fill it with all the debris. For the rest of that day and half the next he piled the rubbish into it. When it was full a phone call from the Hall quickly resulted in its being replaced by an empty one, a different driver this time highly amused that the entire vehicle had almost slid into the quarry. It was being driven away, Piers gathering up rubbish he had found in the garden; tins, plastic bags, a rusting pram, when he thought he heard another vehicle.

Parting the top of the straggling, overgrown hedge he looked down the track. On the left, about fifty yards away, a path led to a ruined barn. He could not see it from where he was standing because both barn and path were hidden by trees. From what he could remember the path was narrow but the ground on either side of it was flat and level, with easily enough space to allow the passage of a car into a small glade. And he was convinced he had heard a car, even above the low-gear growl of the skip lorry in the distance.

He started off down the track, walking quietly, keeping

beneath the cover of the thick hawthorn bushes that leaned right over it. But he had not gone more than a few yards when he heard a car door slam and, seconds later, a red car swerved out on to the track and drove off at speed, its rear wheels sliding from side to side on the muddy surface.

"Which only means one thing," he said out loud. "Someone was watching me from up a tree – using binoculars."

It was now possible to go in through the front door of the lodge and gaze right up into the roof. Miraculously, all the joists seemed to be sound, and downstairs the floors were of stone slabs laid directly on earth. The roof timbers too seemed to be in good condition, only rotten where the rain had entered due to missing slates. That afternoon, Piers was halfway up a ladder he had found in one of the garages of the Hall with a view to do something about these missing slates when he became aware that he had another visitor.

"A skilled business is roofs," said an old man.

"Needs must," said Piers.

"You'll need to take some of the others off first to check what's underneath."

"That's what I intend to do," he said, continuing up the ladder.

"Good pitch though," said the man.

"Splendid," Piers rejoined, not quite sure what he meant.

"And it ain't nail sick by the look of it."

Piers came down again and approached the speaker. Close up he did not appear to be as old as at first impression; a stocky figure with keen brown eyes gazing out from beneath a thatch of unruly thick brown hair.

"You know about roofs?" Piers enquired.

"I've had forty year on roofs," was the calm, proud reply.

"I'd be really grateful for any advice you can give me."

The man shook his head dubiously. "It's a really skilled thing is roofs – not something you can *tell* folks about."

"I'm quite sure you're right," Piers told him earnestly. "But I can't arrange to employ anyone yet. In case I can't carry on with it."

"I know that. Who's talking about employing? The name's William by the way." He came through the gap in the hedge where a gate had once been, stooped to examine the pile of

22

slates that Piers had gathered together from various parts of the garden, grunted and ascended the ladder.

Piers rather felt that William did not notice going up the ladder. Whereas he himself had been aware of every rung and had held on tightly, never having been too keen on heights, William merely rose to the roof, making no more ado of it than if he had been going up on an escalator.

He knows about me, Piers thought. Everyone in the area knows I've been cut off without a penny. And it looks as though they don't approve.

"Coupla days," William called down, "that should take care of it. The chimbleys need a bit of attention too. You'll have to give me a hand with that ruddy great pot though – it must weigh a ton."

"I'm most grateful," Piers said when William had come down the ladder.

"I hate seeing a good home fall down," said William, again fixing him with his keen brown gaze. "But I can't start tomorrow. I've to go to a funeral."

Mentally, Piers floundered. "I say, I hope . . ."

"No one *close*," William said. "An aunt of the wife's. One thing though . . ."

"Yes?"

"I see you've cut down the tree. Can you spare a bit of wood?"

"Gladly."

"I'll send round my son-in-law. He's got a car."

The son-in-law, Eric, arrived early the next morning, apparently on his way to work. A tall, lugubrious-looking individual, he walked in through the open front door of the lodge and did not seem at all surprised to see Piers lying uncomfortably across the ceiling joists over one of the front rooms, snipping off the exposed electricity cables.

"I did remember to switch it all off first," he said, jokingly.

Eric peered through the window at the leaning electricity pole outside and said, "I shouldn't wonder if you'll have to have the service replaced right back to the main road. That looks pretty ropy to me." He went from sight as he crawled under the stairs to look at the meter cupboard. "This lot looks shot away too," he continued, voice muffled.

23

"Shot away?" Piers echoed, thinking along the lines of obscure trade terminology.

"Useless," Eric translated, emerging with black cobwebs in his hair.

"I didn't look too closely," Piers said. "Just switched everything off."

"You should have had someone to look at it first," Eric scolded. "Frizzled yourself likely."

"You wouldn't be an electrician by any chance?"

"Of course. How else would I know?"

Faced with this logic Piers could only smile.

"You having to move in here when the Colonel gets back from his holiday?" Eric said, hastening to add, "I'm only asking because I've got a couple of camping lamps at home I could let you have. And a little stove." He glanced up. "If you put a tarpaulin across the joists it'll keep you snug at nights. And the rain from dripping on you."

"They'd be most useful," Piers replied, really touched. The local people had sat round kitchen and pub tables working out how they could help him. But he could do nothing to repay the kindness, not yet, only load as many logs for William into the boot of Eric's car as the elderly Lada would take.

Thea did not come home that night, phoning to say that she had a dinner date. She hoped to see him the following afternoon, Friday, and be at home all weekend. Piers replaced the receiver, raided a freezer for Cornish pasties, micro-waved them and, when he had eaten, went straight to bed.

He was up and out of the house very early the next morning. It was bitterly cold, his breath steaming as he jogged through the orchard. At the lodge he swept the place from top to bottom, paying particular attention to the room he intended to live in when he was at "home". For although he had to report to Rolt, who would undoubtedly require him to carry on with the assignment intended to put Len Dorney in prison for a very long time, there was no question of his having to stay in London seven days a week. For one thing Dorney did not like people to live on the job, insisting that it attracted unwelcome attention if there was too much coming and going at a premises that advertised itself as an educational video agency.

"My God, you've worked!" William exclaimed when he arrived, staring at the stripped-out shell of the building. He threw down his tool-bag and produced a packet from his pocket. "Missus thought you'd like a bit of cake." As Piers accepted the gift the visitor said, "Lad, your hands . . ."

Piers ruefully gazed at the blisters and cuts. "They'll harden up, I suppose. I haven't done this sort of work before." He poured them both some coffee from the flask he had brought with him and ate the large chunk of fruit cake there and then, all of it, much to William's well-hidden amusement.

"Did you come up the old road or across the fields?" Piers asked.

"Up the road," William answered. "There's enough mud in those pastures to lose a tractor in."

"Did you see anyone?"

"Not a soul. Why, someone been hanging about?"

"There was a car in the wood a couple of days ago. It drove off when I approached."

"After the tools," William said succinctly. "You take my advice and don't leave so much as a nail lying around. There's been a dreadful thieving of tools and garden equipment around here lately. The young devils flog the stuff for next to nothing to keep them in booze and fags – and drugs, ever likely."

Although he had swept up Piers decided to knock down the scullery wall – a recent and shoddily built partition – so that he could make a large and much lighter kitchen. It took him most of the day by the time he had cleaned everywhere up again, and William had gone home when the last shovelful was thrown into the brimming skip.

"Oh, for a chair," muttered Piers, sinking tiredly on to the floor of the largest living room with his back to the wall. It was getting dark, the cold seeping into overworked muscles trembling with exhaustion. He might even have nodded off for a while for when he looked up it was much darker and there was a man standing in the doorway, a shotgun crooked over his arm and what looked like a couple of dead rabbits dangling from one hand.

"Thea mentioned that you were here," said Giles. "What the hell are you doing – holding a seance?" He took something from his pocket that turned out to be a torch, and shone it around the room.

Piers sat quite still as the beam travelled slowly over him. Giles came closer. "Why have you come back?"

"I was offered a roof over my head and a job."

"A job!"

"Mother's found me a job. Didn't you know?"

Giles switched off the torch. "Yes, I remember now, selling mowers or something like that. It had slipped my mind for a moment. Where will you live when you're driving around in your little van?"

Piers had already decided that he wasn't going to lose his temper. "I'm not taking the job. I'd rather work in London. I intend to do up this place and use it at weekends."

The shotgun made a small movement. "Like hell you are," Giles said quietly.

"It's not your decision."

"I shouldn't be too sure about that."

Piers stood up by the simple expedient of straightening his legs, his back sliding up the wall. He was at least a head taller than his brother, the latter a slim, graceful figure with large eyes but small mouth and chin. Rather like Sir Richard of the lace and ruffles who stared down with such disdain from his portrait.

"You're shit," said Giles in a savage whisper. "Look at you, you filthy bastard. Unwashed, unshaven, stinking of sweat. Is this what prison does for you? I thought it was supposed to turn shits into model citizens. Listen to me, brother shit, I want you out of here. Tomorrow. I'll tell Mother you went back to your sewer."

"And if I'm not?" Piers asked.

"You have a criminal record," Giles went on, still speaking softly. "I've no doubt the police will be very interested to talk to you in connection with several thefts we've suffered on the estate this week. A chain-saw, tools, some wood, things like that."

26

"You're lying."

"I'm not. Anyway, whom would they believe – a convicted criminal or me?"

Piers did not throw him out. He just picked him up quite gently, shotgun, rabbits and all, took him outside and planted him on his feet again where the front gate had once been. Then he went back inside, quietly closing the door.

Chapter Three

An hour later, when Piers had walked to the Rose and Crown
in the village, phoned Rolt to confirm that he had no intelligence to impart concerning impending break-outs and had
promised a detailed report listing everything else he had
learned inside prison, he set off back to the Hall. He had also
downed a couple of pints of best bitter and a beef and onion
pasty. The real reason for contacting Rolt, of course, was that
his seven days' breathing space were up and there was not a
chance that he was going to let Giles think he had won. The
Commander had listened carefully – Rolt was a very good
listener – and had granted an extra two days on condition that
the report was on his desk first thing on Monday morning.
Piers was to place it there in person.

He went in through the back, not wishing to take his dirty
working clothes anywhere near polished furniture, oriental
rugs or silken wall hangings. He had removed his boots and
coat in the room reserved for such things and had pushed
open the kitchen door when Thea came like a whirlwind from
nowhere and gave every sign of shoving him out into the
kitchen garden again.

"They're back!" she hissed. "Didn't you see the car?"

"No, I came round the other way."

"Only arrived just this minute. Go back to the lodge. I'll
bring you something hot to eat later."

Piers was not conscious that he pushed her to one side.
Thea herself was aware only that he carried on walking in the
most inexorable fashion and one either got out of the way or
acted the ship's fender. Her real reason for wanting to pre-

28

vent his entry was that their father had come home in a particularly foul temper.

Colonel Mycroft and Mrs Elizabeth Ashley were still in the entrance hall, sorting out luggage and the several parcels of gifts that Elizabeth had brought for friends and relations. Mycroft's bad temper was due to an upset stomach – "Damned foreign cooking" – and the delay in clearing customs. It must be said that for a long moment neither of them recognised the young man who strode through from the rear of the house.

Then, "Piers!" Elizabeth gasped faintly and totally out of character; she never did anything in a faint or gasping manner.

"Get out," said Colonel Ashley. He did not shout, he was the kind of man who did not have to – in his sixties, thick iron-grey hair, powerfully built, still very fit.

"I've no intention of staying where I'm not wanted," Piers said. "It seemed good manners to come and say hello."

"Well, you've said it," rasped Mycroft. "Shut that door when you go out – it's hellish draughty."

"Mycroft . . ." his wife began.

"No, Elizabeth," the Colonel said. "And I hope we aren't going to have to argue this out all over again."

Elizabeth did not feel that she had lost any arguments. "Mycroft, it's perfectly obvious that Piers has been working very hard. I said he could do up the lodge and live there until he found somewhere else. You're not telling me that you can read the lesson in church on Sunday about turning the hungry away from your gate, and send your own son out into the cold."

This piece of news – or homily, whichever way you looked at it – fell on stony ground. And whether Mycroft Ashley merely was unwell, or had had one too many gins on the plane, or really felt that the entire Ashley dynasty was under threat, was unclear. Whatever the reason, he endeavoured to solve the problem in dramatic fashion. He drew himself up to his full height, just a couple of inches shorter than his eldest son, and beckoned to him with an imperious forefinger.

"Come with me."

They all trooped into the Great Hall where the head of the

family removed Sir Richard Ashleigh's sword from the wall. Elizabeth was sure afterwards that she had heard the Ashley shades in the room take a deep breath.

"See this?" said the Colonel.

"Of course," Piers said.

"Well, in case you've forgotten, it was the sword used to kill an assassin who attacked Elizabeth I when she visited Portsmouth to inspect the Fleet. He wasn't just a hired thug but a skilled swordsman. But your ancestor, Richard Ashleigh, fought him to the death and for that he was knighted. There and then, despite the fact that he was bleeding from several wounds."

"I know that," Piers said. "Brave chap."

His father swallowed hard. "I just want to remind you of the calibre of your ancestor. It's what we try to live up to today. There's no place in this family for common felons."

And with that he walked forward. The point of the sword blade went through Piers' sweater, shirt, just a small fold of skin, shirt and sweater again, and then into the linenfold panelling behind, pinning him.

"Did the brave knight make a habit of spitting his sons to the wall too?" Piers asked, feeling amazingly calm.

The Colonel pulled out the sword. "I should make you bleed," he grated.

"You have," Piers told him, feeling the warm blood trickle down his arm. When there was every indication that the same thing was about to happen again he danced out of range and reached for what he had always thought to be the most beautiful artifact in the entire house, an early-nineteenth-century naval officer's sword, obviously as sharp as the day it had been made. He had only held it once before, when no one was looking, and the joy was repeated. It was as though he had practised with it for hours, it was entirely *right*.

"Don't be a fool," his father said sharply.

"Wilkinsons versus an Elizabethan armourer," Piers said. "What odds am I given, eh?" He had, after all, consumed two pints of very strong Old Peculiar. "And I'll tell you something – I'm a far better swordsman than you are. Fencing was on the curriculum of that bloody unfriendly boarding school you sent me to in Scotland."

30

With a roar of rage Mycroft took a wild swipe at the grinning, dust-covered figure before him. Had it made contact the blade probably would have cut Piers into two. As it was, the sword was parried with a steely shock that jarred Mycroft's wrist and he was then forced to retreat, vainly trying to remember the little tuition he had been given as a boy.

Elizabeth Ashley stood quite still. It did not seem to her that her husband was in the slightest danger: the flashing blade driving him relentlessly to the other end of the room not following through with any attacking thrusts. And Piers, bless his flawed soul, was thoroughly enjoying himself.

Thea, prepared to put a lot of money on Wilkinsons on the grounds that they made jolly good razors, viewed the encounter with some alarm. Her brother, she knew, was like milk and honey until he was really upset. When that happened you unpacked the flak jackets and found the brandy. Watching him closely though, she came to the same conclusion as had her mother. He was utterly happy.

It was just as well that neither of them could hear what was being said.

It was doubtful whether Mycroft had used such language since his early army days and it came as a bit of a shock to him that the obscenities poured from his lips so effortlessly. But the knowledge that hostilities would only cease when his son so chose was almost more than could be borne. Earlier crazy intentions apart, he felt horribly guilty about the blood oozing through the sleeve of Piers' sweater.

The engagement ceased abruptly and was neither of the party's doing. In fact, if Mycroft had seen what was about to happen he would have prevented it.

"You unspeakable little rat!" he shouted at Giles, who had crept up behind Piers and hit him on the head with a small oak stool, felling him utterly.

"Piers!"

The voice was insistent but he ignored it. He didn't usually ignore his mother.

"Piers, please wake up."

There was a breath of movement in the air pressing on him.

She was coming close. Then, icy and drenching, cold water sluiced over his face and searchingly down his neck.

"Dear God, it *is* all dirt and he's not really a ghastly shade of grey."

Another freezing drenching. She must have got the water from the lily pond.

"Piers, I'm fairly sure you're conscious. Be so good as to open your eyes."

He opened them. The result was by no means perfect as there were two of everything.

"I'm sure we ought to call the doctor," said Thea's voice from somewhere behind him. She moved and came into his view.

"You've four eyes," Piers told her, his own voice sounding strange to him.

"You'll feel much better when you've had a bath, a hot meal and eight hours' sleep," Elizabeth said. This tended to be her cure-all for everything from boils to chicken pox.

Piers wanted to believe her.

"Get clean when you feel a little stronger. I'll find you something light to eat." She left the room.

"She's as mad as hell with me," Piers said with a groan as he moved his head. "What the hell happened?"

"Giles hit you on the head with a stool," Thea replied. "And she's not mad with you at all – just with Dad and Giles."

"It's all my fault though – I shouldn't have come."

"Surely you don't imagine everything's been sweetness and light while you were away so far as Giles is concerned?"

Piers met his brother on the stairs. The pleasure was all his for Giles stopped dead when he saw him coming and actually went a little pale.

"You're quite safe," Piers informed him. "I don't hit the weaker sex."

"I was a fool," Giles said when they were level. "You're *in* again, aren't you? They're hardly going to throw you out when you're slightly concussed."

A little later, Elizabeth, handing her husband his supper on a tray, the two of them and Thea in their private sitting room, said, "It's important to behave in adult fashion and keep a sense of proportion over this. The boy's home. He has a job and in a couple of days will go to the Midlands for training. I said he could have the lodge and he's started work on it already. To carry on in this spiteful fashion, Mycroft, is quite stupid and not like you at all."

The compliment was lost on Mycroft, who embarked upon cold beef and pickles without speaking.

"I like having Piers at home," his wife continued. "I *want* him here."

Quietly, Thea said, "I'm afraid he's not taking the job."

Elizabeth sat down rather suddenly. "Oh, dear."

"But he's going to spend the weekends doing up the lodge," Thea went on. "He's done an enormous amount of work already."

"Going back to his old game?" Mycroft asked grimly.

"You'll have to ask him," Thea said.

"I'm asking *you.*"

She nodded. "For a while. But he's promised that – "

"Then he can clear out," the Colonel interrupted. "Tonight. I'm damned if I'm giving house-room to a petty crook."

"Piers doesn't look like a crook," Elizabeth said in a faraway voice. "I've always said that you can look people in the eye and know what they're really like. I *know* that Piers has never done anything disgraceful."

"That's why they sent him to prison," Mycroft said sarcastically, savagely spearing a pickled onion.

"Then it was a mistake. He was framed or something." She fixed her spouse with unwavering gaze. "I've really had enough of this business and the way you keep carrying on so. If Piers has to leave, then so shall I."

In the stunned silence which followed this pronouncement the door opened and Piers walked in. Despite feeling very other-worldly he had made a good job of making himself more socially presentable. The overall result, enough to create a warm glow in any mother's bosom, had the effect of making Elizabeth even more determined in her resolve. She got to her feet and made for the door.

"Wait!" Mycroft said, frankly scared witless.

She turned. "Yes, dear?"

"Is there any more beef? Make sure there's enough for Piers though."

She smiled in triumph. "I'll go and see." And went, for some unaccountable reason, humming the *Marseillaise*.

"Have to get the dogs from kennels in the morning," said the Colonel to the room at large. "The place is like a morgue without them."

Thea glanced at her watch. "I'll go now and finish my supper when I get back."

"It's a bit late," said her father.

"I know. But they keep the most odd hours at the kennels. And as you say, the house isn't the same without dogs."

"May I sit down?" Piers asked when the two men were alone.

He was waved to a chair with a fork and there was quite a long silence.

"Nothing's changed," said the Colonel.

"I know. I'll clear out in the morning. One room in the lodge is habitable."

"No. There's no need for that."

"I'd rather not be here. There's too much awkwardness. I don't want Mother to have to take sides."

His father cleared his throat. "There won't be any awkwardness so far as I'm concerned because I'm going to London on business. The business is on Monday but there's a do on at my club tomorrow night so I'm going in the morning. And I don't want it said that I forced my son to live in squalor."

Piers remained silent, deliberately, not because he had nothing to say.

Mycroft said, "I've told Giles to keep out of your way. I very much regret that he acted the way he did. It was a cowardly thing to do and I've told him as much. You won't have any further bother with him."

"He's worried that I might worm my way back into your affections."

The Colonel scrutinised him carefully. "But that's not why you're here, is it?"

"No."

After another silence Mycroft asked, lightly, "When you're – er – working, what do you actually do?"

"I work for a man called Len Dorney. I suppose he can be

34

described as a top-ranking gangster. In a way I'm his right-hand man."

"But what does that entail?"

"Mostly removing rivals who want to take over his manor . . . area, that is."

The Colonel's eyes were like holes in his head as he stared. "You mean, you *kill* them?"

"Oh, no. I've a much better method than that. I hand them over to the police. They're usually wanted for something. You've no idea how effective it is at getting rid of them."

Mycroft nodded thoughtfully. "And word gets round, I suppose."

"Of course."

"And – er – what do you intend to do when you go back?"

"I'm going to put Dorney out of business."

The Colonel was forgetting to eat. "Why?"

"Because he's a blot on the landscape."

"A revenge sort of thing?"

"No, not really."

Frowning in perplexity, Mycroft said, "Wouldn't it have been easier to work for the CID?"

Piers laughed. "They haven't been able to pin him down in twenty years."

As William had said he would finish off the roof the next morning, Saturday, Piers was at the lodge quite early. He had no intention of doing anything too strenuous himself – he didn't feel like it – but would give William a hand with the "chimbley" pot. Another reason for his presence was that he was expecting a visitor, her arrival soon heralded by the appearance of three black Labradors and a Border Terrier. They greeted him joyfully, as they had the previous night – dogs not being concerned about the recent whereabouts of the humans in their lives – and then raced around the lodge, barking excitedly.

"I hadn't realized it was so dilapidated," Elizabeth said when she arrived. She went inside. "My goodness, but you've gutted the place."

"It's got to be done properly," Piers told her. "You can't put carpets over rotten floorboards."

"Heaven forbid that I should suggest you do," she replied. "It's just that . . . Oh, well. But you can't live here, that's for sure. Not until it's been seen to."

"It'll cost a hell of a lot of money."

She turned to look at him. "How much, Piers?"

"At a guess between six and eight thousand pounds. But if you and Dad are happy for me to do it, I'll buy a second-hand caravan and live in that. If I do most of the work myself, it won't cost so much."

"And do you *want* to do that?"

"I'd like to very much. But I'd like some kind of undertaking from Dad that I could have the place on a peppercorn rent or buy the freehold for a reasonable sum."

"Yes, I do see your point. You wouldn't want to spend a lot of money and then have him tell you to get out." She leaned on a door post, arms crossed. "And do you have any means, Piers?"

"I've a flat in Shepherd's Bush, a car and . . . yes, means."

"Mycroft was saying last night that things weren't as he'd thought. You seem to be working in some kind of independent way."

"That's true."

"Do you . . ." Her voice was a little croaky so she began again. "Do you ever carry a gun in the course of your . . . projects?"

"All the time," Piers said softly, seeing William approaching. "Why? Do you need a minder?"

"Yes, I think I do," she whispered. "But we can't talk now." Louder, she added, "There's no need for you to buy a caravan and I'm not sure I'd want to have one of those things stuck here. Take a look at the accommodation over the stable block and tell me what you think. It has all mod-cons and wouldn't cost as much as a caravan to make it really comfortable. And I can find you most of the stuff you'd need to furnish it with."

"Curiouser and curiouser," Piers muttered to himself as she walked away.

"Did you stay here last night?" William said, looking at something in the road.

"No."

"Well, you had visitors."

Piers went to where he was standing gazing down at a set of tyre tracks. They were fresh, partly obliterating those of Kevin's Land-Rover and the skip lorry, frozen solid into the mud of the lane by overnight frost.

"A medium-sized car," Piers said, crouching down to take a closer look. "Worn tyres of a fairly neglected car driven by a fairly bad driver."

"How do you know that?" William asked.

"The front right hand tyre's worn on the inside – it's almost bald, see? So there's probably something wrong with the wheel or the suspension. And the left hand tyre's worn on the outside. That means it gets scrubbed along curbs a lot. The vehicle could also be driven far too fast on rough roads. I'd say the owner's in his early twenties, probably unemployed, and with no real concern for his own or other people's safety."

"That's real neat," William said admiringly. "You could almost be a copper." He went beetroot red. "Sorry, no offence meant. I wasn't trying to be funny."

Piers clapped him on the shoulder. "Don't be such a daft Herbert. Let's get this bloody chimbley pot up."

But half an hour later, a small amount of cement mixed that William had brought with him, they had to admit that they needed help. Piers could easily lift the four foot high pot but going up the ladder with it was another thing, never mind getting it to where William was sitting astride the apex of the roof.

"You'll need to get roof ladders," William decided. "This damn thing moves real drastic like with your weight and the pot."

"I'll see if Tom Jackson's at home," Piers said, not needing to be told these things. "He always has an answer for everything."

The Jacksons had been visiting a daughter in Bournemouth for a week and seemed to have only just returned. Mrs Jackson answered the door. Her husband might always be referred to as Tom and the cook as Madge and David as David, but Mrs Jackson was always Mrs Jackson and that was that. When she saw Piers she looked horrified.

"Is Tom in?"

"I – I – " she stuttered.

"Can he spare a moment?" Piers interrupted.

She was saved from further dilemma by Tom coming to see who it was. "What can I do for you, Master Piers?"

Piers would have rather been called Bonzo than addressed in this courtly and old-fashioned manner but merely smiled and repeated his request. A couple of minutes later the pair of them were on their way back to the lodge, Tom carrying a rope and a short ladder. When they arrived Tom went up the ladder already there like a monkey and from that to the slippery slates of the roof where he lashed the short ladder to the chimney stack at one end and to the long ladder at the other. Piers then carried the pot up the ladder and he and Tom manoeuvred it into place where William could cement it. In all, the job probably took about five minutes.

"Thanks," said Piers when they were all back on the ground. It seemed to him that Tom never looked any older. He was a wiry man of medium height and build and his hair had been thin on top for as long as Piers could remember. In a way he was like a chameleon, exactly fitting the part that he was, at any one time asked to play. Thus when he was butler for the evening when the Ashley's entertained, no finer or more immaculate butler ever trod the Earth. Ask him to take down the paintings in a room that it might be spring-cleaned and the Tate Gallery wouldn't do a more careful job. And when astride a roof, helping with a chimney pot, then he became a master steeple-jack.

"Everything all right, now you're back?" Tom asked.

Piers did not mind the question, the man was part of the family. "Sort of," he replied.

"No one's perfect," Tom said, coiling the rope. "Some people would do well to remember that."

The living quarters over the stable were absolutely ideal. Needing a coat of paint and a good clean, the one-time head-groom's accommodation was just what Piers wanted. There were two small bedrooms, a large living room, a kitchen and bathroom. The heating of hot water seemed to be achieved by a back-boiler behind the living-room fire. As long as this proved to be moderately successful, Piers was happy.

He lit the fire with scrap wood, hunted around out the back and discovered a coal bunker containing at least half a hundredweight of coal. Very soon there was a roaring fire in the grate, the water in the boiler singing as it began to get hot.

Doing these things, and cleaning the flat in the afternoon, his mind was elsewhere, wondering what his mother wanted with a minder. Had she received poison-pen letters? He tried to remember any organisations with which she had connections. Well, there was the Women's Royal Voluntary Service and the Royal National Lifeboat Institution, and she was chairwoman of the local Women's Institute. He seemed to recollect that she was on the Parochial Church Council and helped with church flowers. None of these would attract the attentions of cranks.

At five-fifteen he called it a day, the flat scrubbed out. He was on his way back to the Hall, only a short walk, when he remembered that there were still tools lying about at the lodge. Swearing under his breath, he changed course.

There was great satisfaction in seeing both barley-sugar chimney pots securely in place, William having also attended to the other. He would shortly be receiving a bottle of whisky and a brace of pheasants, only did not know it, Mycroft having agreed to provide them the previous evening.

It was almost too dark to see but Piers gathered together the tools William had borrowed from the things he had brought from home; a spirit level, a shovel, a trowel and a saw. But the saw was William's. Piers locked it up in the store with the rest – the store had a very good padlock on it now – and went back indoors for a last look round.

He was on the point of leaving, walking towards the front door, when he saw a movement outside through the window. Some kind of sixth sense caused him to halt and take a step sideways. The next moment something hit him a hammer blow in the chest. Blackness roared over him and the floor came up to crash into his side.

Chapter Four

Strangely, he remained conscious. The darkness cleared and self-preservation drove him to roll into a corner. When, again, there was a darkening of his vision it was because there was a man standing just outside the now broken window, blocking out the little light there was. The black silhouette was unbelievably sinister-looking and Piers bit his lip hard to prevent fear finding voice. Then, as if it had never been there, the dark shape vanished.

Had whoever it was gone round the back?

Teeth again in his lip, for the top half of his body was one huge flaring agony, Piers wriggled right into his corner and stood up as he had on one occasion before, sliding his back up the wall. Two tools he had overlooked had come into contact with his hands, the large sledge hammer he had used to knock down the ceilings and a chopper he had first used on the dead elm. The sledge hammer was now out of the question, and what use were either of these tools against a gun?

I'm probably dying, was the thought uppermost in his mind. My chest is filling with blood and I'll drown in it. But I'll die with a snarl on my face, just for the bastard outside.

There was silence but for the monotonous dripping of a tap over the scullery sink. Ashley moved, still with his back to the wall, towards the door to this room, gathering the chopper as he did. He paused and then leaned out and pushed open the door wide. An open invitation.

Nothing happened. There was no sound of movement from without.

Then, faintly, he heard a car being driven away.

This could, of course, be a deliberate ploy to bring him into the open. It occurred to him that his attacker had no means of knowing how badly he was hit, if at all. The dirt on the window would have seen to that.

But if you wait too long, boyo, you'll die.

He was never sure how he achieved the journey and afterwards could remember nothing but his actual arrival, a rather dramatic blundering into the kitchen where his father was alone, making tea.

"I never knew you did things like that," Piers said, just before his knees buckled.

The following week was lost to Piers forever. He inhabited a world of dreams where beings dressed in green or white floated close to him and did not speak. They had no proper faces, only eyes in the green or white heads. His own being only seemed to *consist* of a head, he was not aware of a body at all. His brain presented him with several reasons for this. It was possible that he had died and had been reincarnated as the head of Hubert Ashleigh who had lost it for being a strong supporter of Bonnie Prince Charlie. Perhaps, on the other hand, life on Earth was only an illusion engineered by aliens and this situation of his was the real state of affairs. Or he could merely be in Hell.

A little later – if indeed time existed and the word "later" had any meaning – he became aware that he did indeed possess a body but that he had no control over it whatsoever. It breathed on its own – he knew this because he tried to hold his breath out of curiosity and couldn't – and moreover he could not cough or move his tongue to lick parched lips. The only ability left to him appeared to be that of opening and closing his eyes. There was a being in white close by so he tried to communicate with it, opening and closing his eyes as fast as he could.

It spoke.

"Blink once if you hurt anywhere."

He stared stonily at it but the creature did something anyway and he drifted off into nothingness again for a while. His money was now all on the aliens theory.

"I don't really know why he's alive," said a strong masculine voice all at once, so close and so sudden that Ashley was considerably startled. "I think we ought to find out if he can breathe unaided."

There were a few utterly nauseous moments while what felt like a six foot length of tubing was removed from his throat. He gagged, gasping for breath.

"Roll him over!" someone exclaimed.

Not a moment too soon. An extremely bitter-tasting fluid gushed into his mouth and then splashed into a bowl.

"Well caught, nurse," said the man who had first spoken. "God, this boy's so fit I simply can't believe it. He can not only breathe on his own but honk on his own too. Hold his head, there's more yet."

There was too. Afterwards another tube was removed from his nose.

"Now, let's have a look at you."

Lying on his back now, naked, and still host to tubes in places he preferred not to have them, his modesty just preserved by a sheet, Ashley gazed at the speaker. He had recognised the voice instantly. Crispin Blake, private surgeon to just about everyone important in the county, not to mention quite a few in London, was an old friend of the family.

"Better?"

Ashley nodded.

"Can you speak?" Without waiting for an answer the surgeon dismissed the nursing staff, saying he wanted a private chat with the patient. He seated himself on the edge of the bed; a good-looking man, tall and fair-haired, reputedly a womanizer.

"That famous flare of anger in Ashley eyes," he said quietly. "No, Piers, I wasn't suggesting you were refusing to speak to me in some kind of paddy. It's just that some patients find difficulty in talking when they've been on a respirator for as long as you have." He placed a hand over the one of Ashley's that wasn't host to drip tubes. "And I meant what I said. How that bullet missed everything vital, only God above knows."

"Will I be . . . all right?" Piers asked hoarsely.

"I don't see why not. But you'll have to take things very quietly for a while."

Would Rolt keep him on?

"And you actually walked home from where it happened?" Blake said.

"I must have done."

"Did you see who it was?"

"No. Only the dark outline of a man as he looked through the window at me."

Blake patted the hand and rose. "The police want to talk to you when you're a bit stronger. I'll keep them well away from you until at least the day after tomorrow. And who knows? You might have remembered something else by then."

Moments later he had gone and the nursing staff returned to make life uncomfortable again.

The thought uppermost in Ashley's mind was the hope that he would be very much stronger when Rolt came visiting. *If* he came. But Heaven not necessarily answering unjustified prayers, Rolt was the first person he saw when he next opened his eyes. Questions and answers concerning Ashley's immediate worries were quite superfluous for the Commander had not brought flowers but a heavy, cold item that came with its own leather and webbing shoulder harness and which was placed beneath the pillow.

"You'd better not let Leadbetter see that," he said.

"Leadbetter?"

"Inspector Leadbetter of West Sussex CID. He's investigating the case of your attempted murder. Hasn't he been to see you yet?"

"You're my first outside visitor, sir. Have you identified yourself to Leadbetter yet?"

"No. I'm hoping to see him after I leave here."

"I'd rather you didn't."

"*You'd* rather I didn't?"

Ashley was in just a little too much pain to be over-worried about insolence. "I'd rather he didn't know I'm with the police."

"It would have to be a fairly good reason."

"Something's going on at home. There might be a connection with the shooting. But if everyone finds out what I really do for a living, then it's likely that the only people with things to say will clam up."

43

"Give me *some* idea what's going on."

"My mother wants me at home, plus my gangster's Betsy, as her minder."

Rolt looked very thoughtful. "And I take it your mother could be described as one of those backbone of rural England ladies who entertain bishops?"

"Yes."

After pondering Rolt said, "It's not going to make things any easier for Leadbetter if he's not in possession of the full facts."

"I've got all the leads, sir."

"Then I think you'd better tell me about them."

Ashley told him the whole story, including his sister's fears, the suspicion that someone had been watching him, his mother's words to him one morning at the lodge. After he had finished Rolt got to his feet, and with his hands in his pockets, paced up and down the small private room. Ashley knew better than to interrupt his thoughts.

"Do you think it was your brother?" the Commander asked, pausing in his perambulations.

"As far as I know Giles has no knowledge of small arms."

"And you're sure it was a hand gun?"

"I saw someone outside. If he'd shot me with a rifle from that range, I'd have ended up very dead."

Rolt smiled. "And of course the local CID have the bullet, which I understand is .38. Sorry, I was just wondering how much you could remember."

"He looked through the window at me. I'd say he was taller than Giles."

"Could it have been a woman?"

"Yes, I suppose so," Piers said, surprised at himself for not having thought of this.

"Any women you might have upset?" Rolt asked, keeping a straight face.

"No, sir."

"You seem very sure."

"You tend to stay celibate in prison," Piers said.

"Some do, Homage, some do," Rolt observed gently. "Could anyone else be gunning for you?"

"Dorney?"

44

"It's not likely, is it? And the vibes are still strong that he wants you back. Mind you, he'll knock your block off when he does see you for leaving it so long. Which is a good incentive to get well soon, eh?"

When Rolt had gone Ashley hid the gun under a bath towel in his locker. Then he pushed the button that would fetch a nurse, the pain by now on the verge of unmanning him.

"Nice man your uncle, isn't he?" she said brightly when she came.

The business of recovery, Piers soon realized, was furthered by *almost* ignoring how he felt. The main problem was having what felt like a zip-fastener in his chest. It was a curving one, starting about halfway down his breast bone, taking in the entry hole of the bullet and continuing for quite a way around his side between the third and fourth ribs. Blake had apparently undertaken what amounted to open-chest surgery to remove the bullet as it had come to rest actually touching the right ventricle of Piers' heart, and as the surgeon said, "You don't go poking around with probes in that region." The ribs themselves were not too happy at having been prised apart and were very painful, the whole of his side black and blue. But at least he was free now from what he could only describe as captive plumbing.

Half an hour after Rolt's visit and when an injection had taken blessed effect, he was encouraged to get out of bed and go for a short walk down a corridor, supported by two male nurses. Youth being what it is, and Piers' legs being like those of a drunk, there was a certain amount of hilarity taking place when Elizabeth Ashley came upon them. It was a dreadful shock to her, albeit a pleasant one, for during the many hours she had sat at his bedside and when Crispin Blake was refusing to be more encouraging than give the patient a fifty-fifty chance, she had prepared herself for the worst.

"And here you are playing the fool," she said, when he had carefully detached himself from his helpers, placed both hands on her shoulders and kissed her. Just then Crispin Blake pushed his way through swing doors nearby and turned in their direction.

"Ah, the lad himself," he cried. "You're getting the red-carpet treatment. It's me who's going to take your stitches out." He too bestowed a kiss on Elizabeth's cheek, the lady going pink with pleasure.

The helpers were dismissed and the others made their way back to Piers' room. Elizabeth was all for turning tail then but Blake would have none of it, saying that she wasn't squeamish if she lived in the country and did she think twice when faced with drawing game birds?

"Birds' innards aren't the same as holes in your own son," she protested, but he would not listen to her, requiring her to hold the dish.

"You just want my admiration for your handiwork," she said as the small, bloodstained pieces of suture thread were dropped into the dish she had in one hand, her son's hand in the other.

"Be honest," Blake said with a laugh. "It's damned fine stitching. There'll be little or no scar. You do have a lot of inside stitches though, young man, which will gradually melt as you heal. Do anything too strenuous and you'll be back here for a big repair job."

Piers, watching them both as he coped with the lightning and tiny stabs of pain, had an idea that he had solved one mystery. He decided to put the hunch to the test. He said, "I understand, Mr Blake, that I have you to thank for finding me a job."

"Crispin," smiled the man. "A mere bagatelle, dear boy. My brother is managing director of the company in question. But I gather you don't fancy selling the best earth moving equipment in the world."

"The truth is I've unfinished business in London."

"It's not my place to advise you on *that*," Blake said, rather sharply. "But I should imagine that your father's made his views fairly plain."

"Absolutely," Piers agreed.

"So, Elizabeth," said Blake. "Am I to try to find him a place at a local authority nursing home?"

"Good gracious, no!" she cried. "Whatever for? Piers is coming home to us."

"He'll need a certain amount of looking after for a while."

"No problem at all," she assured him. "There's me and

46

Madge and Mrs Jackson, and Thea most weekends. Of course we can manage."

"Then on condition that he stays in bed for most of the time for a week and the district nurse keeps a weather eye on him, you can have him the day after tomorrow. All being well, of course. We've an appalling shortage of beds here right now."

"Splendid," Elizabeth said, handing Blake the dish. When he had gone she turned to Piers, saying, "Don't worry about what I said at the lodge. Just get better."

For answer he opened his locker, burrowed under the towel and drew out the police issue 2.5″ barrel Smith and Wesson. "I'm a damned good shot," he said softly. "Upright or otherwise. What's the problem?"

Understandably Elizabeth had gone very pale. "How on earth did you get that?"

"My boss brought it."

"Threats," she replied, looking around nervously. "But we can't talk about it here."

"To you?"

"I'm not sure. Vague threats."

"By letter?"

She nodded.

"Never by phone?"

"No."

"Why don't you go to the police?"

"I'm not absolutely sure of their discretion. I know *all* the senior policemen around here or, at least, I thought I did, and although I'm convinced they're good at their job there's always the worry about gossip. There's been an Inspector Leadbetter asking a lot of questions since you were shot. He's new and I don't know him at all. He came to the house and absolutely *grilled* us."

"But threats to you might have a bearing on my being shot."

She patted his arm. "Wait until you're home. We can talk about it then."

Soon after his mother had gone a nurse put her head around the door to ask if he felt strong enough to be interviewed by the police. Ashley didn't but wanted to get it over with.

It was Leadbetter himself, as Piers had expected. He had also expected – in the way that one tries to put certain characteristics to a name – Leadbetter to be short, stout and balding and to wear bifocal glasses. Nothing, as it turned out, could have been further from the truth. The Inspector, whose Christian name Piers was later to discover was Julian, was an imposing figure wearing a very white trenchcoat-style mackintosh and a soft black Fedora hat with a wide brim. He introduced himself without smiling and fixed on Piers the bleakest pair of blue eyes he had ever seen.

"I'm much better, thank you," he said, beginning to see the wisdom in Rolt's original intention of giving Leadbetter all the facts. But wisdom did not necessarily go hand in hand with *charity*.

Leadbetter drew up a chair and sat down. "I understand you saw whoever it was who shot you."

"I saw someone outside the window who moved nearer and peered through the glass after a shot had been fired."

"And you're quite sure you didn't recognise him or her?"

"No. It was just a dark shape. The glass was very dirty."

Leadbetter considered for a moment. "Is there anyone it might have been? One of your criminal cronies, for example."

"It's unlikely."

"Why is it unlikely, Mr Ashley?"

"Because my criminal cronies want me in one piece."

"Have you ever grassed on anyone?"

"Not in the way you mean, but I've turned over quite a few mobsters to the police."

"That amounts to the same thing surely?" Leadbetter said with heavy patience.

"Not at all. You were asking me about cronies. These were operators who had shoved their noses in where they weren't wanted."

The Inspector took out a notebook. "Would you care to give me a few names?"

Piers had an excellent memory and gave Leadbetter thirteen names, together with addresses where known, and got so bloody-minded that he furnished details of their past records, how old they were and what they looked like. Leadbetter's notebook was quite full by the time he had finished.

"And any one of these might have it in for you?"

"If they've found out who I am. I don't use my real name in London."

"You might have been followed when you were released from prison."

"Not by one of those whose names I've just given you. Ten are in prison, one died there, and the other two died in a shoot-out last year."

Leadbetter shut his notebook with a loud snap. "How do you know all this?"

"It's my business to know. That's what I'm paid for."

"What about your brother?"

"Giles? What about him?"

"Could it have been him? I spoke to him at length, and although he has a good alibi I'm treating him as a suspect. He has a motive, a strong one. He stands to lose his inheritance if your father changes his mind about who gets the family money."

"It wasn't Giles. He wouldn't have the bottle to shoot anyone. The person who looked through the window was taller and far broader across the shoulders than he is."

"But he could have hired someone to do it."

"What, on his allowance? I know for a fact that what my father gives him doesn't keep him in luxuries. He had to get a job last summer. A contract man would want at least ten grand."

"What about your father?"

Piers had to ask him to repeat the question as suddenly Leadbetter's voice had become faint and strangely buzzing.

"I couldn't help but get the impression how disappointed he is in you," Leadbetter continued when Piers did not immediately reply.

"He'd rather die than creep up on someone and shoot them."

"But he *was* a soldier until he resigned his commission so that he could keep a closer eye on the running of the estate."

"Yes, he was in the Royal Corps of Transport. A wizard at organizing but not really into scampering around waving guns. Colonels don't do much of that sort of thing anyway."

"But he must have received early weapons training."

"So have I," Piers said wearily. "And I assure you that my father could surprise a stone-deaf elephant in the rush hour and that's about all. When he's walking in the country he makes as much noise as one of his bloody landing craft."

"Is there anything else you want to tell me?" Leadbetter said after a short silence during which Piers closed his eyes.

"Only about the red car."

"What red car?"

He had deliberately left this until last. It was a good idea to let the local CID check it out. But as far as he was immediately concerned, it was too late.

"It was parked in the copse near the lodge one afternoon. It drove off when I approached." The next thing Piers was aware of was Leadbetter shaking his arm.

"Wake up, it's very important."

"I don't feel too good. Could you press that button over the locker?"

"When you've told me about the red car."

"I didn't get the number."

"Are you sure you're not telling me this to remove suspicion from your brother?"

"I can't stand my brother but he's not responsible for my being in here. Go to the lodge. There are a set of tyre tracks in the road outside. That's if . . ."

Leadbetter was going backwards, away from him, getting smaller and smaller.

Despite passing out during Inspector Leadbetter's visit and suffering a slight set-back in his recovery the following day, Piers was permitted to go home the day after that. He had been settled into bed in his own room at the Hall for precisely one hour when Thea came in, looking worried.

"I thought you were in London," he said.

"I've taken time off to help Mummy look after you. There's a Commander Rolt downstairs. He wants to see you."

"Then send him up."

"A *Commander*, Piers. That's terrifically senior. And you promised me you'd never done anything really dreadful."

"Really senior fuzz don't call on crooks at all. I expect it's about me being shot." He called her name as she turned to go.

"What?"

"Relax, child. Yer brother loves yer."

Chapter Five

"This is the last time you'll see me until you report for duty," Rolt said as he closed the door. "And I can't stay long. By all that's holy, Homage, I didn't know you lived in a *castle*."

"The gatehouse is the only really old part, sir. The rest is sort of reproduction."

"Did Leadbetter get to you?"

"You can say that again."

Rolt's eyebrows rose slightly. "He's late of Brighton CID and very highly thought of, so I'm told."

"Perhaps you didn't see him in his designer mack and bonnet."

The Commander didn't smile. "He's got a good lead, anyway. Apparently a car – yes, a red one – swerved out of that old road into the main highway at about the time that you were shot. It almost knocked a woman off her bike and she was so angry she took the number."

"Have you spoken to Inspector Leadbetter, sir?"

"Yes, otherwise I'd have remained in the dark as to how he's progressing. But don't worry, I told him I was checking on you from the city end. He'd heard of F.9 of course and was only too pleased to share his findings."

Piers kept quiet. He had noticed on several occasions that Rolt only tended really to make his feelings known when he was on home ground, that is, HQ. It would be too much to expect for him to refer to Leadbetter as a toady here even though his expression had conveyed as much. Perhaps Rolt merely had a lifetime's horror of listening devices, hence the polite attitude when referring to a brother officer.

51

"Who does the car belong to?" Piers asked.

"A man called Colin Morgan. Know him?"

"I'll say I do! He's the son of the estate manager, Charles Morgan. Colin works in the timber yard on the estate."

"He'd reported the car stolen."

"When?"

"That morning."

"But a red car was snooping round before that. And the day I started work on the lodge – I think it was the Monday – I saw a car parked in front of the house when I got home that night. And that too drove off."

"Hold your horses. It might not have been the same car on either count."

"No, I know, but – "

"Retain the professional attitude," Rolt said mildly. "Even when stopping bullets."

"Sorry, sir."

"Leadbetter has taken statements from everyone in the house that night, your parents and sister and also from a Mr and Mrs Jackson whom I understand live at the East Lodge. Are they on the staff?"

"Mrs Jackson's the housekeeper, her husband a sort of general factotum. He was my father's batman when he was in the Army."

"Well, apparently Mrs Jackson watched television all evening and her husband went out for a walk with their dog and ended up in the village pub. He said he heard and saw nothing strange, although according to the barman at the Rose and Crown he didn't arrive until pretty late on. So he must have still been at home while it was all happening. I find it rather odd that neither of them saw or heard the ambulance."

"They're the sort of folk who close the windows and curtains when it's just getting dark, switch on the TV with the radio probably going in the kitchen as well."

"Leadbetter's let your brother return to university but says he's going to go to Oxford to talk to him again. According to Giles he was at a charity ball at Arundel Castle that night and has a fifty quid ticket to prove it. I thought you said his allowance wasn't up to much."

52

"It isn't, but for an occasion like that I should imagine Dad would have coughed up. It would be a question of the Ashley presence at a local fund-raising effort. And neither of my parents likes dancing. They'd regard it as fifty pounds well spent not to have to turn out."

"He said he went on his own. Hasn't he a girlfriend at the moment?"

"You'll have to ask Thea about that. I simply haven't a clue."

"Answer me truthfully – do you think it was Giles who shot you?"

"Leadbetter asked me that. No, I don't think it was. He'd tell lies to get me out of his way or concoct some sneaky little plan, but not take a gun and shoot me."

"I'm going to have to ask you about your father."

"Leadbetter asked me that too. The answer's no again. He'd die of shame if it even occurred to him."

"Have you established why your mother wants you around with a gun?"

"I've only been at home for an hour, sir," he pointed out.

"Then be so good as to find out," said Rolt, not at all contrite. "We'll let Leadbetter get on with establishing alibis and so forth, and checking up on this man Morgan. Let me know about the other business. Write if you don't want to talk about it over the phone. And I'd be grateful for that long-overdue report when you feel like doing it."

"It's in that drawer over there – the top right hand one of the writing desk. The key's here on the key-ring in my bag, if you don't mind rummaging for it."

Without saying anything Rolt found the key, unlocked the drawer and withdrew the envelope with "Bank Statements" written on the front. It went, unopened, into the inside pocket of his jacket.

"The brain wasn't clouded with anaesthetics," said Piers. "I wrote it the night before I was shot."

"Nearly the last will and testament," the Commander said. "What about the Dorney job?"

"He'll have to stew," Rolt said with a shrug.

"If my picture was in the papers . . ."

"It wasn't. And it can't do a tremendous amount of harm if

he does find out who you really are. As long as he doesn't get to know that you work for us. No, let him stew. We rounded up so many of his mobsters on that job when you were deliberately picked up with them that I hear he's having recruitment problems. We'll get him – when you help him arrange his last big one." Rolt stood up. "Get better but don't try and rush it. I've put your name forward for promotion and I don't want to pin it on you posthumously."

Later, bringing his dinner on a tray, Thea said, "That policeman asked me about Giles. You know he went to the dance that night."

Piers said, "It didn't occur to me until just now that he probably hadn't gone out when the shooting happened."

Thea looked shocked. "I know he's a bit of a worm but you don't think he'd go and enjoy himself knowing you were at death's door? Of course he'd gone out. He'd been asked to help with the arrangements. A local drama group were putting on some kind of entertainment, and as our dear brother is a whizz at things like scenery and lights . . ."

"Really?"

"Yes, he's heavily into the theatre. Wants to direct, so he tells me."

"Did he take anyone to the dance?"

"That's what the Commander asked me. No, I'm sure he didn't. I don't think he has a regular girlfriend. But he might have arranged to meet someone there. *Surely* Giles isn't a suspect?"

"Policemen always go for the one with the best motive."

"He was rather nice, wasn't he?"

"Who, Rolt?"

"Umm. I wonder if he's married."

"No, he isn't."

"Piers, you can't possibly know that!"

"No, of course not," he said hastily. "Only guessing."

"Mr Turner's here to see you," Elizabeth said at ten forty-five the next morning.

"Who?" Piers asked.

"Mr Turner. He's been helping you with the roof."

"Oh, William. Shall I come down?"

"You'll do no such thing. I'll ask him to come up."

"Then leave the door open and I can shout directions if he gets lost."

A few minutes later William stood framed in the doorway, looking, as Piers had half expected, utterly bewildered.

"Haven't you been in the house before?" Piers said when William was perched on the edge of a chair. "Very interesting, you know. You must come on one of the open days with your wife."

"It seems a bit nosey," William said, eyeing some frolicsome nymphs painted by the Rubens School. "Like snooping on the neighbours." He sat without speaking for a moment or two, twisting his cap in his hands. "It came as a terrible shock – hearing that you'd been hurt like that. I feel a bit responsible in a way."

"How could it possibly be your fault?"

"For leaving my saw behind. Not *because* I left it behind, but for going back to fetch it and turning back when I realized it was too dark to see and I hadn't taken a torch."

"But it wouldn't have made any difference to the – "

"I haven't finished yet. There was a car parked in that little copse. I could just see it in the dusk. I should have warned you – phoned you or something. But I didn't. I just said to myself that it was poachers or a courting couple."

"Have you been to the police about this?"

"D'you think I should?"

"Yes, it's important. What time did you see the car?"

"I can't say exactly because I busted my watch last week and it's at the menders. But it must have been getting on for five."

"You can only have been there minutes before I went back to the lodge to put things away."

"I feel terrible – honest I do."

"William, I don't want you to give it another thought. It's my fault for not being more careful."

"I tell you who else I saw too – Tom Jackson. At least I think it was him. It's difficult to be sure in the half-light."

"He said he took his dog for a walk, but it was much later than that."

"Well, he didn't seem to have a dog with him. No, perhaps

55

it wasn't him, come to think of it. What would he be doing down there when they always use the main drive?"

"So why did you come in the way you did – down the old road?"

"I live in Maple Drive. That's on the council estate at the far end of the village. It's far closer for me if I'm coming to the old lodge, even though it is a bit rough underfoot in places."

"And where did you see this man who might or might not have been Tom Jackson?"

"Up nearer the lodge than the car. When I stopped and decided that I'd never be able to find the saw because of the light."

"Did he see you?"

"No, he had his back to me, walking towards the lodge. I only saw his outline really – it could have been anyone. For a moment I thought it might be you."

"William, you seemed quite sure when you first told me about this that it was Tom. Now you seemed to have changed your mind."

"Yes, well, it's just occurred to me what's involved. It might have been the man who tried to kill you, mightn't it? Whoever was driving the car for example. I'm not going to say it was someone I recognised and get them arrested for attempted murder. I couldn't even see if anyone was sitting in the car."

"A red car drove away from the old road and almost knocked a woman off her bike at about the time I was shot. It was Colin Morgan's. He'd reported it stolen earlier on in the day."

"That story's been buzzing around the Rose and Crown."

"Have you any comments to make on it?"

"In what way?" William asked uneasily.

"Could the man you saw have been Colin Morgan?"

After hesitating William said, "As I told you just now – I only saw his outline."

"Forget for a moment that he's the son of the estate manager."

William slumped in his chair. "Mr Ashley, you don't half cross-examine a man."

Blame Rolt's recent presence for switching on all the investigative mental processes, Piers thought. He said, "I'm sorry, William, but it's important. What you saw might turn out to be vital evidence."

Following another silence William said, "I suppose it could have been Colin Morgan. Him and Tom are about the same size and build. But I can't see as how . . ." He coloured. "It's none of my business anyway."

Piers said, "The last time I saw Colin Morgan I pushed his teeth down his throat for setting illegal snares, one of which had caught someone's pet cat. There's no love lost between us, none at all."

"I've heard it said he'd skin a cat for the price of a fag," said William scornfully.

"If I were you I'd go to the police and tell them precisely what you saw. Don't name names if you're not sure who it was. But there's no harm in describing the height and build of the man in the lane."

"That's really sensible," William said, relief in his voice, getting up to leave. "I'll do that."

"Don't go yet, this sounds like someone with some coffee. By the way, who was the woman almost knocked off her bike?"

"Sylvia Webb. She's our local artist. She's put Ashleigh Coombe on the map, has Sylvia."

Giles's having returned to Oxford removed one source of tension. Piers realized that he could alleviate the other, his father, by merely avoiding those places where he knew him to be. Mycroft Ashley, when at home, was a creature of habit. He rose at about six, made tea, and then, whatever the weather, walked the dogs for half an hour. He then returned home, had a shower, and then broke his fast on toast and more tea, taking his wife a cup in bed if she was not up by then. His mornings were spent in the estate office, sometimes in the company of the manager, Charles Morgan. Usually, he lunched at the Rising Salmon, the slightly more up-market of the two village pubs and which was his choice only because it was quieter in the middle of the day. In winter, and since the night of the gale, he sometimes supervised tree-planting, the estate having lost sixty percent of the mature timber. Otherwise he exercised his hunter, Nimrod – kept at livery at the local riding stables only for the duration of the Italian holiday – or worked on his autobiography.

It was now the third week in March, and, the next morning, when Piers slowly made his way along the gallery overlooking the Great Hall, bright beams of sunlight were shining through the gothic-style windows, motes of dust suspended in them like tiny specks of gold. The local woman guiding an electric floor-polisher would have preferred to have switched it off and gone to help him down the stairs but, being married, was aware how men hate being fussed over. She was surprised to see him reappear when he had safely negotiated the stairs, coming into the room where she was working. He reached up, took Sir Richard Ashleigh's sword from the wall, weighed it carefully in his hand as though testing how heavy it was, and then, in slow-motion, performed what she could only describe as a one-sided sword fight, as though in conflict with a man she could not see. Then, almost as soon as he had started, he stopped, saluted her gravely with the weapon, and replaced it on the wall.

"Oh, to be twenty again and unattached," sighed the lady when he had gone.

"Piers, I'm sure you shouldn't be up and about to *this* extent," Elizabeth said when her son ran her to earth in the small room where she attended to her correspondence. At one time it had been the butler's sitting room. But any traces of its past use had been obliterated by the woman who regarded it, with its small velvet button-back chairs in deep pink, carpet and curtains to match, knee-hole desk and late-fourteenth-century French armorial tapestry, as her very own.

"Am I disturbing anything?" Piers asked.

"No, of course not. Sit down and make yourself comfortable."

He did so. "Well, I'm here."

Elizabeth sat quite still for on the word "here" he had pulled the gun out from the waistband of his trousers, the weapon hidden until that moment by a baggy sweater.

"Are you sure the safety catch is on?" she enquired.

"Smith and Wessons don't have safety catches."

"Oh, dear."

"You have to pull the trigger quite hard though."

"I see."

"So what's it all about then – these threats?"

"I've been meaning to talk to you about it but never seemed to be able to find you alone or have the time to spare. I don't think you need worry yourself any more."

"Why's that?"

"I had a letter yesterday. It was from the usual . . . source. It said that honour was satisfied. I don't think I'll be getting any more letters somehow."

"But what can that mean?"

"I assume it's a reference to your being shot."

"But it doesn't make sense!"

"No, I think we're talking about a complete crank. Piers, there are some terrible people about."

"Did you keep the letters?"

"No, I always burnt them."

"That wasn't very sensible, was it?"

"On the contrary, I think it was *very* sensible. I had no intention of going to the police about it. I'm glad I didn't. Otherwise it would have been a huge fuss about nothing. And a waste of police time."

"The letters were evidence. Writing people threatening letters is a criminal offence."

"I really don't think you can lecture me, Piers, about criminal offences. It's possible, I suppose, that this madman has a grudge against you rather than me. You must have rubbed shoulders with all sorts of undesirables from the underworld."

He leaned over, winced, and placed the gun on a corner of the desk. "No doubt. But I don't operate under my own name."

"You don't?" she said blankly.

"What kind of a heel do you think I am? Do you imagine I'd rub the family name in the mud like that?"

"So it can't have been that then."

"Tell me the story right from the beginning. From when you received the first letter."

She knitted her brows, staring into space, thinking. "It

hasn't been going on all that long really. I got the first one just after your grandmother died last year."

"September?"

"That's right. It was only a week after the funeral. I remember I went out very early before the postman came as I had to go over to her house to help my brother sort out some of her things. When I got back during the afternoon the letter was waiting for me. It was the same as all the subsequent ones – words cut out of newspapers and magazines pasted on to cheap typing paper. The gist of it – I can't recollect the exact words – was that I'd soon be attending another funeral."

"That was all? No demands for money?"

"No."

"And no demands for money have ever been made?"

"No."

"How many letters have there been in all?"

"Six or seven. I can't remember exactly."

"How were the others worded?"

"Along the same lines really. How I'd need my black hat. Oh, yes, one said that Mycroft would soon be on his own. That's what really frightened me – why I thought of asking for your help."

"And no one has ever tried to contact you by phone?"

"No."

"No obscene phone calls?"

"No, nothing like that."

"It's difficult to see what I can do."

"But you needn't, now. Not after this last letter." Elizabeth smiled at him. "So you see, it's all over. Nothing to worry about."

But he was trained to look beyond smiles and into the eyes of those speaking. She was lying.

Chapter Six

Fitfully, for he was still in quite a lot of pain and the pills he had been given to help counteract this made him irritable and sleepy, Piers goaded his body to recover. He had been told by Doctor Pringle, the family GP, that he could walk for gentle exercise. So he walked, on the first occasion discovering with a shock that he could go no further than two hundred yards before feeling that it was more than enough. And he fenced with his imaginary opponent, using Richard Ashleigh's sword. It was slightly heavier than the other, his favourite, just right for putting strength back into alarmingly weak muscles. He was not aware of it but his morning exercise along this line was observed on the sixth day after commencement by his father, who had returned to the house for something he had forgotten. Mycroft Ashley saw, watched for a moment or two, and said nothing. Swordsmanship of that standard was never taught at any school for boys.

Piers saw little point in badgering his mother about the threats. He wrote to Commander Rolt, setting out what she had told him and intimating that, in his opinion, it was not the whole story. He also reported – aware that Rolt probably knew of the situation – that police investigations into the shooting seemed to be in a state of limbo. Colin Morgan was still sticking to his story of having had his car stolen and Giles's alibi had been made utterly watertight by the Duke of Norfolk himself who had seen him working with lights in the ballroom of the castle at the time that he, Piers, had been shot. The police were now working on the theory that the attacker had been on his way to the Hall with armed robbery in mind.

"Surprise! Surprise!" cried Thea, bursting into his bedroom one Saturday morning and causing him to snatch up a sweater and hold it in front of his nakedness.

"Didn't know you were up," she shrieked, falling about laughing at the expression on his face. Then her smile faded.

Piers gazed at his own reflection in the mirror. "Yes, my chest looks like one of those embroidered Victorian samplers, doesn't it? Perhaps I should have asked Crispin Blake to stitch a Home Sweet Home on there somewhere."

"I'd no idea you were so *bruised*."

"They're fading. That's why they're all colours of the rainbow."

"I've a surprise for you. Can you make it to the stable block?"

"Fair maid, I can make it to all sorts of places. What have you been up to?"

She took him by the hand. "I'll show you."

"Hey, I can't go like this! Kindly avert your gaze while I put some clothes on."

Hand in hand, they went outside into warm, drizzling rain. Thea's surprise had not involved a lot of money – around two hundred pounds or so – but much time and effort. She had started work the night he had been shot, blundering, blind with tears into the one-time head-groom's living quarters over the stable in an effort to get away from other people. The fire he had lit was almost out, and in a kind of fey dream she had approached slowly, taken a piece of wood that he had left ready and placed it almost reverently in the glowing ashes. If it goes out, she had thought, I know he'll die. The wood had lain in the ashes for what seemed an eternity. Then, on her knees, she had blown on it gently and seen the glow brighten. A tiny splinter jaggedly sticking out had flared and she had blown on the wood again, almost screaming when she blew the flame out. Jumping up she had ripped off a piece of the already peeling wallpaper, folded it into a spill and carefully inserted it beneath her kindling. It had blazed up straight away so she had pulled off another piece. Soon the wood was well alight so she put some more on and then some coal. At last there was such a fire that by its flames she could see to carry on stripping off wallpaper, it coming off in huge, satisfying, tearing swathes that curled and rolled around her feet.

"I don't know what to say," Piers whispered, staring around at his new home.

"Do you *like* it though?" she asked breathlessly.

"It's absolutely fantastic," he replied, no louder. "What the hell are you doing running a nanny agency? You ought to be in interior design."

The strange thing was that none of her own personality had imprinted itself on her handiwork. Except for a couple of small items, that is; a picture she had brought from her own flat in London as it was exactly *right* and a bronze figure of a horse Piers had once given her for her birthday which she knew he had bought because he liked it. No, the flat was essentially that belonging to a man with its autumn colours, pine shelving and hessian wallcoverings. The attics of the Hall had been ransacked by Thea and her mother, with the help of Tom, and they had discovered such treasures as a brass bed, a washstand with bowl and ewer, and rust-coloured velvet curtains for the living room. The rest, but for the bed linen, which Thea had bought new, was surplus furniture and fittings from the main house.

She said, "Of course this is all on condition that I get an invitation to the house-warming. Otherwise you sleep with Nimrod, down below."

They were walking back a little later when Piers said, "I hate to bring up such subjects, Sis, but one of the things I've been mulling over the past few days is that I might not have been the intended victim."

"Then who else might they have been after? Daddy?"

"No, you."

"Me!"

"I fully realize that I'm taller and broader than you, but anyone looking through a dirty window might have mixed us up."

"But why should anyone want to shoot me?"

"I was hoping you might be a little forthcoming on that."

"Piers, I haven't any enemies."

"Packed up any temperamental boyfriends lately?"

She stopped dead in her tracks. "I don't go out with men like that."

"I seem to recollect a certain racing driver who swore he would drive over Beachy Head if you didn't marry him."

"That was different. He was merely a silly show-off."

"Nevertheless . . ."

Thea marched off again, chin jutting. "I really don't think it's any of your business."

"Would you rather I asked you or that creep Leadbetter?"

She stopped again. "Are you saying what I think you are? That if I don't give you details of my love life, you'll go and suggest this line of enquiry to him?"

Piers groaned. "No, as a matter of fact I wasn't suggesting anything so low." He grinned. "But I could always give Commander Rolt a ring."

"If you weren't so fragile, I'd box your ears," she stormed.

"So what's this guy's name then?" he asked, unblinking.

It occurred to Thea, a while after this conversation took place, that her brother really had expected her to lash out. She had refrained partly because she had mastered her temper but mostly for the reason that there was the same inexplicable something about him, that she could only describe as a sense of purpose, that she had seen when he had pushed past her to greet their newly returned parents. And why on earth did he show such obvious respect for Rolt, of the same ilk as had put him in prison?

"Lee Haasden," Thea said, setting off again.

"Dutch?" Piers asked.

"South African."

"Are you still seeing him?"

"No. I thought you wanted to know about people I don't see anymore."

"And the parting was acrimonious?"

"Very. We had a row in the Savoy Restaurant."

"Do you mind if I ask – "

She interrupted him with, "Yes, I do, but I'll tell you. We broke up because I found out he was having an affair with someone I'll just describe as a tart. Her name won't mean a thing to you so I won't soil my lips with it. I poured soup all over him."

"Wow," Piers said admiringly.

"But he didn't threaten me or anything. Just raged off."

They went into the kitchen together to find Madge busy cooking breakfast on the Aga.

"Here you are, Piers," she called, and dished up eggs, bacon, sausage, kidneys, tomatoes and fried bread.

"It's almost worth getting shot to eat like this," he said.

"There is one thing though," Thea said to him under her breath, "that worries me a little after what you've just said."

"Go on."

"Lee's a man who might brood over it. He hates being made a fool of. And he belongs to a gun club – he used to tell me about it."

Lee Haasden, however, had to wait. Piers wrote a quick note to Rolt about it and a couple of days later received a post card from Frinton, Rolt signing himself just with his Christian name after a few words to the effect that their mutual friend was out of the country. So Piers could only fret, attend the out-patients clinic at the hospital for check-ups, read, watch television, and take a little more exercise every day.

One afternoon, when he had been living in the flat over the stable for two weeks, he heard Nimrod's hooves in the yard below and looked out of the window. He was just in time to meet Mycroft's gaze, looking up. He opened the window.

"I just wondered how you were getting on," said the Colonel. From his elevated position on the hunter's back his head was only about three or four feet below.

"Not too bad, thanks. But I feel utterly useless."

"Can't drive yet, eh?"

"Not really. I can't swing the wheel for tight turns."

Mycroft came to a decision. "I wouldn't object if you wanted to plod around on this old fellow. He's as quiet as a lamb now. You wouldn't need strength to ride him."

"I might fall off him though," Piers said with a grin.

"Nonsense! You were a damned good rider as a boy." He cleared his throat and smiled awkwardly, understandable really when one remembered that his face wasn't called upon to do it very often. "Blake gave me hell over that sword cut in your arm."

"How did he know?"

"I naturally assumed that you'd told him."

"No. But I might have rambled on when I was under the anaesthetic."

"What, with all those tubes down your throat?"

"Perhaps he asked me outright and I nodded."

"That sounds like him," the Colonel observed sourly. "He's been a friend of mine for years but I sometimes think he's too fond of knowing everything that goes on here."

"Have you heard how the police are getting on with their enquiries?"

"No. Not a word. And I don't expect we shall." And with that he turned the horse and rode out of the yard.

Piers gave no more thought to the conversation until the following morning when he was crossing the yard and saw Nimrod tethered to a ring in a wall while David mucked out his box. The horse whinnied, and when he went closer, nudged his pockets for sugar.

"Just don't shove me in the chest, that's all," Piers told him.

David, who had been carefully told that Piers could ride his charge, was only too pleased to help him saddle up the horse. On cold frosty mornings he preferred sitting in the kitchen with his aunt drinking coffee and reading comics to leading Nimrod around country lanes for exercise. The animal was of an age – almost seventeen – when if not gently exercised he became stiff and prone to lameness.

There was a mounting block so Piers used it, Nimrod standing quite still while girths were tightened and stirrups adjusted. It only took a quiet, "Walk on," from his rider to set him off out of the yard.

After twenty yards or so Piers realized that he had done the wrong thing; every stride of the horse seeming to vibrate right to the middle of his chest. Then, and possibly unconsciously, he ceased to sit like a sack of potatoes, his body remembering what it should be doing. Sitting up straight, his weight suddenly supported by his spine and down through his knees to his feet, pain ceased to be a major problem.

They progressed sedately down the oak tree-lined main drive, the horse on a long rein, ears pricked, his rider noticing all at once that it was a fine morning, frost glittering where sun beams shone through trunks and branches. Piers took a deep careful breath and shortened the reins slightly. Nimrod responding by picking his hooves up a little higher.

"The odd thing is . . ." Piers said aloud, one large chestnut ear swivelling to listen ". . . that I was never allowed to ride you in the past. You could only be controlled by your master. That was all of a year ago."

He reined in when they came to the main road, Piers having a feeling that his mount would have stopped anyway and looked right and left of his own accord. They turned right, towards the village. When they came to a wide grass verge Nimrod indicated that here they usually trotted but Piers made it clear that any trotting would be at his own behest.

"No," he said suddenly. "First of all we'll see exactly where that car emerged."

Nimrod wasn't too sure about this change of routine but allowed himself to be neck-reined around and set off in the opposite direction. They went right past the main entrance, along the road on the opposite verge for half a mile or so, branched left down a lane and then came to the almost forgotten track that had once been a busy turnpike road. It still had a reasonably good surface in the centre but the edges were churned up by the hooves of horses and cattle. And this, Nimrod made perfectly plain, was where he was permitted a jolly little gallop.

Piers simply could not hold him and did not try. All he could endeavour to do was to stay in the saddle. By the time the horse slowed and dropped back to a walk, his rider was past the swearing stage and hanging on grimly to his mane.

"You old ginger bastard," said Piers through clenched teeth. He reined the horse to a complete standstill and tried to stop shaking and get his breath back.

From where he was he could see the twin chimneys of the lodge sticking above the trees. Anyone wanting to keep watch on the place would have to go a lot closer, at least as far as the copse where he had seen the car. He nudged Nimrod forward.

"If you so much as sneeze I'll take you to the knacker's yard on the way back," he threatened.

The tyre tracks in the copse could still be seen, deep in one muddy patch where the wheels had spun. There were several sets of tracks, all, by the look of it, made by the same vehicle. The copse was the only place where any tracks could be clearly discerned; police vehicles had churned this stretch of the old road into a morass, now frozen and just starting to thaw as the sun rose higher.

"I'll go and talk to Sylvia Webb," Piers told his mount.

Naturally, the horse attracted attention. He was quiet in traffic so the Colonel quite often rode him through the village, often stopping at the Post Office and bank and tying his mode of transport to a handy lamp post, woe unto anyone who fed him sugar. Now, seeing the animal with a different rider, the citizens of Ashleigh Coombe gawped and nudged one another, attention that Piers could have well done without.

"Excuse me," he said politely to the police constable on duty by a school crossing. "Can you tell me where Sylvia Webb lives?"

PC Peter Anderson knew perfectly well who was addressing him. He had not been in the district long but had heard all about the ne'er-do-well son of the local landowner who had recently got himself shot. Up until that very second of shading his eyes against the bright sunlight and looking up at the man he had nursed the conviction that ne'er-do-wells deserved what was coming to them. What he saw destroyed utterly his preconceived idea of a wealthy yob with a sneer to the mouth and a choice of several fast cars. Here was a very pale invalid trying to get fit by riding his father's horse. He had earnest blue eyes and was asking after the local and highly respected lady artist.

"You know where the Cross is at the other end of the village?" Anderson said.

"Yes."

"You go straight ahead for about five hundred yards and take the first turning left. You'll come to several cottages. It's the one with the cats."

Piers thanked him and nudged on Nimrod. Like most of the Ashleys he was not a cat lover and had visions of calling on a latter-day witch, a premonition strengthened when he approached the cottage. It stood on its own, the last of three, and was separated from its nearest neighbour by a ten-foot high copper beech hedge. The cats were real and otherwise; a large fat tabby sunning itself on a mossy wall, a Siamese squinting at him from the lower branch of a lilac tree and

68

several others painted on the walls of the cottage. These were nothing out of Disney; white cats with black tails, striped cats smiling, spotted cats chasing butterflies. Surreal cats, all with a strange malevolence.

The drive and gateway were wide, a six-bar gate in fact, and it had one of those catches you could open while on horseback. She probably had it put in specially, he thought wildly, after she looked in her crystal ball and saw that I was coming to see her. She's spitting mad with me for being partly responsible for her getting a bad fright and almost falling off her bike. I'll be the only toad in the world that answers to the name of Piers Ashley.

It was rather disappointing then to behold a Citroen 2CV parked to the rear of the cottage and a very ordinary wheelbarrow on the lawn filled with prunings. When Piers had opened the gate and ridden in Nimrod was not at all happy about the wheelbarrow, stopping dead and regarding it with the deepest suspicion.

"Put him in the garage," said a woman's voice suddenly, making both horse and rider start. "It's a stable anyway so he won't mind."

She emerged from an overgrown mock-orange bush shedding twigs and clutching a pair of secateurs. Piers supposed she might be in her middle thirties but the gaze she held him with might have been that of a child, the eyes green and very large, like pools of clear water with the sun on them. Just then he noticed nothing else about her.

"Well, aren't you stopping?"

"If I dismount I might not be able to get on again."

"Is that what your ancestors said in the heat of battle?"

This stung Piers to say, "And if I don't care a monkey's about ancestors, wounded or otherwise?"

At this she laughed outright. "Spoken like a true Ashley. Most of them never cared a toss about anyone." She dropped the secateurs into the wheelbarrow. "I'll make some coffee."

"If I could dismount on that low wall . . ."

"Certainly. But don't you dare let him eat my winter jasmine. Here, I'll hold his head."

Nimrod was manoeuvred to the low wall that bordered the lawn and Piers carefully slid off, forced to turn his face away from her as he coped with the consequences of having all his weight momentarily on his chest.

"Good," Sylvia Webb said lightly. "I'll go and put the kettle on."

Nimrod was lured into the rather dark stable-cum-garage with several apples, long-stored and wrinkled but sugar sweet.

"He'll be all right," Sylvia said. "He'll be able to see us through the window." She glanced at Piers quickly. "Come in and sit down – before you fall down."

The kitchen was at one end of a huge modern extension, invisible from the road. The rest was taken up by an artist's studio; a glorious conglomeration of easels, paints, blocks of stone and bags of plaster of Paris. Several blank canvases leaned against a table upon which were eight small bronze figures, mostly of nudes. Piers sank on to a couch that was along one wall, first removing a length of black velvet that was draped across it.

"Don't move," Sylvia said softly, picking up sketch pad and charcoal. "No, your lips were slightly parted. As you were, please." She made swift movements with the charcoal for a couple of minutes and then, the kettle whistling in the kitchen, thrust the sketch pad into his hands and left him. Almost immediately she put her head around the door to say, "Have a look round when you feel better. It's not one of those don't touch places."

"You and who else?" Piers asked when she returned with the coffee.

"Well done!" she cried. "A man of perception. I've had people in here who thought I did all of this. It's just me and a few friends. We call ourselves the Ashleigh Coombe Art Club. A bit snobbish, I suppose."

"The bronzes are yours."

"What makes you so sure of that?"

Piers looked again at the sketch of himself. It was a very good likeness, the face in greater detail than the rest of him. It was a study of exhaustion. He said, "There are the same kind of lines in both. Depth of expression I suppose is the nearest I can get to it."

Sylvia smiled. "Have you had any training in art?"

70

"No. And there's another thing about them. They're down to earth. Frank. The male figures have had a lot of trouble taken with the genitals. But unlike the sketch the faces could be anyone."

"From life," she said with a broader smile. "His face *was* very nondescript. Here, drink this while it's hot. Hungry?"

"I can never lie about that kind of thing."

"No," she said thoughtfully. "You have very expressive features. Hot buttered toast?"

"Have the police caught him yet?" she asked when he was eating.

"Not so far as I know. The investigations all seem to have come to a dead end."

"Even though I took the number of the car!"

"It was Colin Morgan's car – he'd reported it stolen that morning."

"So I heard. Do you believe him?"

Covertly, Piers had been watching her as she had made the toast. When one was not looking into those marvellous eyes she could almost be described as ordinary. Her fair hair was fine, shoulder-length, and kept off her face by a dark blue bandeau. The face itself was strong and not particularly feminine, the mouth and chin very determined.

"No, I don't think I believe him," Piers said. "I knew him when we were both a lot younger and he wasn't famous for telling the truth then. That's why I came to see you – to ask if you'd seen who was driving the car."

"The police asked me that – a dreadful designer cop wearing *Concours d'Élégance* aftershave. I told him no, it all happened too quickly."

"*What* aftershave?"

"God knows. But like those things you hang in cars to get rid of the smell of dogs and curry farts. There!" Sylvia exclaimed. "You look really super when you laugh."

He couldn't remember the last time he had laughed.

Sylvia said, "I hope you're not playing cops and robbers and trying to find who shot you."

He nodded slowly.

"I'm a firm believer in letting the police deal with that kind of thing."

71

"It'll give me something to do."

"It's your life," she said dismissively. Her expression softened. "You wouldn't like to model for us in between your investigations I suppose?"

Piers had never been slow-witted. "In the nude, you mean?"

It was her turn to nod.

"I don't *think* so."

"Please don't get the wrong idea. We really are serious about our art and drawing sessions. The standard's very high. There's an annual exhibition in Chichester and most of the work is sold."

"So I'd be on half the living room walls in West Sussex."

"No one would know who it was, silly boy. You make the features sort of indistinct."

"I'm not the sort of bloke who takes his clothes off in company, that's all."

"Heaven preserve us! You undress behind that screen in the corner and come out wearing the bath robe that's hanging there. Then, when everyone has decided what kind of pose is required, you remove the robe. If you're really coy you can insist on rear views only. And I always have a small electric fire on in the winter near the model – no one can draw the shivers."

"Look, I'm a real mess. My chest looks like a relief map of Mars."

"The rest's all right though," she declared stoutly.

He laughed again. It was only later that he was to ponder on the enthusiasm with which this had been uttered.

"I just thought a little pocket money might come in handy until you get a job," she said with a sigh.

"Money?"

"Of course. You don't imagine we old fogies expect the youth of Ashleigh Coombe to waste their evenings for nothing? They get ten pounds a sitting. And a bite of supper afterwards with a glass of wine."

"I'll think about it," Piers promised.

"Let me know by Tuesday if you're interested. We have life drawing once a fortnight on a Thursday."

"Haven't you anyone for the next session then?" he asked, deliberately in innocent fashion.

"Only someone whom the members are fed up with drawing."

"About that car . . ." Piers said pensively. "I don't suppose you noticed how many people were in it."

"Only the driver, I *think*. But you can't really tell in a bad light with modern cars – they all have these head rest things."

"And you saw no one else in the area?"

"Only William Turner. I had to push my bike home because the chain came off when it fell over. I caught up with him just as he reached his turning."

"Are you sure it was William?"

"Of course. We spoke. He helps me with some of the heavy work in the garden."

"Did you mention what had happened to you?"

"No. To be honest I felt a bit of a fool, with my tights laddered and oil all over my hands. And of course I didn't attach any importance to the car at the time."

"That's strange. I spoke to William and he didn't mention that he'd seen you."

"I'm not surprised. Poor William had a slight stroke just over a year ago, and although he's recovered his memory is a little dodgy sometimes. I have to leave him notes as to what I'd like him to do in the garden. He forgets otherwise."

"Thanks for the toast," Piers said.

"Come again. Even if you don't want to model for us."

He remounted Nimrod by the simple expedient of standing on the dustbin. Their return home was faster than he would have wished, a spanking trot, but he solved the problem by standing in the stirrups the whole way.

Chapter Seven

"Colin Morgan's car's been found," Thea said.

"Where?" Piers asked.

"In London. It was burnt out – weeks ago, according to Inspector Leadbetter."

"Well done the Met," Piers said sarcastically.

"No, apparently it was in a derelict garage and the car was found when contractors turned up to clear the site. The inspector thinks that strengthens the case for whoever shot you being a London gangster with a grudge."

"When did he contact you with this information?"

"Just now. He spoke to Mummy."

It was the afternoon of the day he had been to see Sylvia Webb, a Saturday, and Thea had only just got home, having had to spend the morning in her office.

"And where does Lee Haasden live?" Piers asked.

"Hyde Park Gardens."

"Just off the Bayswater Road?"

"Yes. Piers, I hope you aren't going to go and see him."

"I can't at the moment. He's still abroad."

"Who told you that?"

"Rolt."

"Inspector Leadbetter didn't say anything about Lee."

"I don't suppose he's following that line of enquiry."

"Then why does Commander Rolt know? This is terribly confusing."

"Rolt's from London," Ashley said, wishing she would stop asking questions. There was one way he could divert her thinking. He said, "Oh, by the way, I've got a little job."

"Great! Doing what?"

"Posing in the buff for an art club."

"What!" Thea shrieked.

"You heard," he said, grinning.

"Where?"

"Here – in the village."

"Oh, you mean Sylvia Webb's club. That's all right."

"So I have your permission then?"

"I didn't mean it like that. Sylvia's quite famous. Daddy wants her to do a bronze for the park."

"Me, eh? No fig leaves."

She grabbed his arm. "That would be *super*. Can't you see his face at the unveiling? No, seriously for a moment – I came to ask you to dinner tonight."

"At the house?"

"Yes. Wear all your frillies, the Lord Lieutenant and his wife are coming."

"Thea, how the hell have you engineered this?"

"I haven't. Mummy made it perfectly plain that you are invited. But she wanted to make sure you're well enough. Are you?"

"If I can stay on Nimrod, I can wear a bow tie."

"You didn't go riding!"

"How else do you think I went to the village?"

Thea threw up her hands in despair.

Fortunately the gun harness was of the kind with no strap across the chest. Otherwise Piers would have had to put the weapon in a pocket, something that he hated doing as it smacked of the amateur and always risked a dangerous delay. For there was no doubt in his mind that it was not just his company that was desired by the hostess. She was not only hazarding a little social awkwardness in inviting him but had almost certainly somehow overcome enormous resistance from her husband. Not worth the candle in ordinary circumstances and with such illustrious guests.

So he presented himself at the approved time, snowy-white ruffles on his evening shirt unmarred, and gravely accepted a glass of dry sherry from his father. The introductions were made. As it was, neither the Lord Lieutenant nor his wife appeared to be aware of any skeletons in the Ashley cupboard, or, if they were, had chosen to forget for the evening. Also present were Hereward and Veronica Brimley, the son of the local MP and his wife, and Justina Causeley, the novelist. (It must not be thought that Elizabeth Ashley had included her son amongst the company with match-making in mind with regards to Miss Causeley, the lady being in her seventies and slightly batty.)

"You look so *nice*," Elizabeth said when Piers found her in the dining room making last minute checks on the table's glittering silverware and glass. Madge had been brought in for the evening to cook and Tom had put on his butler's uniform to take people's coats and a daughter of one of the cleaning ladies had come to wait at table, but Elizabeth always satisfied herself tht everything was perfect.

Such was the tone of tragedy in her voice that Piers almost told her the truth about himself there and then. But no, there were more important things at stake than his reputation.

"Have you had another letter?" he asked quietly.

"Yes."

"When?"

"This morning."

"I hope you kept it this time."

She withdrew a folded sheet of paper from the pocket of her long black evening skirt.

"It's a demand for money," he said, having quickly scanned the crude lettering that intimated that the next dinner party would be a wake.

"I didn't tell you the truth, Piers."

"So there have been demands for money before?"

"Right from the beginning," she whispered.

"And you paid?"

"Yes, I sold the jewellery my mother left me."

There wasn't time now to ask all the questions. "Who else knew you were entertaining tonight?"

"I might have mentioned it to any number of people. And of course . . ."

"Quite," Piers said. "The florist, the grocer, the milkman . . . They must all be aware when you're having people here. It says here 'the usual place'. Where's that?"

"A litter bin in Arundel, along by the river."

"But they can't expect you to pay up *tonight*."

"No, not at all. I – I just wanted you to be nearby. I feel safer."

"We'll talk about this early tomorrow," Piers said, squeezing her shoulder. "You can give me the rest of the details. But tonight . . ."

"Yes?"

"Don't worry."

"And I lied to you about something else. I didn't get a letter saying that honour was satisfied. I just wanted you to get better and not have to worry about anything. Piers, I've been an awful fool."

"The important thing is that I know now."

"And I must have been responsible for your being shot. I ran out of money so I ignored a letter." Tears welled in her eyes. "I'm so terribly sorry."

He carefully removed a rose from an arrangement on the table and tucked it behind the diamond brooch pinned on her blouse. "You'll ruin all that blue stuff on your eyes. Fret not, your son is armed to the teeth and enjoys slaying litter bins."

"Are you planning on shooting whoever it is?" his mother asked in all seriousness.

"No," he answered evenly.

"Surely – "

"No," Piers said again, and then clicked his tongue disapprovingly. "What, when your own daughter has a crush on a policeman?"

"Not Leadbetter!"

"No, Rolt."

"Is he the man who put you in prison?"

"Yes, I suppose you could say he was."

When Elizabeth recalled their conversation much later that night and when dinner had been a success, the conversation scintillating and Mycroft hadn't fallen asleep before the guests had departed, she felt very ashamed. At that moment she had recognised that there could be a very fine line indeed between right and wrong. And Piers, of all people, had kept her firmly on the side of right.

Piers was pretty sure that no attack would be made on the

family that evening but took no chances. He checked that all the curtains were tightly closed and then roused the dogs from in front of the Aga in the kitchen and sent them into the garden with cries of "Rabbits!" Unused to being permitted to run riot after dark like this they behaved in fairly idiotic fashion, as only dogs can, raced around barking, stampeded a herd of bullocks in a neighbouring field and at the same time quartered every inch of the grounds. Piers rested content, convinced as he wiped muddy paws that anyone lurking nearby would have been sent packing. To be absolutely sure, he locked all the outside doors.

To his relief no one asked him what he did for a career or living. This might have been because everyone knew he had been shot and the questions were merely discreet enquiries about his recovery. As the evening progressed Veronica Brimley became a little less discreet – it was probably something to do with the Barolo they had been drinking – making Piers the subject of her rather stagy attentions.

"Do tell me," she said to him at one point. "Is it true that when something *ghastly* happens to one, all one's past life flashes through one's mind?"

Piers delicately speared a piece of Stilton from the cheese board. It was on the tip of his tongue to say "No, one was too busy saying 'Oh, shit'", but he refrained. Instead he said, "Not really – I was too furious with myself for being careless, and scared that he was going to come in and finish me off."

"Did you make your peace with God?" asked Justina Causeley.

"You do that when you've accepted that you're going to die," Piers told her.

She chuckled. "You're one of those who are dragged kicking and screaming into Hell."

"The Moslems have a good saying: 'Trust in God but tie your camel down first'."

"Oh, I *like* that!" Veronica cried. "And is it true that Crispin Blake saved your life?"

"Yes, I understand there had been a bad road accident with several casualties and his colleagues were all very busy. He heard what had happened and volunteered to come in. Otherwise I might have been shunted off to another hospital and . . . well, it might have been too late. How did he find out incidentally? Did someone here phone him?"

"I didn't," Mycroft said. "It wouldn't really have occurred to me."

"Nor did I," said Elizabeth. "The only person I rang was my brother."

"It might have been on the local radio," Thea suggested.

"Not until much later," Hereward said. "I was listening to the radio on my way home from a meeting. I have it on for the traffic news really. The announcer said something about reports just coming in about a shooting here."

"What time was that?" Piers asked him.

"Round about six-thirty, I should imagine."

The conversation then went off on another track, Mycroft smoothly steering it around to the reason he had requested the pleasure of the company of his guest of honour, to discuss the venue for a prestigious trade delegation luncheon that was being planned in order to draw commercial attention to redevelopment in a run-down part of Brighton. By the end of the evening he had got what he wanted.

"We must attract more visitors," he told his wife when the guests had gone home. "Put this place on the map. Otherwise we won't keep our heads above water."

"Are times hard?" asked Piers, who had overheard.

"Times are always hard for people who live in big houses," his father replied shortly.

Under the pretext of taking him a hot breakfast Elizabeth presented herself at her son's front door at eight the following morning and tapped lightly. She was admitted to find him shaved, fully dressed and making a brew of coffee. The breakfast was very much welcomed though and given first priority.

"Now," he said when he had finished eating, "the truth, the whole truth and nothing but the truth." He placed two chairs so that they faced one another.

"There's no need to make me feel like a criminal, surely," Elizabeth said, never at her best after a late night.

Piers seated himself. "That wasn't my intention at all. Subconsciously I might have been reminding you that this will all end up in a court of law."

She swallowed rising panic. "Thank you for coming last night. I'd forgotten how good you are at dinner parties."

"The pleasure was all mine," he assured her.

"Perhaps I ought to have asked you if you wanted to bring a young lady."

"There isn't anyone at the moment," he told her with a smile.

Elizabeth left it at that. He was hardly the sort who would have any trouble in finding girl friends.

Piers said, "How much money have you handed over to this blackmailer so far?"

She dropped her gaze. "I'm not sure why I said I'd sold my mother's jewellery. I suppose I was worried about the evening being a disaster. No, I *gave* him the jewellery, in dribs and drabs. Now, I know you're convinced that your mother is a terrible liar."

"Stress," he whispered in conspiratorial fashion. "And the fact that you gave him the jewellery is good news. It can be traced."

"I couldn't sell it. I'm so well known round here people would have gossiped."

"How much do you think it was worth?"

"About five thousand pounds."

Piers whistled. "And what is this person holding over you? What's the big secret?"

"It's nothing like that. They're just making threats. And carrying them out, by the look of it."

"That was added incentive to make you pay up. Most women would tell their husband what was going on. Why didn't you?"

"You know what your father's like. He would have hit the roof. Besides, he has enough to worry about right now." When she had said this Elizabeth met her son's gaze and immediately wished that she hadn't. She actually felt her skin crawl.

"It's about you and Crispin Blake, isn't it?" Piers said. "Someone's found out you had an affair."

She nodded slowly, twice, feeling the ice blue eyes searching her very soul.

"The affair's been going on until quite recently."

"Piers . . ."

"I watched you at the hospital when he was there."

"How can you understand how – "

"You feel?" he interrupted. "Easily. All of my lady friends so far have been older than me. When it comes to . . ."

"Passion?" she suggested when he stopped speaking. "That's the polite word for it."

"Thank you. When it comes to that . . ." Unusually for him, again he floundered.

"The older ones leave the youngsters standing?"

"Precisely."

His tact, she realized afterwards, had been staggering.

"So who else knows?" Piers asked.

"I've no idea. I simply can't begin to guess."

"How about his wife?"

"Naomi? She's so vague she hardly knows what day of the week it is. But there's no malice in the woman. And what would she want with my jewellery?"

"Did the blackmailer ask for it specifically?"

"No, but he said it would *do*."

Piers refilled her coffee cup. "We're talking about someone very close to the family. Somebody who knew you'd been left the jewellery, who knows when you entertain, and about you and Blake. Have you said anything to him about it, by the way?"

"About being blackmailed? Heavens, no!"

"Why not?"

"What would it achieve? What could he do?"

Piers reserved judgement on both those points. "Do you think Dad would divorce you if the truth came out?"

Elizabeth thought about it carefully for a moment or so. "Yes, I think he would. My behaviour wouldn't have come up to the Ashley norm." Her voice was remarkably free from bitterness. "So it's just you and me, Piers. We have to sort it out ourselves."

"What are the arrangements for handing over the money?"

"The same as when I gave him the jewellery, I suppose. There's a park by the river in Arundel – quite close to the Town Bridge. I have to leave the package in the third litter bin along from the entrance."

"When?"

"On the first Monday morning after I receive the demand between the hours of nine and ten."

"Okay, do it. I'll keep watch for whoever collects."

"But I can't get hold of five hundred pounds just like that! Monday's tomorrow."

"Don't use real money. Cut up some paper and put it in an envelope so it looks like notes. I'll see to that, if you like."

"But he'll immediately know we've set a trap for him."

"No. Think. He won't stand and count it out there and then. As soon as I see someone take the package from the bin, I'll follow them."

"They might see you."

"Not even *you* will see me," he asserted.

Elizabeth was sceptical about this but discovered that she was feeling very calm. "Are you coming to church?"

"No valid excuse leaps to mind," he said ruefully.

"I shouldn't think so either."

"Do you think Dad would lend me his car tomorrow?"

"We can go in my car."

"No, we mustn't be seen arriving together. Besides, I'll want to get there quite a while before you."

"I'm sure you shouldn't drive."

"I'm sure too. But a Jag with power-assisted steering should be all right."

"Ask him. I think he might agree if you tackle him directly. What reason will you give?"

"I'll just tell him I want to go and take a walk in Arundel Great Park."

Mycroft agreed readily, mainly, it must be said, because he recognised that the sooner his son was able to drive, the sooner he might leave. He felt rather guilty about this for he was forced to admit that he had nothing to complain about. None of his worst fears had materialised. No dubious people had come to call – one could hardly include a pleasant and forthright senior policeman in this category – neither did it appear that Piers was planning any further breaches of the law from the safety of home. He wasn't worried that his car would be driven recklessly or suffer damage for, unlike Giles, his eldest son hadn't gone through a "speed crazy" stage. So he handed over a spare set of keys with a brief smile and merely urged caution. But by Monday afternoon, when Piers had still not returned, he began to get very worried.

As soon as he had eaten breakfast on that morning, Piers left. To his surprise he felt nervous. He analysed this carefully as apprehension was not something that happened to him very often. After a few moment's reflection he decided to treat the morning's work as a rehearsal for his return to F.9 – it would be dangerous to become too emotionally affected just because his closest family was involved. Dangerous, that is, if he was tempted to take the law into his own hands.

He had briefed Elizabeth carefully. She would do exactly as she had done before; feed the ducks and then place the bread wrapper with the envelope in the litter bin. Then she would leave the park, do a little shopping, have coffee in the café where she normally did, and then go home. He had impressed on her that under no circumstances was she to try to spot him in the park.

The car was no problem at all as long as he remembered to corner slowly. In fact he soon forgot about his handling of the vehicle and concentrated on strategy instead. There were a pair of good binoculars in the car and he intended to use them. When he reached Arundel he parked the car well away from the river, leaving it in a car park near the castle entrance. This was important as the vehicle had personalised number plates.

The park, one of several in this most attractive town, was bounded by the River Arun to the south, by the castle grounds to the north and by the main road to the coast in a westerly direction. Upstream, it petered out in watermeadows but one could still carry on walking along the tow path, the river being a navigable waterway for several miles.

Piers made his way to the park, walking steeply downhill through a series of footpaths between the houses and shops. He did not enter the park by the main entrance – near the Town Bridge – but walked for fifty yards along a road that led to the boating lake. It was a simple matter to take a short cut around tennis courts and a bowling green, climb over a low

83

wall and drop, for the ground was far lower on the other side of it, amongst a group of tall ilex trees. These evergreen Holm oaks were hundreds of years old with massive crowns. One of them was to be his observation point.

Climbing into the tree of his choice produced several nasty moments. He was suitably dressed, dark old clothes and training shoes, but present circumstances forbad that he launch himself into it with the same verve as he had at army assault courses during training and over which a high standard was a requirement for final acceptance into F.9.

At last, at some thirty feet above the ground, he wedged himself into a reasonably secure position and waited until the tearing pain in his chest had abated. It did eventually lessen, a fact that he found reassuring. When he felt better he wriggled up the broad branch upon which he had been sitting, stood up on it and, leaning on the branch above, carefully parted the foliage.

"Perfect," he whispered.

As he had thought, the park was very narrow at this point, his vantage place only a matter of twenty yards from the river bank. He had a clear view of the entrance, a picnic area with rustic tables and chairs and several boats moored to stanchions. And, of course, a row of five litter bins.

Piers broke off a few small bunches of leaves in order to see more clearly and fixed a couple of them to the binoculars for camouflage. Then, using them, he slowly and painstakingly examined the whole area. He could see nothing suspicious.

The minutes ticked by. A jackdaw investigated the contents of one of the litter bins but was frightened away by a dog being taken for a walk by a woman and young child. Another woman pushing a pram paused to watch the ducks and moorhens on the river. Traffic thundered and roared over the bridge. Half an hour went by.

At ten past nine Elizabeth came into view. Piers willed her to act naturally. Other than looking at her watch a trifle nervously as she entered the park he could not fault her subsequent behaviour as she crumbled bread for the waiting birds, a couple of bold mallard drakes actually leaving the water to yank on the hem of her skirt when they felt they were being overlooked. When the bread had all gone Elizabeth screwed up the wrapper and walked over to the third litter bin. As she reached it she took the envelope with the 'money' from her coat pocket and dropped both in together. Then she left, not turning her head to glance behind her.

Piers waited for over three hours but nothing happened.

Finally, frozen to the marrow, he came down from his perch. It seemed inconceivable that anyone would leave it this long as there was every chance that the litter bin would be emptied by a council worker. It also seemed inconceivable that an interested party had seen him arrive. No houses overlooked the area and no curtains in the boats had so much as twitched. But he made sure of this, visiting each one in turn. All were unattended, the cabin doors securely pad-locked. There was no one in the other Holm oaks either.

It was time to go and talk to Colin Morgan.

Chapter Eight

The estate timber yard was situated to the north of Ashleigh Hall and had its own approach road. In the wake of the gale every last foot of space was taken up with the trunks of the mature trees that had been blown over that night. If the high winds had been a local freak of nature Mycroft Ashley would have had a very valuable harvest on his hands but the gale had raged across the whole of the south of England. Oak and beech were being given away by some land-owners as firewood. The only saving factor was that two very fine walnut trees, up-rooted in the gardens, had gone to furniture craftsmen in Scotland, the scarcity of this wood resulting in a handsome cheque.

The main product of the estate was softwood for the building industry, mostly fast-growing pines and spruces. There were also acreages of ash and larch trees used for fencing materials. All this was properly managed and there was a constant replanting programme. And, fortunately, very little of this bread-and-butter timber had been brought down in the gale, the trees, unlike the Hall which was on a hill-top, growing in a sheltered part of the Sussex Weald.

Piers parked his father's car by the office next to Charles Morgan's Ford. The estate manager looked out of the office window as he approached and Piers did not imagine the frown. But if Morgan intended to be unpleasant he was disappointed for Piers changed track, having spotted the person he had come to see.

Colin Morgan glanced up from re-fuelling a chain saw and then gave every indication of concentrating on what he was doing. He was a thin, pale man who looked a lot younger than his twenty-six years, appearing to be no more than a youth. He had wispy sandy-coloured hair and very bad skin.

"I hope he knows you've got his motor," Colin said with a smirk. At one time he and Piers had been good friends. A long time ago.

"Too right," Piers said. "I haven't borrowed anything of his without asking since he leathered me that time for turning his favourite fishing rod into a long-bow."

"You couldn't sit down for two days," Colin said with a guffaw.

"But I did though – when he was there. You do, don't you?"

Morgan screwed the cap back on the fuel can. "I thought someone put a bullet in you."

"That's what I want to talk to you about."

"Because someone pinched my car to do the job?"

"Are you sure it was stolen that morning?"

"Of course. Why shouldn't I be sure?"

"Someone in a red car had been hanging around the lodge before that."

"There are thousands of red cars."

"It's a bit of a coincidence though, isn't it?"

"Look, I'm the one who's dipped out," Morgan said angrily. "The bastard made off with it and turned it into a bonfire in London. How much do you think I'll get from the insurance company for a ten-year-old car?"

"I'm surprised you had it insured."

Morgan stared at him in amazement. "You stand there having just been let out of the slammer and preach to *me*?"

Piers knew very well what he was doing. "Yes, but there's a difference between making a mistake and paying for it, and living your whole life in dodgy fashion and hardly ever being found out."

"And what exactly do you mean by that?" Morgan said through his teeth.

"You know very well what I mean. Not bothering with car insurance. A little bit of poaching now and then. Illegal snares. Having a job and still taking dole money. I remember you bragging to me about *that*."

"So, what of it, Mr Holier-than-thou?"

"If someone offered a fiver for the last Golden Eagle in Scotland, you'd go and shoot it."

"Now look here – "

"If someone offered you money to put a bullet in me, you wouldn't think twice."

Morgan went white. "You're out of your skull. The police questioned me for hours."

"I know you better than the police. You'd always do anything for money. What were you doing that night?"

"I went to the pictures with my girlfriend."

"At what time?"

"Just before seven – we went for a drink first."

"I was shot round about five-thirty."

"So I was getting ready then – and having my tea. Why don't you ask my parents? I still live at home."

"And what did you use for transport?"

Morgan jerked his head in the direction of his father's Ford. "That."

"So your alibi rests on the word of your girlfriend and your parents?"

"What of it? Their word's good enough, isn't it?"

"Would they say the same in court under oath?"

"Get out of here!" Morgan yelled shrilly. "Leave me alone!" His voice dropped to a whisper. "Say what you like, I'll never go inside. Never have to shit in a bucket and have the stink of it in my nostrils all night."

He was perfectly correct.

In the pale afternoon sunlight the cats on the walls of Sylvia Webb's cottage looked even more surreal, as though at any moment they would come to life – or he would awake from a dream – and they would run about the garden and rub themselves against his legs. One real cat did greet him as he opened the car door and got out, one he hadn't seen before, a gigantic ginger tom. It stood waiting to be let in as he rang the doorbell.

"Marmaduke, where the hell have you been?" Sylvia said severely when she opened the door, noticing the cat first.

"Been up to London to see the Queen," Piers said.

"I haven't clapped eyes on him in two days," Sylvia explained. "Do come in. For some reason I thought you were the milkman."

"Does he have a Jag too?"

She laughed. "Don't mind me. When I'm working I'm not on this planet. Tea? Or are you one of those awful people who drink coffee in the afternoons?"

"Tea, please. But I don't want to stop you working."

"It does me good to stop sometimes. Then I remember to eat and things like that." She removed a paint-smeared overall and tossed it into a corner. "Well, what have you been doing with yourself since we met?"

"Fulfilling my responsibilities as son but not heir."

"Oh, being polite to the Lord Lieutenant, you mean. What a bore for you."

"Sylvia, does *everything* the Ashleys do get bandied around the village?"

She turned her bright gaze on him. "God knows. Only the Ashleys can answer that. But I suppose when you entertain what the folk around here call 'nobs', then the answer must be yes. Blame those who work below stairs, as it used to be referred to. There are at least six cleaning ladies, aren't there?"

"Point taken," he said, following her into the kitchen.

"I do sympathise though. I'd hate everyone to know my business."

"What do you know about Colin Morgan?"

The hand holding the tea-caddy paused for a moment in mid-air. "So you're still doing a spot of private sleuthing."

"I still think he's lying."

"He's the sort who might be worth putting the frighteners on."

"That's what I've been doing this afternoon."

"Be careful of his father."

"Why?"

"It's not something I can put into words. You just get a gut-feeling about some people. I've often wondered if he has your father's interests as a priority."

"Gossip?" Piers asked gently.

"Not really. I don't call William a gossip. It was he who said something about lorries late at night loaded with Christmas trees and a lot of pheasants in the butcher's that the proprietor refused to give the origin of. There's probably nothing in it at all and everything's perfectly above board." She handed him a loaded tray. "Take that into the living room, please."

There was a log fire burning in the hearth, proof that Sylvia had not spent all afternoon in her studio. Piers placed the tray on a low table and looked about the room. It was very warm, the soft and yet vivid hues from the silk shades on the lamps making small oases of colour that drew him closer in a way that was almost magical. On the floor were scattered huge cushions to match; jade green, burnt orange, cobalt blue. Like the colours on an artist's palette.

When Sylvia came in, he said, "You were expecting me, weren't you?"

She grinned in boyish fashion. "Well, you said you'd let me know about being a model for the drawing class before Tuesday and as I know you're a man of your word . . . Milk and sugar?"

"Can I smell Earl Grey?"

"Yes."

"In that case neither, thank you."

"Well?"

"Oh – yes. I might do it once. Before I go back to London."

She had removed the bandeau from her hair so he could not see her face as she poured the tea. "And when will that be?"

"Soon."

"Going back to your old life?"

"Not in the way you think. I'll probably be here for most weekends. I'm going to do up the old lodge."

"Not in the way I think?" she repeated slowly. "What is that supposed to mean?"

"I've learned my lesson."

Sylvia shook her head impatiently. "My mother always said I had second sight. What you said just now was true. That isn't."

"I'm not saying any more," he told her quietly.

"Second sight," she whispered. "Piers Ashley, if you've done anything wrong in this life, may God strike me dead."

"Don't say another word," he begged.

"What's the matter with all of them? Are they blind?"

Their gaze met.

"Yes," Piers said. "But it's serving a very good purpose at the moment."

"Then I won't say another word. And have no fear, there are bigger secrets in my mind than your chosen career."

They talked: of art, music, the theatre. Then she took him into her studio to show him the painting she had been commissioned to do of a leading actress. When they returned to the living room, it was getting dark.

"Stay and have supper with me?" Sylvia asked,, drawing the curtains.

"I'm sure you're desperate to get back to work."

"No, not now. The light's gone. Besides, I always work better in the mornings."

"In that case . . ."

"Make yourself at home then while I have a quick shower. Then I'll get us something to eat."

While she was away Piers walked with light step to the car and locked the gun and its harness in the glove compartment.

They ate fillet steak and salad, and then relaxed in the soft lamplight, drinking coffee. Sylvia, who had changed into a long flowing robe, and who had been staring pensively into the glowing ashes of the fire now raised her head and looked at him. He was already watching her, smiling in a way she had seen men smile before.

"I don't allow myself to be seduced," he said.

Sylvia laughed softly. "We'll see about that."

He stood up. "No, I mean it. Women might boss me around and organise my life for me. They might decorate my flat and cook my meals, but they don't seduce me."

"Really?"

Piers pulled his sweater over his head. "No. In bed I'm king."

There was nothing she could say to this.

"Have you ever seen the giant carved into the chalk of a hill at Cerne Abbas in Dorset?" he asked in conversational tones as he removed his shoes and socks.

"No, but I've seen photographs of it. Why do you ask?"

"We were on holiday in the area when I was eight years old.

91

Looking at it answered nearly all the questions I had concerning the birds and the bees."

Piers removed the belt from his trousers, rolled it up and then pulled out his shirt and commenced to undo the buttons slowly. Halfway down them he glanced up and smiled.

The woman stirred restlessly, breathing a little faster now, a pendant she wore between her breasts flashing jerkily as it caught the light. She went so far as to draw the robe around herself slightly and that she had deliberately left loose. When the strong brown hands went to the fastener of his trousers the movement she made was involuntary. But she stopped herself in time. Not that he had not noticed and was right now coming to sweep away the robe and her pretences.

Not long afterwards she uttered a loud, glad cry.

The very last thing Piers was expecting was to find his parents waiting up for him. He paused when he saw a light still on in the private sitting room and as he did so Elizabeth came out.

"We've been so frantic with worry," she said. "When you didn't come home we thought . . ." She came closer. "I told your father. I simply can't keep this from him any longer."

He put an arm around her shoulders and they went into the room together.

"So who took the bait?" Mycroft said as the car keys were dropped into his waiting palm. His mood, Piers decided, could only be described as murderous.

"No one. I sat in a tree for three hours."

"You might have rung," his mother said. "I really thought something had happened to you or that you'd followed someone to the ends of the Earth."

"I'm sorry. I thought you might both be out and I didn't want to leave a message with anyone."

"So that's it then," Mycroft snarled. "We're completely at the mercy of this bastard unless we go to the police and thereby suffer a huge scandal."

"By no means," Piers said quietly.

"What are you suggesting then? That I send your mother to live abroad? She might prefer that, come to think of it."

"No, Mycroft, no," Elizabeth moaned.

Piers said, "I distinctly remember you telling me on several occasions in the past that in moments of crisis the Ashleys stick together."

"Yes, but – "

"And I'm *sure* you once said that Sir Richard's wife had an affair with a wealthy Scottish merchant by the name of Jameson."

"That was – "

"Hundreds of years ago? Of course it was. But what's changed? I'm merely saying that you're not the first Ashley who's not too exciting in bed."

Mycroft's face went a rather alarming shade of puce.

"I suggest," Piers continued, "that we tackle this in practical fashion. There is the distinct possibility that the fish wasn't hooked today because he knew we were on to him." He turned to Elizabeth. "Did you even hint to anyone that we were *both* going to Arundel this morning?"

"No, I spoke to no one about it."

"Not even in the most innocent fashion? Did you say anything to any of the cleaning ladies? About me, for example? About how I was well enough to drive?"

"No, Piers. But anyone might have seen you drive off in your father's car."

"I went early. Before any of the outside staff arrive. Not even Madge and David were here when I left."

"Perhaps someone was watching in the grounds," Elizabeth suggested.

"So are we hiring you to sort this out?" Mycroft said all at once. "That's your line of business isn't it? A sort of hit-man."

It was doubtful what Piers might have said to this had he had time to reply. As it was there came a thunderous knocking on the front door, the like of which probably hadn't assailed Ashley ears since feudal times.

"Who in Heaven's name is that?" Elizabeth cried.

"The police," Piers said, who had parted the curtains to look outside. "Good God, its Leadbetter and he's brought the Tactical Support Group with him."

Inspector Leadbetter, it seemed, was taking no chances.

Let in by the master of the house they made straight for Piers, who although he stood quite still and offered no resistance, was grabbed, slammed into a wall and made to stand facing it while he was searched for weapons.

"This is a very serious matter," Leadbetter said to Elizabeth when she protested. "Colin Morgan has been found dead, murdered. Your son was seen talking to him today and apparently threatening him."

"How was he killed?" Mycroft asked, after exclaiming in horror.

"Someone battered out his brains. With a stone, by the look of it."

"Piers has been wearing those clothes all day," Elizabeth declared. "I can't see any blood on them, can you?"

"I'll answer that when they've been to the forensic lab," Leadbetter said. He waved a hand impatiently. "Take him away."

"I'm not sure that Leadbetter was acting legally," Mycroft said slowly when he and his wife were on their own. "I thought that suspects have to be cautioned."

"I don't think he was arresting Piers," Elizabeth said.

"Then he had no right to remove him by force. I've a good mind to get on to that Rolt fella – he left me his phone number."

"What shall I do with this?" Elizabeth said, taking the Smith and Wesson from beneath her full-length skirt.

"Where the hell did you get *that*?" asked Mycroft, appalled.

"From Piers. While you were answering the door."

The Colonel snatched it. "I'll hide it. Throw it in the pond."

"Calm down, dear. The Inspector said that Morgan had been battered with a rock or something."

"Or this."

"Mycroft, you're simply not thinking clearly. Even I can see that it's loaded. Who would hit a man with a loaded revolver if they wanted to kill him? What's that badge on the leather bit?"

He found his reading glasses. "It's a coat of arms."

Elizabeth had a look. "The things the lions have in their paws – are they scrolls?"

Mycroft sat down suddenly. "No, tipstaves."

"I thought . . ."

"Yes, it's a police revolver. It belongs to the Metropolitan Police."

"He had it in hospital. He said his boss had given it to him."

Mycroft hurried off to the phone.

Chapter Nine

"I'm surprised you're not bleating for your solicitor," Leadbetter said.

Piers shifted on his chair. "I thought it would be a good idea to keep this cock-up of yours just between our two selves. And all your subordinates, of course."

It was very late – just after midnight – and he was functioning strictly on will-power. He had also got to the stage where he hoped that if he gave Leadbetter enough rope he might hang himself. There was quite a coil of it already, the Inspector having obviously let it be known that he had a "record" to the men transporting him to the police station in a van. The journey had not been pleasant. The treatment of suspects was something that particularly interested Commander Rolt and often F.9 operatives were unloaded "drunk and disorderly" in police areas where members of the public had made complaints. As he was already of a rank equivalent to sergeant and recommended for promotion, Piers rather felt he was beyond that stage.

He said, "As I've said several times, I went to see Morgan because I thought he might be involved with the business of someone gunning for me. I still think so. He was the sort who would do anything for a fast buck. I'm not making any secret of my suspicions. He denied having anything to do with it. But I know him of old. He was lying. I also think he was killed to keep him quiet."

"It was his father who saw you talking to him. He said Colin seemed afraid of you."

"Perhaps he merely looked guilty," Ashley retorted.

"There's a chance that Colin contacted someone after I'd gone and told them about my suspicions. It might be a good idea if you checked on his movements later that day."

"We are," Leadbetter said. "Have no fear about that. I'm also checking on yours. Where did you go after you left the timber yard?"

"I called in to see Sylvia Webb and stayed to supper. I've already told you this."

"Why did you go to see her?"

"To tell her I'd model for the art class."

"Into that sort of thing, are you?" the Inspector asked with a curl of the lip.

"No."

The door of the interview room opened and a constable entered with Piers's outer garments in a plastic bag. "Clean as a whistle, sir," he said.

"Try knocking next time," Leadbetter said grimly.

"Sorry, sir," said the man, colouring.

"I hope there's a proper written report in the pipeline and I don't just have to take the information on hearsay."

"On its way, sir."

"When?"

"Sometime tomorrow morning. Or rather, this morning, sir."

"Good," Leadbetter said. And then to Piers, "You can stay here until it arrives."

"You haven't a shred of evidence," he said, getting up to put on his clothes. It was very cold in the room, Leadbetter having turned off the radiator.

"I haven't said you could put that lot back on."

"What time was Morgan killed?" Piers said, ignoring this.

"Round about seven-thirty."

"Killed with several blows to the head?"

"That's right."

"Where was the body found?"

"Not far from his parents' home."

"So it looks as though he'd gone out to meet someone."

"That had occurred to me," Leadbetter observed sarcastically.

"Well, that person wasn't me. Has the murder weapon been found?"

"*I* will ask the questions," Leadbetter told him.

There was a knock at the door, a rather loud one.

"Come!" the Inspector shouted.

The same constable put his head in. "Phone call for you, sir. From the Chief Super."

"Stay with him for a minute," Leadbetter ordered.

When he had dressed Piers put his head on his arms on the table and tried to sleep. He must have succeeded for the next thing he was aware of was Leadbetter shaking him.

"You can go," he said.

"Go?"

"You heard me. Get out. It seems you have friends in high places."

Piers stood up. "Lend me the cost of a taxi fare? I didn't have time to bring any cash."

"This is a police station – not a charity shop," Leadbetter replied stonily.

"I can let you have it back later today."

"Get out," the Inspector said again.

By the door Piers paused. "Untouchable, eh?"

"So it would *appear*."

Piers followed the smell of chips frying and soon found himself in the canteen. In a corner were the half dozen members of the T.S.G. who had been in the area on an exercise and whom Leadbetter had "borrowed". To be fair it must be said that they were still trying to work out why. Piers approached the six, firmly telling himself that the intimidation he had suffered had been mainly of the verbal and heavy stare variety. That's if he discounted being tripped as he got out of the van. He knew precisely which one had tripped him.

"I swear we didn't touch him," one of the group assured Leadbetter when he had been summoned to the affray to behold two prone bodies. "Honest to God, sir," the man went on frantically. "We never so much as laid a hand on him. He came in here, flattened Jamie, and then just keeled over."

"Put him in a cell," Leadbetter ordered, having satisfied himself that both would awaken sooner or later. "Carefully.

Cover him with a blanket. Don't even breathe too hard on him."

"What's all this then, sir?" asked the sergeant in charge of them.

"Those who ask no questions get no lies," Leadbetter ground out.

David Rolt decided that it couldn't be allowed to go on. Too much was at stake. People's lives. As soon as he had replaced the receiver after speaking to Mycroft Ashley, the Commander came to a decision. Thus he made a phone call and, after a while, another to Leadbetter. Later that morning, but still far too early by Piers Ashley's reckoning, he made another. Three hours elapsed before the knock came at his door that he was waiting for.

"I understand you're still convalescing," Rolt said.

Piers kept his mouth shut. There was a dangerous glitter in Rolt's eyes.

"Not only beating up the T.S.G., but spending several hours with a lady well-known to enjoy the company of young men."

Rolt did not use the word "company", utilising a more basic anatomical noun instead.

The Commander went on, "I had an *in depth* conversation with Leadbetter. I thought that as he's now investigating a murder it was about time he was in possession of the full facts. And if you're curious, it was your father who got in touch with me because he was concerned that Leadbetter had acted in questionable fashion. In that I agree with him and it's just about the only thing that goes in your favour. Sit down."

Piers sat.

Rolt said, "I don't expect my people to lose their tempers – however provoked."

"Sorry, sir."

"Even when they're picked up by those they would normally regard as colleagues and who use unnecessary force."

"No, sir."

"Under no circumstances are you to carry on investigating this matter until I say you can break your cover and do so in an

99

official capacity. We daren't risk ruining the Dorney job because of it. The criminal world has long ears, Homage, and I don't want two year's work thrown away because you're messing around with a domestic case all on your own in the sticks. Is that understood?"

"Yes, sir."

Rolt took a deep breath. "Good."

Piers took a sealed envelope from his pocket. "That's what I've discovered so far."

The Commander hesitated, frowning, and then slit the envelope open and extracted the contents. There was utter silence while he read. Finally he said, "This will have to go to Leadbetter."

"There's every chance that the blackmailer will either bolt or carry out a few more threats if the local plods start crawling all over the place."

"Spoken like a true crook," Rolt said with the ghost of a smile. He leaned over and tapped a few keys on the computer terminal on his desk. "I want you to move back up to town. Keep right away from Sussex until I say you can return." He stared intently at the information displayed on the screen. "Lee Haasden flew into Heathrow from South Africa yesterday morning. So he can't have written any notes demanding money or have been in Arundel, can he?"

"No, that would have been someone like Colin Morgan. But Morgan wouldn't have thought up something like that on his own, he wasn't bright enough."

"Haasden isn't entirely without blemish. He was involved in a fracas at a club in the West End when a bouncer was thrown through a plate glass door. That is not to say that he did it. But he was implicated in the fight – he had grazed knuckles and someone had hit him hard enough for him still to be in the vicinity when the police arrived."

"And he does belong to a gun club."

Rolt gazed steadily at his subordinate. "Doctor Miller, the police surgeon, is on the premises and I've asked him to give you a check-up. I want to know when we can get on with this Dorney job. But meanwhile, and until I give you further orders, there's no reason why you shouldn't go and see Haasden in the capacity of being your sister's brother, if you follow me. Tell him your suspicions. Confront him in the rather boorish way some of the upper classes conduct their business. Let me know what his reactions are. And be *careful*."

When he was in the UK Lee Haasden jogged in Hyde Park every morning. It was very convenient for him as his flat was in the Lancaster Gate area and all he had to do was cross the Bayswater Road. He was a man who prided himself on his physical fitness and he ensured that he spent sufficient time in his native country during the British winter to retain a tan. Slightly vain he might be, but the thought of resorting to sunlamps appalled him. There was more to life than behaving like a slice of bread. In his view too many of the Brits resembled the dreadful substance they consumed with such gusto: limp, pallid and stodgy.

On this particular morning – a beautiful Spring-like one, willow tips greening, the tulips coming out in the park, all the daffodils in full flower – Haasden was infused with a feeling of well-being. All was good with him and the world was a wonderful place. Little normally upset his equilibrium, he was the sort who could jog with serenity through a Cairo slum or perform press-ups alongside a drunk prone in the gutter. So when another jogger fell into step just behind him along a straight stretch near Rotten Row he merely felt slightly irritated and speeded up a little. The other runner kept up. Haasden turned and received a bit of a shock.

"Don't I know you from somewhere?" he asked the stranger, stopping dead.

"She must have made some impression on you then," Piers said.

"My God, of course! Thea. You must be twins."

"No, as a matter of fact she's a bit older than me. I'm Piers Ashley by the way. It's why I want to talk to you – about a possible mix-up of identities."

Haasden glanced at his watch. "Look, I'm late already. Can we talk about this another time?"

"I'm not letting you out of my sight until I'm satisfied that you didn't take a shot at me thinking it was Thea."

Haasden stared at him. "Me? Take shots at people? Are you crazy?"

"We can either talk about this in adult fashion and you'll tell me where you were on February 15th or we can have a rather untidy brawl. And that wouldn't go too well for you, would it? Being as you've already been in trouble once before."

Haasden had already come to the conclusion that the brawl, if it came to that, would not be untidy in any sense of the word. He envisaged being laid out very neatly on the ground by this blond-haired Englishman. And, as far as Thea Ashley was concerned, his conscience was not its usual blithe self. But he was quite innocent of what she had accused him of.

"I *do* have an important engagement," Haasden pleaded. "But if you run back with me to my place, we can talk while I get ready."

"Okay," Piers said.

He never forgot that run. He was in pain before they had covered five hundred yards, Haasden having set a fast pace, his long legs striding effortlessly. Neither spoke. After a while Piers discovered that if he ran on the soft sand of the Row itself the jarring to his chest was not so severe, even though it was harder work. By the time they had turned left and were running in a northerly direction across the grass of the open park he felt that he was being slowly impaled with a white hot sword. Afterwards he was not sure how he had completed the run, vaguely aware that they had slowed, waiting for a gap in the traffic of the Bayswater Road. Haasden walked the rest of the way to his flat, to cool off.

"I can't give you very long," the South African said, running lightly up the short flight of steps to the front door of a Regency terraced house. "I've a lunch date too."

Piers discovered that arriving first at the door and taking hold of a handful of the front of Haasden's track-suit was no problem at all. Neither would have been rattling the man's head smartly against the shiny black surface. But he desisted, saying instead, "Whereas someone who almost *died* simply doesn't matter at all."

"Do you have to be so bloody aggressive?" the other said after nervously licking his lips.

"I'm very fond of my sister," Piers said, releasing him. "And if I thought that anyone took a gun . . ."

Haasden opened the door, his movements jerky and agitated. They entered and went up a wide staircase to the first floor. There, Haasden turned to the right and unlocked the door nearest to the top of the stairs.

"Come in," he invited without enthusiasm.

Recollecting all too well Doctor Miller's injunction that he must refrain for a while from all strenuous activity Piers followed Haasden into a light, bright living room. On the walls were large framed photographs of the South African veldt, studies of sunsets and early morning mist scenes with zebra drinking at a water hole.

"Take these yourself?" he asked.

"Yes, it's a hobby of mine," Hassden muttered.

"You don't have much of an accent."

"It doesn't do you much good to have an Afrikaner accent in this country." He had taken a Filofax from a briefcase and was flipping through it. "Did you say the 15th of February?"

"That's right."

"I was in Brighton for the day. A friend has a yacht in the Marina."

"What time did you leave?"

"Not until the Sunday morning."

"And in the evening – what did you do?"

"We dined out and then went to a recital at the Pavilion. Brahms."

"Brighton is only about an hour's drive from the scene of the shooting."

Haasden turned to look directly at him. "I'm fully aware of that. Your sister invited me home on several occasions. But I assure you I was not the person who shot you."

"You parted from my sister on very bad terms."

"That is true. But I'm not the sort of man to take revenge on people, least of all on a woman."

"You told Thea you belonged to a gun club."

"Yes, but at home. Not here. Everyone does at home. If you live on a farm you have to. But I don't shoot here. For the simple reason that . . ."

"Go on."

103

Haasden shrugged. "I don't want you to think me offensive, but over here gun clubs often draw the wrong sort of people. The very last people who should know how to use weapons."

"But how do you *know* that?"

"From friends. From my friend with the yacht in particular. He shoots. He has a small estate in Yorkshire."

"Perhaps you'd tell me his name."

"The Honourable George Smythe. His wife was with us during the weekend too – in case you think I'm peculiar."

"Oh, I know you're not like that," Piers said sweetly. "Thea told me *why* the pair of you split up. What kind of business are you in?"

"So many questions," Haasden murmured. "I've already told you that it couldn't possibly have been me who attacked you. Who knows? Perhaps you were the target after all."

"The police are working on that angle," Piers told him. "I'm just following up a few ideas of my own. I've no doubt the police will interview you sooner or later."

"But why should they?"

"Because the case is a complicated one. You've just told me that you were a visitor to the Hall. I understand that you were quite close to my sister for a while. So in view of the fact that we're also talking about another murder . . ." He broke off, smiling bleakly.

"But I've been out of the country," Haasden protested. "How could I possibly be involved?"

"You left the country pretty smartly after I'd been shot. Tell me . . ."

"Yes?"

"Is your name pronounced as in 'ass' or 'arse'?"

"As in 'hazard'," was the tight-lipped reply.

"What does Lee Haasden do for a living?" Piers asked.

Thea glanced up from pouring coffee. "I'm not sure. He was a bit cagey about it. He always had plenty of money though."

They were in Thea's office at the Kensington nanny agency. Piers had gone straight there after leaving Haasden's apartment.

"Didn't that bother you at all?"

"Not really. I suppose I thought he might be involved in something like sanctions busting in the arms trade. To be honest I didn't give it a lot of thought."

"But what gave you that idea?"

"Piers, I don't *know*," she replied, irritated. "I suppose when he mentioned the gun club and the fact that he didn't really want to tell me what he did I put two and two together. You don't always question people closely. It looks as though you don't trust them."

"But, arms?"

"Nothing illegal, silly. I wasn't even sure if we had any trade sanctions with South Africa. I was thinking of things along the lines of sporting rifles and so forth. Not munitions. Why do you want to know?"

"I've just been talking to him."

"How was he?" she enquired eagerly.

Piers took a mouthful of coffee, regarding her over the rim of his cup.

"You're a pig," Thea said with feeling.

"I didn't realize that you still liked him."

"So I'm interested in how he's keeping," she said in off-hand fashion.

"How many times did you take him home?"

"I resent this inquisition," she retorted.

"It's *important*."

"All right. On several occasions," she said defiantly. "There was a time when we were going to be married."

"Look, I want you to think carefully. Do you think he could know that Mother was left that jewellery?"

"Grandmother's jewellery?"

"Yes."

"It's possible, I suppose. Yes, I remember now. She was wearing a sapphire and diamond brooch one evening that had been Grandma's and I said how it suited the dress she had on. I'm sure Lee was there."

"And was he ever there when Crispin Blake was too?"

"Oh, yes. That's easy. Last Christmas. At the big party we have on Boxing Day."

"And you broke up with Haasden soon afterwards?"

Thea nodded slowly. "I can't imagine why you're asking me these questions."

"Mother's being blackmailed."

"Is that why she wanted you at home?" she gasped.

"Yes."

"But – "

"Someone has found out she had an affair with Blake."

This rendered Thea speechless for a moment. Then she said, "Well, I knew he meant something to her but imagined it was all in the past. Oh God, how awful for her."

"She's given whoever it is the jewellery."

"And she told you all this without your having to put pressure on her?"

"Of course. She wants me to sort it out for her. So does Dad."

"Mummy rang last night and said that Colin Morgan had been found dead. Is his death something to do with it?"

"Only if my being shot is connected too."

"And you suspect Lee?"

"It's just a line of enquiry. If you chucked him, and he had guessed about Mother and Blake and also knew she had the jewellery . . ."

"I still don't see what this has to do with your being shot."

"The blackmail notes made threats of other deaths following Grandmother's – as well as making the affair public knowledge. So it's fairly immaterial whether the blackmailer thought it was you or me in the lodge."

"What would you say if I told you that I thought I was being followed?"

"I'd treat the statement with great seriousness."

"I'm not sure, but they – "

"They?"

"Two men. I have a feeling there are two. They might even hang around all day in the street. If you come to the window, I'll show you what I mean."

Thea parted the vertical blind a little. "There. See that man leaning on the wall reading a paper? I'm convinced he followed me here from home this morning. Sometimes another man's with him."

"And they follow you home at night?"

"I *think* so. But everywhere's so crowded, of course."

Piers sat down again. "It's all right, I know them. The one reading the paper's called Tony."

This enraged her. "Part of your little criminal empire?"

"No. As a matter of fact they both work for Special Branch. I met Tony when he and I – "

"I'm sure you bloody well did!" Thea shouted. She rarely shouted like this. "Well, you can call them off. If you don't, I'll go down there and have a go at them with a knife or something. How dare you!"

"You're too upset to think straight," Piers told her. "They're there to protect you in case this person tries again. Besides, do you imagine I'm in a position to tell the police what to do?"

He had obtained permission from Rolt to tell her the truth if it became absolutely necessary and had been about to do so before she interrupted him.

"They're *policemen*," he went on gently. "Another two watch your flat at night."

"How do you know this, Piers?"

"Commander Rolt told me."

"Oh." She went pink with embarrassment. "Oh." After another silence she said, "Silly of me. Sorry I shouted at you."

He held out his cup. "The penance is another cup of coffee."

"Are you going to help Mummy over this blackmail business?"

"I've done what I can. But now Morgan's been murdered the police will have to be told about it. It risks people's lives not to."

"She was relying on you rather."

"I'm aware of that. What do you want me to do? Go gunning for whoever it is?"

"Isn't that better than a dreadful scandal?"

Piers said, "So everyone has an attack of the vapours when I go to prison for six months for driving a getaway car but it's okay if I'm sent down for life for murder trying to keep the Ashley name pure."

He walked out.

Chapter Ten

Len Dorney's "manor", in Hackney in the East End, an area of some twelve square miles and roughly bounded by Graham Road to the north and the Grand Union Canal to the south, was all urban, the only green open spaces worth mentioning those of London Fields and Well Street Common. It was near the latter that Dorney lived, in a red brick Victorian semi-detached house in a cul-de-sac.

One did not, however, arrive at the house unannounced if one valued a long and healthy life. One did not, for that matter, go to the house at all, business being carried out at an office over a shop in Mare Street. It was to these premises that Piers went. Rolt had not sent him, he had made the decision after having a conversation with a man in a pub in Soho.

Dorney had decided, rightly, that a business purporting to be an educational video distributors would not attract many casual callers. Those who climbed the narrow stairs were either expected, having appointments, or had already been spotted by the lookouts who had warned those within. Piers had not made an appointment. It would make no difference if he had.

The lookout – Vince, on this occasion – was standing talking to Jacko, a disabled man who had a flower stall on the corner of Bush Road. Vince went from sight as soon as he caught sight of Piers, not even waiting to see if he was heading for what Dorney liked to describe as his HQ. Piers knew that he had gone down the alley into the car park behind the shops, run up the fire escape, probably two steps at a time, and from that climbed through a window into a room used as a store. Len Dorney's office was next door to this.

Bracing himself, Piers mounted the stairs. He wondered who would be on duty and how many of them there would be. Too many probably. They might be waiting for him in the small, dark space at the top of the stairs just in front of the lavatory door.

They were, men he had never seen before.

"Okay, let's leave it at that for a moment," Dorney said a while later. He stared with the intensity of a cat at Piers as he was hauled up from the floor.

"Still got that rebellious look on your face?" Dorney asked. "Yes, I think you have." He signalled to his henchmen.

It was the mildest retribution he could expect: being held while his face was slapped until he either passed out or vomited. Both of the goals were well in sight when he received what he knew were the final blows, back-handers, the rings on the man's finger splitting his lips like over-ripe plums. Then he was allowed to fall to the floor again and find a corner where he could retch in comparative privacy.

"I told you to report to me when you were released,"Dorney said after a while. No one seemed to be in any hurry.

Piers crawled to a chair and used it to pull himself up. "You still have the same methods," he said with difficulty, mopping the blood with his handkerchief.

"D'you want some more? Answer the question."

Piers sat on the chair. "You didn't ask me one." When Dorney raised a hand in another signal he added, "I was shot, you stupid bastard."

Dorney's small eyes almost disappeared into his head in amazement. "Shot!"

Piers nodded.

"You could still have got a message to me."

"With the police sitting at my bedside?"

Dorney dismissed the other three.

"Who are those vermin?" Piers asked furiously.

"New recruits."

"Recruits! Since when have you employed such riff-raff?"

"Beggars can't be choosers," Dorney said uneasily. "It's only snouts who are rich men these days round here. All the best people went down with you. I'm doing this last job and then clearing out."

"The jewellery snatch?"

"How did *you* hear about it?" Dorney hissed.

"Now you're adding insult to injury," Piers said. "I seem to remember being your right-hand man. It's my business to know everything that goes on."

Dorney eyed him narrowly. "How do I know you're telling me the truth about being shot? You look all right to me."

Piers pulled off his track suit top and tee shirt.

"Holy Mother," Dorney muttered.

"I'm waiting for an apology. I resent being treated like some little erk who's done something wrong. Setting those three on me was the mark of a petty gangster, not the sharp businessman you keep telling me you are."

"Drink?" Dorney asked nervously.

"Not with this mouth, thank you. When's the big job?"

"It'll only happen if I can get the personnel."

"You give me a few names of likely candidates and I'll get them on the pay roll."

"It's not as easy as that," Dorney said, sitting in the chair behind his desk. "They're simply not available."

"Then let us two do it. We're worth ten of that rabble you've got now. Where are they from – the other side of the river?"

"Sub-contracted from Gerry North's lot. I was thinking of getting rid of them to be honest."

"So we do the jewellery job them?"

"I never get involved personally."

"If it's your last job, it'll prevent a lot of loose ends to be taken care of. No people to be paid off who might talk. No one to *know* about it in detail but us two."

"I'll think about it," Dorney said. He opened a drawer of the desk and withdrew a thick wad of money. "This is your wages for while you were doing time. But don't count on any apologies. I expect people to do as they're told, getting shot or not. If you step out of line again you'll get the same, only it'll go on a lot longer and might spoil your pretty face for always. Now get out. I know where to find you."

Piers took the money and stuffed it in his pocket. "My little bird also said that it was the Van den Hooper diamonds you were keen on lifting. When they come to this country to be displayed in a Bond Street jewellers. It'll have to be real pros for that job. With hardware – good shots. If you rely on yobbos you'll be finished."

"I know where to find you," Dorney said again.

Piers took two taxis to reach Woodford with a very short bus journey in between. This, of course, was to shake off anyone tailing him. He explained his appearance to the taxi drivers as resulting from an attempted mugging. Rolt, however, expected a more accurate account than this and it was only after Piers had gone into great detail that he summoned the resident medical orderly to attend to his injuries. He was, in short, angry.

"You could have jeopardised the entire operation by such hasty action," the Commander said, tossing the wad of money that Piers had given him into a drawer.

"My information was that the job was next week," Piers said. "I met someone in the Sun and Thirteen Cantons who's given me useful info before. It seemed important to follow it up immediately."

"The Van den Hooper Collection is due to arrive here in a fortnight's time. It would have been a good idea if you'd checked up on that first."

"Dorney's temper wouldn't have cooled if I'd left it any longer – if anything the reverse."

Rolt was the first to recognise that it took courage to go somewhere where you knew you were in for a hiding. He just wished that sometimes the man before him would act in less impetuous fashion. He said, "I'd like you to look at some mug-shots while you're here. If we can put names to those faces that Dorney's hired, we can keep track of them."

"He said he was thinking of getting rid of them."

"Is he now? Then our Len'll have to be careful. They're an ugly bunch in more ways than one."

"What's the secrecy?" Sylvia whispered as Piers slipped past her out of the darkness into the hall and quickly closed the door.

"I'm not supposed to be here," he replied.

"I heard the car and wondered who it was."

He removed his overcoat and she took it from him and hung it up.

"I'm sorry about Thursday – I couldn't come."

Sylvia exclaimed in horror as she saw his face in the much brighter light coming from the kitchen. She touched his mouth with one gentle hand.

"That wasn't really why I couldn't come," he explained. "I'm not going to use it as an excuse. It happened afterwards."

"Come in the warm." She led the way, having made a lightning visit into the kitchen for a bottle of wine and two glasses.

"You haven't seen me if anyone asks," he said. "I'll be hung, drawn and quartered if the boss finds out I came here."

"I'm flattered that a man should risk so messy a death for my company," Sylvia said with a grin. "Oh, damn, I've forgotten the opener."

Piers took the wine bottle from her, went into the kitchen, found the corkscrew and opened it. It amused him that his visit seemed to have flummoxed her a little.

"Your health," Sylvia said. "I hope you're going to let me paint you."

"D'you have special rates for ex-cons?"

"Poppycock! About you being an ex-con, I mean. I charge one thousand pounds and it's worth every penny. That's framed, of course."

"Done."

"Are you serious?" she said, eyes round with surprise. "I wasn't touting for trade."

"You denigrate yourself. I'm very honoured. And I hope there won't be any unseemly arguments if I insist on giving you half the money at the first sitting."

"What kind of backdrop would you like?" she wanted to know, unable to prevent herself thinking about lighting, whether he should be seated, if it should be a study indoors or out.

"Oh, I was thinking of something along the lines of most of the stuff at the Hall. You know the sort of thing – cherubs and flowers and just a whisp of material to cover the naughty bits as one wafts through the air." He chuckled.

Sylvia, who believed in being utterly direct in such matters, said, "So in other words you feel like taking everything off right now?" When she had spoken thus she rather wished she hadn't as she saw the expression that flitted over his face.

"London was ugliness and pain, argument and bad feeling," he whispered.

"Then come and make pleasure," she invited, holding both arms out to him.

Pleasure there was, she thought later, breathlessly accommodating plentitude. No woman could ever accuse him of being a selfish lover. There was also the merest tinge of earthiness, a facet that made her wonder if the woman who had initiated him into the art of lovemaking had been French or Italian. After these reflections, the very lavishness of what he was doing robbed her of any constructive thought whatsoever.

"I assume you don't want celestial virgins," she said softly into his ear quite a while afterwards.

"In the painting?" he enquired.

"At any time."

"No, I've no time for blokes who sleep with young girls and get them into trouble. Mature women are far more interesting too. Girls giggle."

"How about someone your own age?"

"I haven't met anyone yet."

"How old are you, Piers?"

"Twenty-four."

"How long have you been in the police?" When he did not reply immediately she said, "I know because you relax when you're with me. You are yourself. That's why you came to me tonight – because the strain of being someone else was too much for you after you'd been hurt."

"Five years," he said. "A special undercover unit. I actually wanted to go into the army but at the interview said I was also interested in the police. I was immediately asked a lot of questions and then they shunted me along the corridor to talk to a shrink. He got it out of me that I'd also wanted to go on the stage. Well, after more interviews, medicals and so forth,

I was asked if I wanted to join a new police unit. That's how the department recruits. You have to actually attain a standard that would get you into the SAS. You're trained for a while by them. You go to drama school for three months in order to learn how to pretend. There's no attending the police college at Hendon, no passing-out parades, no uniforms, and utter secrecy. If you get involved with really important jobs you can't even tell your next of kin what you're doing. I opted for that straight away. I suppose it was a way of getting my own back for a rigid upbringing. That's very childish – I know that now."

"Why are you telling me if it's so secret?"

"Because I think you'll keep secrets. And soon I'll be able to come into the open a bit. You're not permitted to walk through the criminal underworld for too long. There's always a danger of being found out and ending up in the Thames. I nearly told Thea the truth the day before yesterday but she was more concerned with the family name than my welfare."

"Don't be hard on them. It's too much of a shock for some people when trouble strikes. I take it you're talking about Colin Morgan being murdered."

"Investigations might let a couple of skeletons out of the family cupboard."

"So they want the crook of the family to take care of it for them?"

"You did say you had second sight."

"Pooh! It wasn't difficult to work out at all. Incidentally, you know we were talking about Charles Morgan and I said I had a funny feeling about him? Well, he has unlikely friends."

"Unlikely?"

"Yes, I'm sure I saw Crispin Blake's Rolls-Royce parked outside his house the other night. I couldn't see what colour the car was – you know how those orange street lights make everything look brown."

"When, exactly?"

"I can't be too sure. Two days ago perhaps."

"Other people have Rollers."

"I'm sure they do. But Morgan's not the sort of man to know folk with Rollers. Unless it belonged to a top-line crook or somebody like that."

"You really have a knife in him, don't you?"

"Not at all. I just think he's up to no good. I think you should warn your father about him."

"Dad might have asked him to drop something off at Morgan's house."

"Yes, I agree. Anything's possible. It's just that I've ignored my feelings about people before and regretted it afterwards. Like the woman who once came to clean for me. I didn't like her at all even though she was very pleasant and worked very hard. She stole my gold watch and I never saw it or her again."

"About this painting . . ." he said dreamily.

"Have you thought any more about it?"

"A sporting scene, do you think?"

"Look at me," she ordered. When he had done so she said, "You astride a stallion gazing at hounds working a covert in the distance?"

"It would have to be a stallion."

"Naturally. Did you know that the entire horse's penis is called a yard?" Then, when he had come close to her she added, "You don't need much encouragement, do you?"

His answer was forthright and entirely practical, action sometimes being a lot more satisfactory than words.

Chapter Eleven

The phone was ringing. Piers turned over and tried to go back to sleep, hoping that Sylvia would answer it. The realization – it being one of his rules never actually to sleep the night with his lady friends – that he had not only driven back to London, but that it was a whole twenty-four hours since he had waved goodbye to Sylvia and that he had spent a day watching someone's front door for Rolt, penetrated his wits slowly. And the phone kept on ringing.

"Hi," he said at last into the mouthpiece, having failed to find the lamp switch and groped for the phone in the dark.

"Thank God!" Thea sobbed. "I really thought you weren't there. Piers . . ." She broke down completely.

"Tell me!" he barked, now very much awake.

"It's Giles. Someone's tried to kill him. Mummy's just rung. He's in hospital."

"Where are you?"

She seemed to have put down the phone.

"Thea, answer me! Where are you phoning from?"

"Sorry, trying to find a hankie. Here. In town."

"At your flat?"

"Yes. That man Tony – the one from Special Branch – knew your number."

"I'll come round and pick you up. Give me fifteen minutes." He crashed back the receiver, raced into the bathroom and put his head under the cold tap. Then he snatched up the phone again and dialled.

Rolt's stand-in, Inspector Ellis, came on the line. "Commander Rolt's in Hackney," he said crisply. "Reports came in of shooting and a fire at Dorney's place. He's probably looking for your body right now. Where are you?"

"At home, sir. I wanted to talk to him about something else."

"Can't it wait?"

"No, it's very important."

"I'll try and get hold of him for you. But I can't promise anything."

"Don't worry, sir, I'll see if I can contact him over the radio in my car."

Thea was waiting for him on the pavement outside her flat, huddled into a huge padded jacket with a hood. As soon as he stopped the car and got out two men appeared at her side, placing themselves in front of her as he approached. Tony, clearly, had been relieved by two colleagues, neither of whom Piers knew. He couldn't remember the last time he had shown anyone his warrant card. It had lain in the safe in his bedroom where he normally kept his police revolver for the best part of a year. The result of this was that the passenger door of the car was opened for Thea and she was carefully ushered within. Piers made the first stop, a few minutes later, an all-night café.

"We mustn't stop," Thea protested.

"For you hot tea," he told her. "Something to eat. My handkerchief. In reverse order. But I want to make a call first. Give me the main details."

Ellis must have succeeded in contacting Rolt for the Commander responded to his call-sign immediately. Piers recounted the story as Thea had told it to him: how Giles had been at home nearly all week with a suspected recurrence of his glandular fever but had felt well enough to go out for a drink with a couple of friends. They had walked to the Rising Salmon. On the way back a car had driven directly at them, knocked Giles down, almost hit a tree and roared off without stopping. Giles's injuries were regarded as serious.

Piers finished by saying, "I feel I must take Thea home, sir, because she's not fit to drive herself – she's too upset. If you wish I'll come straight back to town."

Rolt said, "You told Ellis you weren't in Hackney tonight. Is that true?"

117

"Yes, sir."

"I did have to ask you because someone's burnt down Dorney's little hideaway with him in it, plus half the row of shops. At least, there's a charred body in the remains of the shop downstairs. I've a feeling there are several bullet holes in it too. I think I could understand it if you'd decided to tidy things up a little but I can't see you lobbing a petrol bomb in afterwards. I suppose we shall have to start looking for those three who wiped the smile off your face the other day. No, stay in Sussex. See what you can do to clear the problem up. I'll give Leadbetter the nod."

"Thank you, sir."

"Go and talk to that surgeon – Blake, is it? Lean on him a little. I saw him on television once and it struck me that he was a bit glib. If your sister with you now?"

"Yes, sir."

"Bring her back to London as soon as possible. It's far easier to keep an eye on her here than in the wilds of Sussex."

When he had replaced the mike Thea said, "It appears that everyone's been really *thick*. I just can't imagine why I didn't put two and two together when Commander Rolt came to see you at home. As though a senior policeman would visit an ex-con."

"I've a feeling he might have been trying to drop a few hints. He gave me a revolver with a Met badge on it as large as life. Come on, let's find a phone and discover what's happening."

Giles, it appeared, was in no immediate danger of dying. Both his legs were broken and he had three fractured ribs. It was thought he had internal injuries and this was the only real cause for concern.

After hot food Thea stopped shivering despite the fact that she had discovered to her mortification that beneath the thick padded coat she only had on her skimpy pink satin pyjamas.

"What will people *think*?" she agonised on the way to the car.

"No one'll know as long as you keep the coat done up," Piers said.

Her eyes filled with tears again. "Poor Giles. He simply won't be able to cope with this. That's if he lives."

"He'll live all right. He's Sir Richard all over again. Small and wimpish-looking but as tough as hell underneath."

"D'you really think so?" Thea said, brightening considerably. And then, when he just smiled broadly at her, said, "Isn't it odd? Not so long ago I was saying that I was the one who always bathed your grazed knees. Now it seems that everything's the reverse."

"Sleep," he ordered when they were in the car. "If you arrive all distraught and haggard-looking you'll only make it worse for Mum. We shall have to be the strong ones."

At just before four a.m. he swung the car into the main drive of the Hall. There were no lights in the Jacksons' lodge, something that surprised him slightly. Perhaps they didn't know what had happened. Perhaps, on the other hand, such practical people saw no point in losing sleep over something they could not help with.

To begin with things were difficult. It was possible that when he first joined F.9 as a trainee at the age of nineteen he had had a rosy vision in his mind of some day in the future when he would confront his family with the truth and glory in their guilty expressions. Truth rarely goes hand in hand with daydreams. As it was, Mycroft had guessed already and was only hoping for confirmation. He got it when Piers handed him his warrant card.

"You could have hinted," he said reproachfully.

"I thought about it," Piers said. "But you must remember that you once hired a private eye to check on a friend of mine. You always insisted on knowing everything that I was doing. I'm in the sort of job where the wrong word – just a hint – would have resulted in a bullet in my back. It still could. So please, if anyone asks about me, just say that all the trouble is in the past and I have a good job in London. And by "anyone", I mean relations and also close friends of the family."

"And the staff?" Elizabeth asked.

"*Especially* the staff. I'm afraid that you'll have to do quite a lot of pretending until this business is over and you might have to field a few complaints. I shall be asking a lot of questions."

By ten that morning Giles was conscious but on a dialysis

119

machine as his kidneys had ceased functioning. The specialist looking after him would not commit himself but hoped that this was only temporary. He was also hoping that there were no serious internal injuries, only massive bruising. But there was no question of his having visitors, not even brothers.

Piers went home again but returned to the hospital that afternoon, found a ward sister and exerted a little charm. Five minutes later he was at Giles's bedside. Hollow-eyed misery lay supine, but in a mood of brooding anger.

"Thank God for a human face," Giles said weakly.

Piers made a play of looking over his shoulder.

"Idiot," Giles whispered, albeit with a faint smile.

Piers drew up a chair and sat down. "You and I have something in common at last."

"I chickened out of coming to see you though. I never know what to say when people are in hospital. Someone always comes along and asks them how their bowels are while you're there, and you don't know where to look."

"I'm not looking at all the plastic tubing," Piers assured him. "And before I say anything else, I want you to know that I think it's about time the pair of us grew up and made peace with one another."

"Yes, feuding within families is a bore, isn't it? Piers, old man, we can't shake hands as I don't have one free of hardware at the moment. We'll have to rub noses or something like Nanook of the North." After Piers had kissed his cheek he said, gruffy, "It's been sort of preying on my mind how I welted you over the head with that stool. Bloody vicious thing to do. Sorry."

"You might wish you'd hit me a bit harder when I tell you what I really do for a living . . ."

"And you're investigating all this?" Giles said breathlessly, a couple of minutes later when Piers had given him the essential details, also mentioning the blackmail.

"Yes. So I'm now going to whip out a little notebook and ask you questions. One thing though, brother mine. You keep what I told you to yourself. Okay?"

"Sure. What do you want to know? I didn't see who was driving the car, if you were going to ask me that."

120

"Not even what sort of car it was?"

"No. But you could ask the other two – they might have noticed. It happened too quickly."

"Apparently they didn't, according to what Inspector Leadbetter told Dad. One of them – Peter, I think it was – is convinced only that it was a dark colour."

"Not an up-market car either, come to think of it. I mean, it didn't have the kind of brilliant headlights you see on a Rolls or Jag. And they weren't that wide apart either so it wasn't a big car. I only saw the lights, you see."

"And it came from behind you?"

"Yes. We'd left the street lights of the village behind. But it's only a short distance that you have to walk in the dark before you reach home."

"Where had your friends left their cars?"

"Parked outside the Hall. It's better to walk. And I've a feeling that the fuzz – sorry, police – watch the pubs especially for the likes of us. We always play it like that. Then if anyone really gets canned I ask Dad to run them home and they pick their cars up the next day."

"I thought you were supposed to be ill and that's why you came home."

Giles smiled wanly. "No – well – I'm thinking of dropping out of Oxford and don't know what to tell Dad."

"We'll talk a bit more tomorrow," Piers said, seeing a nurse beckoning to him. "One last question. Did you tell anyone that Dad had stuck a sword in me?"

"God, I don't know. I might have done. Yes, I remember now. I said something to Charles Morgan when I saw him the next morning. He commented that Dad was in a very bad mood and I jokingly suggested he put on a suit of armour."

Piers remembered something else. "That evening you came to the lodge with a view to frightening me off with your shot-gun . . . who told you that tools and a chain saw had been stolen?"

"That was Charles Morgan too."

The nurse practically bundled him out of the ward. "Sister says you shouldn't have *really* been let in."

"Tell her I'll come and ask her again tomorrow," said Piers with a grin.

The Morgans lived in a detached house not far from the main drive to the Hall. Recollecting what Sylvia had told him about seeing a Rolls-Royce parked outside, Piers drove up to it slowly. The house had quite a large front garden with a tall cypress hedge bordering the road. But the drive was wide and it was very easy to see what vehicles, if any, were parked by the double garage. A new Audi stood on the quartz gravel at the moment, its bonnet warm under Piers's hand as he walked by.

"My husband's at work," Mrs Morgan said when she opened the front door.

It occurred to him that she might not know him by sight so he introduced himself. Her face hardened.

"It's you I'd like to have a word with," Piers said.

"I don't know how you have the effrontery to come here," the woman said venomously. "Not with our poor Colin buried yesterday."

"I'm very sorry about Colin," Piers said quietly. "And I assure you that I'm here with my father's blessing." Perhaps "knowledge" would have been nearer the truth.

"Oh," she said, opening the door a little wider. "That's different."

"May I come in or shall we talk on the doorstep?"

She darted a glance left and right. "Yes. All right. I suppose you'd better."

"Good cars," Piers said, waving in the vague direction of the Audi. "Is it yours?"

"Charles bought it for me for my birthday," Mrs Morgan replied, apparently unable to keep a defensive tone from her voice.

The three-piece suite in the living room looked brand new as well. He sat down without being asked to on the settee and gave her what he had been told by others to be his best milk-curdling smile. It had the effect of rattling the woman to the extent of making her trip on the edge of a Chinese rug.

"What time does your husband get home in the evenings?"

122

She glanced at her watch. "In about an hour. He finishes at about five at this time of the year. Later in the summer, you understand. There's more work to be done then."

"I'm sure," Piers said. "Look, I'm sorry to have to ask you questions that concern Colin but I think it's very important to build up a picture of his movements to help discover who killed him."

"It's for the police to do that."

"My father is most anxious that I talk to people on the estate itself. He's worried about everyone's safety. We're both convinced that employees will be more forthcoming with us than the police." This was straight off the top of his head but very reasonable, he thought.

"But if any information you get is given to the police anyway . . ." Mrs Morgan said, openly puzzled.

"Well, I know that and you know that, Mrs Morgan, but obviously it must be seen that everyone's being interviewed. That's why I've come here first seeing as your husband's in such a senior, trusted position . . ." Piers broke off with quite another kind of smile altogether.

"Oh, I see," she gushed. "Of course. Yes."

"I want to go back to the night of February the 15th. The night I was shot. Where was Colin that night?"

"He went to the pictures."

"No, I mean before he went out. Round about five-thirty."

"He was here – having his tea."

"Can you remember what he ate?"

"No, of course not. Not after all this time."

"But didn't the police ask you that?"

"I – I don't know. I can't remember."

"They should have done. What time did he go out?"

"About a quarter to seven."

"Isn't that rather early?"

"They said they were going for a drink first."

"They?"

"He went with his girlfriend, Jane."

"And Jane was here while Colin ate his tea?"

"Well, no, not exactly. She arrived when he'd finished and was getting ready."

"And where does Jane live?"

"I don't know precisely. Only that her parents keep a shop in the village."

"Come now. Surely parents find out everything they can about the young ladies their sons go out with."

She coloured. "They'd only met that week. You can't be too nosy to start with, can you?"

"He'd reported his car stolen that morning so how did they get to Littlehampton? I assume it was to Littlehampton they went."

"Colin took his father's car. Yes, it was Littlehampton."

"Did he see Jane again after that night?"

Her hands, although clasped tightly in her lap, were shaking. "No, I don't think so. I think they broke up."

"Don't you *know*?"

"No. Not with Colin. He was very close, was Colin. I never knew quite what he was thinking and doing."

"What time did he come in that evening? Before he had his tea."

"He'd been in all afternoon, watching the football."

"While the person who stole his car was sitting in it not even two miles from here. Doesn't that strike you as rather strange?"

She just stared at him.

Piers said, "And don't you think it's strange that someone stole a car in the same district that they intended to commit murder? People nearly always steal vehicles many miles from the place of the crime."

"Perhaps he wasn't very bright," Mrs Morgan suggested with a kind of forced cheerfulness.

"Or was *very* stupid and used his own car?"

"Are you calling him and us liars, Mr Ashley?"

"I'm suggesting that Colin had been out that afternoon and came in at a little after five-thirty. And although he'd reported the car stolen he had actually lent it to someone who hid it for the day and then picked him up at some time in the afternoon. This same person drove the car to London afterwards and set fire to it to make it look as though the gunman lived there."

"Rubbish! And you haven't one bit of evidence," Mrs Morgan said.

"No, only the way he couldn't look me in the eye when I tackled him about it. Tell me, do you know Crispin Blake the surgeon?"

"I think I met him at one of the Christmas parties that your parents give at the Hall."

"Has he ever been here?"

"No, why on earth should he? I mean, he's not the sort who moves in our social circles. Why are you asking?"

"Someone I spoke to said they thought they saw his car parked here one might. Perhaps they were mistaken."

"No, you're right. I've just remembered. He did call in to see my husband one evening not all that long ago."

"Do you know why?"

"No. I just assumed it was because your father had asked him to for some reason. Now, have you finished with your questions and blackening my poor son's character?"

"Surely you've asked yourself why he was killed? What possible motive could anyone have had for killing him? It wasn't robbery and it didn't look as though there'd been a struggle. No, he knew whoever killed him. Personally. I think you do have suspicions but you're frightened that your husband is involved. We have a real live murderer in the area, Mrs Morgan. Don't you think it's your duty to tell the police what you know?"

"But I don't know anything."

"First I was shot, then your son was murdered. Now Giles has been knocked down by a hit and run driver. Who's next? Thea? My mother?"

"But I hadn't heard about *Giles*," the woman cried. "Oh, how awful! I hadn't realized there might be a connection. Charles said . . ."

"Yes?"

"Charles said that it was one of your criminal cronies who had shot you and you were blaming Colin because you hated him."

Piers went so far as to lean over and take her hands. "Look, if Colin did do anything it wouldn't have been his idea. Someone either forced him to or paid him a lot of money. I didn't hate your son. I only fell out with him because he was setting snares that caught a little girl's pet cat."

"He never really aspired to things that were worthwhile," Mrs Morgan said with a faraway expression on her face. "In fact, when you think about it he always went against his father and me. Here was Charles manager of a large estate, and his son behaved like a poacher. He got in with the wrong crowd, that was Colin's trouble – he wasn't what you called a strong-minded boy. As long as he had enough money to spend in the pub at weekends, that was all he wanted. In my heart of hearts I know he didn't even pull his weight with his job at the sawmill."

"Did he know how to use a hand-gun – a pistol, for example?"

Still in a dream, she nodded. "I'm fairly sure Charles showed him how to use one once."

"Do you have a gun in the house?"

"Oh, no. I wouldn't stand for that."

"Then which gun did your husband use to demonstrate for Colin?"

"I really couldn't say. This was years ago, mind. When we first came here. Colin was only in his teens then."

"Mrs Morgan, please tell me the truth about that Saturday afternoon when I was shot."

She fixed him with her rather weak blue gaze. "But the police'll automatically think he did it. That's what Charles said. He told me that if we said that he'd come in directly it happened, the police would arrest him as a chief suspect. As it was Colin had to go to the police station for hours and hours because of the car."

Gently, he said, "But it doesn't make any difference to Colin now, does it?"

Her mouth trembling, she whispered, "I couldn't bear to think of him as a murderer."

"But he wasn't. I didn't die. The worst that people will think is that he was manipulated by someone ruthless. I'm sure that's what happened. Money might have been involved as well, but a fair amount of bullying must have gone on."

After a long silence she nodded very slowly. "He did stay in for a while during that afternoon watching football on the television. But then he went out. He came back about a quarter to six. I thought he'd had a row with someone. He was flushed and out of sorts and went straight upstairs. He had a bath and changed and then came down again. I didn't ask him what was wrong as I knew he'd have only bitten my head off. So I just gave him his tea."

"And when did Jane arrive?"

"He didn't have a girlfriend. We made that up as it sounded better. But I don't think the police checked up on it."

Or failed to trace her, Piers thought, and assumed she'd moved away. A black mark for Leadbetter.

"Will I be arrested for concealing evidence?" she asked nervously.

He stood up. "I can't answer for the police." This was not the right moment to confront Charles Morgan. It seemed likely that he was very much involved and that some kind of coercion had been used. Like someone discovering he was defrauding his employer, for example.

"That was Rolt," Piers said, returning from the phone in the hall to the dinner table. To Thea he added, "He asked me if you were back in town yet and I had to give him my word that I'd put you on a train first thing in the morning."

"Like a parcel," she said, wrinkling her nose.

"Red Star," Piers said. "He's meeting you at Victoria. All I have to do is let him know which train you're on."

"How *kind* of him," Elizabeth cried.

"Is that why he rang?" Thea asked, trying not to smile.

"No, as a matter of fact he phoned to say that Lee Haasden's in the clear. He works for a security firm that escorts works of art around the world. It's all a bit hush-hush, that's why he wasn't more forthcoming. And his alibi's been thoroughly checked out. He was with who he said he was and where all that day and until the following morning."

"Good," Thea said. "I'm glad he's not a suspect now."

Outwardly all was as normal. It seemed that everyone was making a tremendous effort, for Giles's sake, if nothing else, to be as natural as possible. Elizabeth and Thea had been to see him in the late afternoon and had only been permitted a couple of minutes with him. Elizabeth had returned from the hospital looking very white and drawn.

"Can I have a word with you in private?" Piers asked Mycroft when dinner was over.

"Come in the study," his father replied. When they were seated in the leather wing armchairs he said, "You want to ask me what I'm going to do about your mother."

"It was one of the things I was hoping to talk about," Piers told him. "I think from the point of view of her coping with this nightmare you have to make your intentions plain. And looking at her this evening, I'm not even sure that you've discussed it with her."

Surprisingly, Mycroft chuckled. "She threatened to leave me if I threw you out. Where does that leave a man? Alone," he added, answering the question himself. "Quite alone. I don't think I could live alone after all this time. And she's a very good woman except for this stupid business with Blake. To be honest I don't know what to do about Blake." He rose from his chair. "A drop more port?"

"Thanks," Piers said. "But first go and tell Mother what you've just said to me. It'll help."

"You think so? Yes, perhaps that would be a good idea. Clear the air a little." He left the room, not intended to see his son's eyes go ceilingwards and the shake of his head. When he returned with the bottle of port he was looking almost happy. "There, that's done. Should have said it before really."

"I'm glad you've changed your mind about things," Piers said, holding his glass up to the light to admire the ruby-like glow of the contents.

"Fell off Nimrod," the Colonel muttered. "Haven't fallen off a horse since I was a lad. I lay there in the mud with that damn fool nag staring down at me with I'll swear a grin on his face, and it sort of brought it home to me. All at once I saw the real life behind the portraits and banners. I thought of Sir Richard's wife having her jolly with her Scotsman. I mean, damn it all, he probably groped the serving wenches when she wasn't looking. And folk lived like pigs in those days, you know, filthy. But under our civilised veneer these days we're just the same – human beings."

"Absolutely," Piers agreed, secretly quite astounded. "And we all mourn the lack of serving wenches in these modern times."

Mycroft guffawed.

"How much does Charles Morgan get paid?" Piers asked a while later.

As predicted, this took Mycroft back a little. "Well, I – "

"I'm not merely being nosy," Piers interrupted.

"I'd have to look at the books for the exact figure but it must be in the region of twenty thousand a year. Plus the house of course – and a car. There are a few other perks as well."

"Does his wife work?"

"No, I'm pretty sure she doesn't. Why are you asking?"

"I deliberately didn't ask you how much he *earned*. I'd say, having been in their house today, that he earns more than that. There was a brand new top of the range Audi outside that she said was hers, and the furniture and carpets in their living room have cost thousands. She was wearing a lot of jewellery that hadn't come from Woolworth's either."

"Are you suggesting he's on the fiddle?"

"There are rumours in the village that stuff is going out through the back door. I think you ought to check."

"I do have an accountant."

"An accountant can only examine the books as they're given to him. Does he check that every Christmas tree that's planted comes to maturity? That all the pheasants which are reared and shot are sold to the game-dealers for *your* profit?"

"That wouldn't account for much loss," Mycroft said thoughtfully. "We'd be talking about a much bigger fiddle than that. No, Charles doesn't have a lot to do with the running of the home estate – I took that over some time ago. But he does run the three farms and they've been doing quite badly. It's funny, but I was actually on the point of doing a little investigation of my own about this. I know that agriculture's in the doldrums at the moment but those farms are on some of the finest land in the county. Two of them breed beef cattle for export and there's no reason in my mind why they shouldn't be making a good profit. One of our bullocks, a Hereford called Ashleigh Thunderer, won the Championship at Smithfield last year and overseas buyers have been flocking to buy animals of the same blood line."

"Do it soon," Piers urged. "If necessary, call in a firm of auditors."

"Do you think he's connected with this blackmail business?"

"I think it's likely. I got out of Mrs Morgan this afternoon that they concocted Colin's alibi for the afternoon that I was shot. And Morgan's in the ideal position to keep watch on this family and know our movements. But I wouldn't have thought he'd kill his own son."

"Are you going to talk to him?"

"No, I think I'd prefer to let him stew. That can do no harm for a while, especially if you start checking on his activities at the farms."

"There's something you ought to know about Blake," Mycroft said after a short pause. "He doesn't know that I know about him and Elizabeth. That's obvious because he's still as nice as pie. But yesterday he asked me for a loan."

"Oh, brother," Piers whispered. "How amazingly interesting."

"Why? What's wrong? Why are you looking like that?"

"I'll tell you in a minute. How much does he want?"

"Two thousand. He admitted he had gambling debts."

"That still doesn't tell us who killed Colin Morgan," Piers said, mostly to himself. "I can't see a surgeon hitting someone over the head with a rock. But otherwise we have a fairly watertight case."

Chapter Twelve

Through Crispin Blake's secretary Piers tracked down the surgeon the next day to the Pelican Inn at Arundel, where he was having lunch. This hostelry was more commonly known to the local people as the Filofax and Firkin on account of the lifestyle of most of its clientele. Piers wouldn't have said that the tone of the place was quite that which Blake would hunt out, rather that it was a bolt-hole where a busy man would go, knowing that none of his colleagues would seek him there. And the food was reputed to be excellent.

Blake sat at a small table right in a corner of the saloon bar, *The Times* propped up before him. As Piers entered a waitress brought Blake's order and he folded away the newspaper, seeing Piers as he did so. He waved him across.

"Sit down, my boy! Have you eaten? The steak and kidney pie here is food for the gods."

"I have eaten, thanks," he replied. "Let me get you another glass of wine to go with it."

"I won't argue," Blake said. "It's the house red – quite quaffable."

Piers fetched the wine and a pint of bitter for himself.

"How's the chest?" Blake enquired.

"Almost like new, thanks to your skill."

"You have the constitution of a horse. But don't push your luck – no real exertion." He sipped the wine appreciatively. "A bad business about Giles. Especially after what happened to you."

"Have you seen him at all?"

"This morning, as a matter of fact. But only as a friend, you

131

understand. John Timpson's looking after him – a good man but touchy. I didn't want him to think I was interfering."

"How was Giles?"

"Quite poorly really. But it's what I expected. Timpson's optimistic that his kidneys will start functioning again soon. There's no damage as far as they can tell. Nature has a way of shutting things down after a huge shock like that."

"There might be a connection between me being shot and what happened to Giles."

Blake looked appalled. "You mean it might not have been an accident?"

"No. You see, Mother's being blackmailed."

Blake laid down his knife and fork. "Elizabeth? Being blackmailed?"

"About you and her."

"Did she tell you this herself?"

"Of course. It was why she wanted me to stay at home – to protect her from whoever it is. She's given him all her mother's jewellery."

"Does Mycroft know?"

"Not yet. But he'll have to be told eventually. And so will the police."

Blake grimaced.

"I know it's awkward for you but it can't be allowed to go on."

"It's not awkward – it's a disaster. Can't we frighten off whoever this person is?"

"I was hoping you might be able to give me a few clues."

"But I haven't the first idea who it could be!"

"*Someone* must know. How about your wife?"

"Naomi knows nothing about it," Blake snapped.

"Nor about the other women in your life?"

"Now, look here – " he began furiously.

"It's no good making suitable noises," Piers interrupted affably. "My mother is attractive but not a *femme fatale*. I'm sure you were delighted to liven up a side of her life that's no doubt been sadly lacking, but it wouldn't be enough for you. Somewhere there's a little piece with silk under-pinnings and a nice line in copulatory positions. Or are you a leather and whips man?"

Nostrils flaring, Blake pushed his plate to one side. "You don't mince words, do you?"

"Just thank your lucky stars you're not talking to my father."

There was silence between them for a moment or two and then Blake said, "I admit there is someone else. But even if she knew about your mother she wouldn't care – she has other interests of her own and is quite the last sort of person to indulge in blackmail. She's a woman with the world at her feet."

"A celebrity?" Piers drawled. "Lucky old you."

"And Naomi wouldn't do anything like that either. She's not the type."

"A kind woman? The doting sort? Knits you big sweaters to keep you warm and stays up so she can make you a nightcap when you're home late?"

"Yes, something like that."

"You're a real bastard, aren't you?"

"It's not your place to make judgements on me."

"I don't think you realize the seriousness of all this. I have a notion that the blackmailer hired or bribed Colin Morgan to take a shot at me. Then Morgan was murdered. Can't you think of anyone who might be responsible? Someone with a grudge against you?"

Blake frowned deeply. "No, I can't."

"What about Charles Morgan?"

"What the hell has he to do with it?"

"You do know him, don't you?"

"Only because he's your father's estate manager. I suppose we've met once or twice."

"So you've never been to his house."

"No. Of course not."

"Not even to drop something off for my father?"

"Look, I won't be grilled like this. Mycroft isn't in the habit of regarding me as an errand boy."

"Okay." Piers drained his glass.

"This is all very irregular," Leadbetter complained.

"No, it's not," Piers said. "And when you have an F.9 branch of your own, you'll think it's hunky-dory. Regard me as a dress rehearsal."

133

Leadbetter glowered at him. "Frankly I'm not even sure of your status."

"Forget all that. We don't have the same rank structure, and even if you were the Chief Constable I wouldn't call you sir. We only acknowledge our own officers. It's downright dangerous to have conventional forces giving orders to people like us. And be fair – would you give orders to Special Branch personnel without consulting *their* senior officers? No, of course you wouldn't. Too much goes on that you don't get to hear about."

"All right," Leadbetter said. "Point made. What do you want to see me about?"

They were strolling through Little London in Chichester, a quiet haven of narrow lanes free from traffic and about five minutes' walk from the Inspector's office.

"I just thought I'd bring you up to date on what I've discovered so far," Ashley said. "To be honest, I'm hellish scared that someone else is going to get killed."

"That might be a trifle over the top. There's no evidence that points to anything but a genuine hit-and-run as far as your brother's concerned. Has your mother had any more letters?"

"Not so far."

"I thought that might cease. And I can't help but think that Colin Morgan's killer's right out of the district by now. There was a lot of trouble at Brighton and Seaford that weekend with bikers. Who knows? Perhaps one of them was short of money and did a tour of the area looking for someone to mug."

"Did anyone report motor-bikes in the village at about the time he was killed?"

"No, but one wouldn't have drawn much attention."

"I've broken his alibi for the night I was shot. Mrs Morgan admitted to me that he'd actually come in at about five forty-five. In her own words he was flushed and out of sorts, and she thought he'd had a row with someone. And there was no girlfriend – they made that up to make it look better. I presume your people couldn't trace someone called Jane whose parents kept a shop in the village?"

"Sergeant Johns was working on that. He didn't mention it."

"Another thing that Mrs Morgan said was that Crispin Blake had been to see her husband one night. But when I asked Blake if he'd ever visited them, he denied it. It's worth mentioning too that Blake doesn't know my father's aware of his affair with my mother. A couple of days ago Blake asked him for a loan to pay off gambling debts. That looks very suspicious to me."

"You mean you think *Blake's* the blackmailer?"

"The theory's got a lot going for it."

"But it wouldn't stand up in a court of law."

"Too right it wouldn't."

"I can't quite understand the connection with the Morgans."

"My father once said to me that Blake always liked to know what was going on in the family. He might have made it his business to discover why Mrs Morgan drips with expensive jewellery, even during the day. He might also have listened to local rumours that Morgan's on the fiddle. They're certainly doing very well but the farms he's responsible for aren't. It's possible that Blake used that as a lever to get Colin Morgan to put a bullet in me."

"But why should Blake, an eminent surgeon, get involved with such dealings?"

"Well, he's admitted to gambling debts. If he owes a lot and it's to a really dodgy establishment, it's possible that they're leaning on him quite hard. Still, I don't have to tell you the methods they use to force people to pay up."

"I wish we could trace that jewellery your mother parted with." Leadbetter said wistfully.

"It might come to light yet."

"And who killed Colin Morgan?"

"That's why I'm worried. I don't know. I can't even begin to guess."

The Inspector shook his head sadly. "I'd like to agree with you – really I would. But when you've been a detective as long as I have you'll realize that you can write scenarios like this for nearly every case. It's neat. Too neat. I agree that the business of Colin Morgan's alibi needs looking into but you must bear in mind that people do lie through their teeth to save their kids from possible suspicion. The first thing the Morgans would have thought of was that he might be a suspect because of the car and the fact that there was no love lost between the two of you. As for Blake – would he really have the brass neck to ask your old man for money if he was the blackmailer?"

"If he was desperate he might."

"And the man saved your life. Can you really see him getting Colin Morgan to have shot you in the first place?"

"Yes, if he told him to miss and I moved."

Again Leadbetter shook his head. "It won't do, Ashley. I'm sorry but it really won't."

"I still think that Colin Morgan was murdered because he reported back to someone that I was on to him, and that person killed him to keep him quiet."

"Who, Blake? Would Blake hit him repeatedly over the head with a rock?"

"Was it found? Was it a rock?"

"According to the pathologist there were pieces of sandy stone embedded in his skull. There are thousands of rocks of suitable size in the bed of a nearby stream. That's almost certainly where it came from and where it ended up. The stream was in spate that night because it comes from the reservoir and they'd opened the sluices to lower the water level – a waste of time even to start looking."

"No, I don't think it was Blake. Unless the method of killing was deliberate to put you off the scent."

"You need *evidence*, Ashley. Find some and I might be more interested."

But there was encouragement for Piers when he got home, a message from Commander Rolt to contact him immediately. Rolt was off-duty when he rang but he spoke to Ellis.

"Following a tip-off we've traced a car that *might* be the one that knocked down your brother. It had been cleaned but the radiator grille was dented and there are traces of cloth and human hair in the windscreen wipers. The Commander's contacted Leadbetter asking for the clothing your brother was wearing and a small lock of his hair."

"Who does the car belong to?" Piers asked.

"The proprietor of a gaming club just off Tottenham Court Road. It's not actually the car he drives personally but a

Volvo the staff use as a general runabout. He's adamant that whatever's happened to the car is nothing to do with him. The staff are being questioned."

"But a tip-off though."

"I know. It's a bit odd really. And if it is the car, it will be the second involved with attacks on your family that has been found in London. That does rather point away from involvement with people at your end."

"That might be how it's intended to seem. Any chance of a look at the membership list, sir?"

"You'll have to ask Rolt about that. I'm a bit involved with other things at the moment."

"What sort of reputation does the club have?"

"Not too good from our point of view."

"Is it the sort of place to employ heavies to hound people who owe the club money?"

"Almost certainly."

As Piers replaced the receiver and turned to go back into the sitting room where he had been talking to his father – for he had been living at the main house since returning on this occasion – he saw, out of the corner of his eye, a movement. A door in the gloom to one side of the main staircase had closed soundlessly. The reason for the lack of light, he saw when he approached, was that the lamp in one of the wall-lights had failed.

The door led into a corridor to the kitchens that had, in days of old, been used solely by servants. On impulse, he opened it and stepped into the dark, narrow passageway beyond. Again, the reason for the darkness was that the sole illumination for this length of the corridor, a single bare bulb, appeared to have failed. He pushed the door open again slightly in order to utilise what light there was, and saw that the bulb was in fact missing.

There was a faint smell of cigarette smoke in the air.

"Who would want to get the proprietor of a gaming club into hot water?" Piers muttered to himself as he set off along the passage. Answer: someone who owed him money and was being leaned on. Someone who would borrow a car belonging to the club and use it to knock a man down in a little on-going plot of his own. Someone who would then tip off the police.

Piers started to run lightly, making no sound on his soft-soled shoes. The next light bulb was functioning normally and by it he saw that here the passage split. He could not remember this at all from childhood games of Murder in the Dark and closer examination revealed the reason for this. A door had been removed from what was now, in effect, the left-hand passageway. The door had always been kept locked.

Curious as to who had been in the entrance hall, he went a short distance down the left-hand passage and sniffed the air. Yes, whoever it was who smoked had come this way. David didn't smoke and neither did the cook, his aunt. Both the Jacksons did and so did his father. The latter was instantly ruled out, Mycroft only smoked cigars. The cleaning ladies worked only in the mornings.

He came to a steep flight of steps that led downwards and suddenly remembered the reason for the locked door during childhood years. This was part of the original moated Ashleigh Castle; deep cellars, a vault that was reputed to be haunted, and a well that local legend insisted was bottomless. The present Ashley family believed neither in ghosts nor bottomless wells but had preferred to keep their offspring away from such a tantalising playground.

The stairs brought him to a small room some twelve feet square. The single bare electric bulb, very dim because of a thick layer of dirt, was behind an iron grille in the ceiling. As Piers's gaze came to rest on it, it went out.

"The White Rabbit didn't smoke," he said into the darkness, his voice echoing hollowly around the walls. "It's you, Tom, isn't it? Joke's over."

The light came on again and Tom Jackson emerged from a doorway on the right-hand side of the room. He was grinning broadly.

"Just like old times, eh, Master Piers?"

"We weren't allowed down here as children."

Tom did not reply, just grinned more broadly making Piers wonder if he had been referring to more recent events.

"What are you doing down here, anyway?" he said.

"I check everywhere," was the reply. "D'you want to come on a tour of inspection with me?"

"If it doesn't take too long."

"It's too bloody cold to linger," Tom said. He eyed Piers up and down keenly. "You've got over being shot in quick time. That makes folk eat their words who said you lead an idle life."

"Youth helps."

"You train though, don't you? It stands to reason. I thought that when I saw you carry that soddin' heavy chimney pot up the ladder." He led the way through the door he had entered by. "This next bit's the place that's supposed to be haunted. I don't believe a word of it personally – I just think ghosts are invented when people have a cellar of fine wine they want left alone."

"Does it adjoin where my father keeps his wine now?"

"No, but it might have done at one time. Personally I think there were a lot more underground places here in the old days. More than likely most of them were filled with rubble when the place burnt down and was rebuilt. And a good job too – like as not nasty things went on in dungeons and so forth."

They entered a long low vault with a curving roof. The floor was of dry, chalky earth, the walls rough-hewn stone blocks, and the ceiling, oddly, in finely done brick-work. There was a feeling of timelessness in the room, as though it had existed from the moment the world began.

Piers said, "Did you see William Turner the night I was shot?"

Tom turned to look at him. "Can't say I did. Unless he was in the pub."

"No, earlier than that. Late afternoon."

Tom chuckled. "I was indoors. And you don't want to take too much notice of what William sees these days. His eyesight's not all that good since he had a slight stroke." He ducked down and went through a low opening. "Mind your head and watch your feet."

The ground sloped downwards for a few yards. It was very uneven, worn stones sticking up through the earth floor. Then they were able to stand upright, Piers more cautiously as he was several inches taller than Tom.

"That's the well," Tom said, indicating a round hole in the floor with a grating over it. The hole was at least six feet across.

"Some well," Piers commented, bending down to look.

Tom took a flash lamp from a shelf on the wall and shone it down. The beam was lost, petering out into blackness in the depths.

"*How* deep is it?" Piers asked.

"Dunno."

"But if you drop something down you must eventually hear a splash."

"No, you don't," Tom said. "You don't hear a sound."

"But dammit-all, Tom, someone must have *dug* the thing."

"The locals say it's natural, and at one time it was a spring and the water level dropped when they tapped the chalk springs further down the hill. It's possible, I suppose."

The cellar that housed the well was about twenty feet by fifteen. Around three sides were worn stone platforms where servants had rested water containers.

"Of course it was only used in time of drought," Tom Jackson said. "Or when the castle was under siege."

"And during times of plague and pollution," Piers added. "Thousands upon thousands of buckets have been dumped down on those ledges while people waited and chatted."

"Maybe," Tom said.

"Who has the key?"

"Key?"

"The key to the padlock that locks the grating."

"Oh. I do."

"I'll suggest to my father that the door's put back on in the passage to the kitchens. There might be grandchildren around before too long. Not me," he continued when the other gazed at him with curiosity. "But Thea might get married before too long."

"That's if she ain't number three," Tom said morosely.

"You said you weren't superstitious," Piers reminded him, probably speaking more sharply than he had intended.

"Superstition nothin'. There's someone got it in for you. It's obvious."

"Any ideas?"

"Not one," Tom said dismissively, brushing past him to put the flash lamp back on its ledge. "That's the emergency lighting by the way."

There was one further, short tunnel that ended suddenly in a pile of rubble. In stark contrast to the area they had covered already this was wet, water trickling down the walls to form greenish pools on the floor before it soaked away. The large stones that blocked further progress were covered in a dark-coloured slime.

"This is why I have to check," Tom said. "I have a notion that the moat – when it existed – was fed by a stream, and that when everything was rebuilt the water had nowhere to go. The Colonel's dead worried it's going to flood but apart from getting a bit worse after heavy rain there doesn't seem to be a real problem."

They retraced their footsteps, Piers glad to get back into the warmth of the house as he was only wearing a thin sweater. There was little point in trying to contact Commander Rolt until at least ten o'clock when he would be back on duty. But Rolt rang him at nine forty-five with the news that fibres from Giles's clothing – taken to London in a squad car – matched those found in the windscreen wipers of the Volvo and that the human hairs appeared to be the same as his too.

"I've told Area Eight I'm handling this," he went on. "It's important to get the investigation on an official footing at this end. To be frank I want a solution to this business so it can be got out of the way. We'll raid the club. You can do it, tomorrow. I got Ellis's message that you said you'd like a look at the membership list. It's the sort of club where there are probably several lists of members and it'll take unconventional methods to dig them out." Rolt broke off and laughed softly. "Sorry, I didn't intend that poor joke. The club's called The Boneyard. I'd like you back in town tonight and at HQ first thing in the morning. If you're at all worried at leaving your parents at home on their own, I suggest you bring them with you and they can stay at an hotel."

"That reminds me," Mycroft said when Piers had told them of his immediate departure. "Blake rang me at the office late this afternoon and asked me out to dinner tomorrow night. I think the beggar's trying to sweeten me up because he's after the money. I said I'd let him know by tonight. What do you think I ought to do?"

"I wish you'd mentioned this before," Piers said.

141

"Sorry. Slipped my mind for a while."

"Accept. See what he has to say."

The Colonel went off to phone.

"It's positively archaic only having two phones in a house this size," Piers said to his mother.

"You know what he's like," Elizabeth said. "Hates modern technology. He won't have a computer to help with the estate. I'm sure poor Charles has to carry all the facts and figures around in his head." She gave Piers a sharp look. "I wasn't aware that Crispin had asked your father for money."

"Gambling debts, apparently."

"Gambling debts! How stupid of him."

"Did he ever mention a club he went to in central London?"

"No, never."

"Do you mind if I ask you a very personal question?"

"Probably not," she answered slowly.

"Where did your affair with him take place?"

"In Brighton or Eastbourne," was the immediate reply. She uttered a light laugh. "Brighton of all places. Isn't that where everyone goes for dirty weekends? It was usually when there were Mothers' Union outings or some bunfight for the WI. That's where I told Mycroft I was going, anyway."

"Do you still love Blake?"

"I don't think I ever loved him. Fond of him, yes. I'm sure you think I'm very silly but I suppose he could give me a little of the excitement and glamour that being the wife of an Ashley could have brought and never has. Women *are* silly creatures in that respect and I've accepted it. Crispin has been my one wild fling in life – a once and for all kicking over the traces. I'm not sorry, just very grateful to Mycroft for being so understanding. That was the big dread, of course, that he'd find out and divorce me."

Mycroft returned a few minutes later. He was smiling.

"Well?" Piers asked impatiently.

"You have to hand it to the scoundrel. First it's dinner in the West End and then he's taking me to this club of his. I've an idea he wants to use me to show he has landed gentry friends. D'you still think it's a good idea, Piers?"

"Did he give you the name of the club?"

"Yes, he said I mustn't mind the name. It's called The Boneyard."

After a short silence Piers asked, "Did you see much action in the Army?"

Mycroft's eyebrows shot up. "What an extraordinary question. Yes, even though I was on the transport side of life, I saw a fair bit. Why?"

"You'll see a bit more tomorrow night." To Elizabeth he said, "Where did you hide the shooter?"

Chapter Thirteen

The night was fine and cold, a thin icing of frost on the roofs and windscreens of parked cars. Anyone seeing the four men – and few did as it was a little after one a.m. – might have assumed them to be junior officers from Chelsea Barracks. For Piers, in command of the group, had decided that they would not behave in uncouth fashion, bursting into the club as though it was an East End rock and drugs dive, but behave like gentlemen. To this end all four were in evening dress, and Stuart, code-name Pretender, had been ordered earlier in the day to get his hair cut.

The club was so named because the basement premises where it was housed had at one time been part of a much older building and, in the time of the Plague of London, had been used as a charnel-house. The modern building – a modest two-storey structure with a Greek restaurant on the ground floor, offices above – was painted white, in fact the work of re-painting it had only been completed the previous week. Piers knew this and also exactly the lay-out of the premises on all floors. And as usual the Fire Brigade had been most helpful in giving the whereabouts of emergency exits and fire-escapes. Time spent in thorough ground-work was never wasted.

"A charnel-house?" Oarsman said as they strolled down Percy Street. "Are you sure?" His real name was Martin and he had rowed for Oxford.

"I did a little homework," Piers told him. "All this area was part of lands belonging to a merchant. During the plague his servants collected the bodies of the dead in carts and buried them in lime-pits. But they couldn't dig the pits fast enough so the corpses were dumped in disused buildings until they could be dealt with. There were other mass burial sites in Soho."

"The good old days," Dark Horse, Phil, said with a laugh. Rolt himself had bestowed this alias when the speaker had emerged with top marks in his group in the selection course for F.9 having started as a rank outsider. Dark Horse's problem – if it can be described as such – was that he *looked* stupid. To F.9 this was his greatest asset, bone-headed thugs always being much in demand in the criminal underworld.

Piers said, "The emergency exit leads into an alley that comes out at the side of a pub in Windmill Street. According to the department's photographer who took a few pictures for me this morning and who's been in this area at night on another job, the door's usually left open for ventilation purposes as it's right next to the kitchen. Yes, the place does have a restaurant – I forgot to mention that earlier."

"Someone'll be watching the door," Pretender pointed out.

"Of course," Piers replied. "And we must assume that he's like the side of a barn and with a brain in inverse ratio. But he won't be there all the time. He'll wander through to one of the bars or answer a client's query. He might even have to watch the front entrance as well. The important thing is to take him out. Even more important is to do it so quietly that no one misses him, or if they do they assume he's gone to the john. Stuart, old man, you can do that."

"Right," said Pretender with, it must be admitted, relish. Stuart did everything quietly. Physically, he was one of the bastions of F.9. This is not to say that he was of big build for in actual fact he was not as tall as Piers. His strength was in his hands and long arms; gangland heavies having discovered to their cost that they only had to come within his reach to be gathered, almost lovingly, and rendered very unconscious. When it came to trouble it took bullets to put him down, not fists or knives, and there had been one occasion still very vivid in Piers's memory when as a probationer he had fled, literally, to the man from three members of a Triad gang when they were both on an assignment in Chinatown. The one armed with a knife and clearly intent on slitting both of them from stem to stern had finished up with a broken neck, the other two out cold on the pavement. Stuart had had plenty of energy left to box Piers's ears afterwards for being careless. But he had no ambition to lead, quite content now to take orders from his one-time protégé and when off-duty to go home to wife and baby daughter.

"Then what?" Oarsman asked.

"You *were* at the briefing," Piers reminded him. "We don our masks as soon as we're inside and preferably before anyone's seen us. The manager's office is up a flight of three stairs near the kitchen and actually above it, the kitchen being lower than the rest of the premises. We make for that, get him to open the safe if he's there, do it ourselves a little more noisily if he isn't, all the while repelling borders from the door. We'll have ten minutes before the closing team arrive, ostensibly in response to a witness of our arrival having dialled 999 at that phone box over there. That will be what Mr Ricardo will be told afterwards. The main thing is to get what's in the safe and search Ricardo's office from top to bottom. Martin, I want you and Phil to get on with that while I grill Ricardo, and give Stuart a hand if necessary. Rip up the carpet and tear down the walls if you think there are other hiding places – especially if nothing's in the safe."

"Then we finish pulverizing the opposition, pinch a few watches and wallets from the clients," Dark Horse said, "and make our escape only to fall into the arms of our brother officers. I hope they don't make it too realistic – I ended up with a black eye once."

"Very good for your cover," Stuart told him soothingly.

Piers halted. "We're here. That's the pub over the road. I propose that we just breeze in through the back door of the club as though we're slightly canned Hurray Henries. There's no point in causing instant panic amongst the clients on our way *in*."

"Or alerting any undercover Special Branch bods in the place as has happened before," Stuart added.

There was muffled laughter, Pretender having been called to explain himself once as to why a Special Branch sergeant also working undercover had suffered a broken jaw, and defending himself by saying that the injured party had been the biggest oaf present. There was quite a lot of not too good-humoured rivalry.

They walked down the alley, Oarsman singing in a very cracked tenor voice a university chant that they had heard before but which always made them titter. The smell of cooking wafted to meet them and Stuart groaned in appreciation. He was forever hungry.

There was no doubt about it, the bouncer was standing at the end of the alley, taking the air.

"Put him where he'll be found by the closing team," Piers whispered. "And by that I *don't* mean down a manhole."

Stuart smiled reflectively at the stars and flexed his wrists.

"That's Sid," breathed Dark Horse. "We've met before."

"Hide yourself then," Piers ordered.

"He's a bad lad, Stuart. Dangerous. Watch yourself."

Oarsman commenced to treat them to the second verse of his song, *fortissimo*, under cover of which Pretender said, "Suspected of having been responsible for putting two young Met. constables into hospital for quite a while but nothing could be proved. I'm beginning to dislike this Luigi Ricardo already."

"I don't want him crippled," Piers said grimly. "No, *this* one," he added, seeing the expression on the other's face. "Stuart, I'm warning you . . ."

"Your wish is my command," Pretender said sarcastically, going forward.

Such was the excellence of the semi-inebriated gestures – a forefinger tapping a wrist, Stuart tripping over his own feet as he tottered in the man's direction – that the bouncer looked helpfully at his watch. To no avail, it was too dark, so he went closer to a street lamp, half turning away from the one who was supposedly asking him the time in order to see. Ten seconds later he was insensible, gagged with his own handkerchief, hands and feet tied together with his own shoe-laces. He was bundled unceremoniously behind a pile of beer crates at the rear of the pub.

Entry to The Boneyard was ridiculously easy. One chef did glance up from chopping vegetables, the kitchen being almost opposite the rear entrance. From the total lack of interest Piers deduced that it was commonplace for clients to come in this way. The stairs to the manager's office were just to the left of the kitchen. Adjacent to them was a small bar manned by a young woman in an off-the-shoulder evening dress. She was talking to a dark-haired giant of a man who was obviously bouncer Number Two. He yielded utterly and in complete silence to a little more science from Pretender, who had by now pulled on his mask. The girl opened her mouth to scream but no sound emerged.

Piers ducked under the bar flap, grabbed her rolled-up coat and handbag from a bottom shelf, took her hand and hustled her through the door into the open air. "I've just accepted your resignation. Go and get a job in a place that's on the straight and narrow."

The girl gaped at him for a moment and then turned and ran.

By this time the other three were on a small landing at the top of the three stairs. Around the corner to the right was the door to the office. At a signal from Piers, Stuart knocked politely and when a man's voice bade him enter, went in.

And all the while the muted sounds of cutlery tinkling on plates, the click and whirr of the gaming tables, continued unabated. As Piers ran up the three stairs there was a burst of laughter from the direction of the restaurant and a group started to sing *Happy Birthday to You*.

He had assumed that Blake and his father would be somewhere at the front of the building in the casino. Positively the last thing he had expected was the tableau before him now: one man behind the desk, standing, obviously Ricardo, another two by his side, one holding a gun and pointing it uncompromisingly at Mycroft Ashley's temple as he wrote a cheque, seated, Blake at his side, utterly ashen. The group remained motionless, like a wax-works display, for one split second longer and then came to life as the silenced gun in Dark Horse's hand coughed and the Mauser trained on Mycroft Ashley fell to the floor. A few spots of blood followed it down but no one noticed.

"I've paid!" Ricardo yelled shrilly. "This is a mistake. I've paid, I tell you. It's – "

"Shut up," Piers told him, pitching his voice anywhere but at its normal level. He ignored the heavy thump as Stuart

148

wrung to the carpet the man standing nearest to him and leaned over to take Mycroft's cheque book. "Extortion, sir?" he asked silkily.

"God, if I'd have known that this would happen," Blake burst out. "Mycroft, I just don't know what to say to – "

Piers was not a vicious or violent man and contented himself with shoving Blake and his chair over backwards. There was no doubt in his mind that the "this" that Blake had referred to was the business of the gun, not what was taking place now. In other words, Blake was trying to save face.

"The combination of the safe?" Pretender requested of Ricardo, moving in that gentleman's direction with the inexorability of a mowing machine.

The Italian's hands were fluttering like handkerchieves on the line in a Force Ten. "I've paid, I tell you. They came last week and I paid them." He uttered a dispairing wail as he was garnered and lifted as though weightless to where a large picture on the wall was swung out like a door to reveal the safe in the wall behind it.

"Just tell me the numbers and I'll do it," Stuart said encouragingly.

"Who?" Piers asked. "Who came last week and you paid them?"

"Lenny, of course. Aren't you from Lenny?" Ricardo squeaked.

"No, we're free-lance," Oarsman said. "Get a bloody move on."

"What the hell *is* this?" Blake roared, having picked himself up.

Ricardo went into a positive shimmy of tiny shrugs, his thin moustache keeping time.

"Don't listen to *them*," Pretender shouted in his ear. "Give me the numbers."

Piers held out his hand to Mycroft who shrugged angrily and removed his Rolex watch, holding it out for Piers to take. All in the cause of authenticity.

"Go to hell," Blake said as Piers turned to him.

It seemed unlikely that Mycroft was worried that Blake might recognise the man facing him, balaclava helmet notwithstanding, for Piers had applied black mascara to his blond eyelashes. In fact it was more than possible that all his anger and resentment surfaced at this point. The straight left he gave the surgeon was not particularly stylish but it served to propel him backwards for the second time in so many minutes. Only on this occasion Blake stayed down.

The safe was open, Pretender shoving the contents into his pockets. The man who had had the gun shot from his hand still stood motionless, holding the hand, blood dripping slowly through his fingers. He flinched visibly when Mycroft approached him and was just as clearly flabbergasted when his wounded hand was snatched and rapidly bound up in an exquisite small square of printed lawn.

"Lenny who?" Piers asked Ricardo as his team commenced to tear the room apart. Stuart had moved to the door and had opened it slightly, watching and listening.

"I don't know. They don't give their names. Just Lenny."

"How much money does Crispin Blake owe you?"

"Who?" The Italian tore his gaze from a filing cabinet that was yielding, reluctantly, to Oarsman's ministrations.

"Him. The one with the nose bleed who's asleep."

More little jumps of the shoulders. "I don't know – two thousand perhaps."

"Did he borrow your car? The Volvo?"

"A lot of people use the car."

Piers grabbed the lapels of the dinner jacket and shook Ricardo. "Tell me the truth!"

"Why you want to know that?" Ricardo stuttered.

"Someone used it to knock down a friend of mine, that's why."

"The police – "

"I'm not interested in what the police have done," Piers interrupted. "Did Blake borrow the car that night?"

"He could have done. It was parked nearby."

"Was he in town? Had you seen him?"

"I had seen him in the morning of the day the car went missing."

"Where are the keys to the car kept?"

"There are two sets. One is here in my desk drawer, and the other usually with the chef. He uses it to go to the vegetable market."

"So which set were used?"

"I don't know. The chef was ill that night. There was terrible chaos."

"But you must know if your set of keys were missing."

"They were in my desk drawer when the police came to ask me about it. But I could not say if someone had borrowed them and then put them back."

"Did Blake come in here on that morning?"

Ricardo nodded. "I asked him to come and see me."

"In connection with his gambling debts?"

"Yes."

"Fuzz!" Stuart announced. "Inside. Not who we're expecting."

Piers swore. "Give me your gun." When it had been handed over he grabbed Mycroft. "Sorry about this – you'll have to come with us for a short way."

"Someone's boobed," Stuart muttered in Piers's ear as they moved towards the top of the stairs. "West End Central's actioned the call."

"Surprise, surprise," Piers said through his teeth, seeing that Blake was now conscious. The last thing he wanted was to have the mask pulled off in his company. That little surprise would come during Blake's interrogation.

The area car crew were at the bottom of the stairs, a sergeant and two constables, all in uniform.

"Just step quietly to one side," Piers told them, holding the barrel of the pistol to Mycroft's head. "Then no one will get hurt, your good selves included."

The trio chose instead to walk in front of them. A grim procession, Piers sweating inside his mask, they progressed through the restaurant and casino.

"No one has a go," Stuart said all at once as two waiters moved in their directioin.

"You wait until we get you outside, laddie," said the sergeant under his breath.

"Precisely," Piers whispered. "Where the *pre-arranged* arrests will take place."

Oarsman blithely recited, "Once upon a time there were three little foxes Who didn't wear stockings, and they didn't wear sockses . . ."

The sergeant spun round. 'F.9!'

"Just walk through the door and away from the club," Piers told him.

"But they all had handkerchiefs to blow their noses, And kept their handkerchiefs in cardboard boxes . . ." Oarsman warbled when they were in the night air.

Suddenly the street seemed to be full of police who advanced not at all slowly.

Piers gave the gun to his father. "You may now overpower me and thus earn a place on the front pages of the national press."

"They lived in the forest in three little houses, And they didn't wear coats, and they didn't wear trousies . . ."

As was traditional the four gave the other team a run for their money. Gaping bystanders – and it was quite amazing how so many people had mustered from nowhere – were treated to a fairly brisk and business-like display of law and order triumphing over evil-doers. When it was all over one of the later could still be heard, muffled, but doggedly proclaiming: "They ran through the woods in their little bare tootsies, And they played 'Touch Last' with a family of mouses."

"With deepest apologies to Mr A. A. Milne," Piers said to Rolt who was looking down at him as he sat on the kerb. "Pretender has his pocket full of my mother's jewellery, sir."

Although it would be incorrect to say that police personnel at West End Central started a new calendar with Year One on that early morning when Commander Rolt and his retinue arrived with several suspects, or that forever afterwards it was referred to as The Night The Shit Hit The Fan In New Burlington Street, there were nevertheless lingering shockwaves. And Rolt was quite within his rights, of course. People were never taken for questioning to the secret HQ near Woodford, in fact hardly any outsiders visited it at all. So, really, when it came to this kind of situation, the Commander was a man without a home base. His brief therefore permitted him to take himself and his officers to the nearest – as nomenclature has it – nick.

The first thing that Rolt required was the name of the

person who had actioned an unforeseen 999 call from a member of the public who had seen Piers's team deal with the first bouncer instead of abiding by standing orders issued to cover the 'raid'. When this proved to be a probationer three months out of Hendon who had been left unsupervised while his sergeant tutor had gone to the canteen for coffee to keep them both awake on account of their having not been relieved – half the station being down with flu – several more senior officers breathed out slowly and sent for the hapless probationer.

"Are you awake *now*?" Rolt demanded, clearing clutter from the top of the desk in the office he had commandeered by the simple expedient of sweeping everything into the wastepaper basket.

"Yes, sir," whispered the man.

"Speak up, I can't hear you."

"Yes, sir," louder.

"Good. Sit down. I'm going out for a few minutes. If Blake is brought in for questioning while I'm away, just stand over there by the door and keep an eye on him. If he makes offensive remarks, ignore him."

Blake did make offensive remarks when he was brought in. The probationer stonily stared at the opposite wall, quite unaware that the ones who had so cheerfully sent him to the slaughter were at this moment mustered and – with Rolt's own staff looking on but being careful with their faces – listening to a gut-wrenching account of their own shortcomings.

"Right," said the Commander on his return. "Yes, you can stay here, Rawlings. It won't hurt you to learn about interview techniques. Find a pencil and paper, sit over there and make a note of anything that interests you and that you want to ask me about afterwards."

"Then you need another officer in here, sir," observed Rawlings without really thinking if the offering was wise. "I mean, if I'm not here in an official capacity."

"You're quite correct," Rolt told him solemnly. "And I had already thought of it. He'll be along at any moment."

Blake said, "I want it put on record that I object to being used as some kind of lecture exhibit."

153

"Come now, sir," Rolt said gently. "I should imagine that you've had trainees under your tutorage. Just think of yourself as the patient for once." He seated himself behind the desk. "And no record is being kept. Not just yet. Any notes that young Rawlings makes will be destroyed afterwards. If, however, you choose to make a proper statement, then it will be written down and you will be requested to read it through and sign it."

"And it will be used in evidence against me?" Blake said derisively. "What the hell is all this crap?"

"No, I'm not cautioning you," Rolt said. "The department I work for doesn't have much to do with that side of things. I'm merely an investigating officer. And right now I'm trying to clear up this business of the blackmail of a certain Mrs Elizabeth Ashley, the attempted murder of her eldest son Piers, a hit and run attack on her other son, Giles, and lastly, and by no means least, the murder of a man by the name of Colin Morgan."

"You're out of your mind if you think I'm connected with any of that," Blake shouted. "And I'll have you know that the Chief Constable of Sussex is a very good friend of mine, and when he hears that I've been assaulted and arrested on false pretences I can't imagine what his reaction will be."

"You can forget that rubbish," Rolt said calmly. "Mycroft Ashley volunteered the information that he hit you without any prompting on my part. Under the circumstances I think he behaved with incredible restraint. You seem to forget that you were responsible for him being a victim of attempted extortion."

"I didn't know they'd turn nasty like that," Blake said sullenly. "I merely thought that if I took Mycroft to the club, he'd agree to give me a loan."

"A bit audacious, don't you think? Seeing you'd been having an affair with the man's wife."

"I haven't the slightest intention of endeavouring to justify my behaviour to you."

"It has a direct bearing on the case. That was the reason for the blackmail. I suggest to you that no one knew about the affair but yourself and Mrs Ashley, and it was *you* who made demands for money."

"I have made no demands for money," Blake said, banging his hand on the desk at every word.

"You said that the jewellery would *do*."

"What jewellery?"

"Mrs Ashley's mother's jewellery. It was found in the wall safe at the gambling club. I believe you were unconscious at the time."

"You can't possibly know whose jewellery it is in so short a time."

"But we do. It was identified by both Mycroft and Piers Ashley. There's a locket, I understand, with initials, and a picture of Mrs Ashley's father who was killed in the War." Rolt smiled bleakly. "Dodgy stuff to accept in lieu of blackmail money. Jewellery can be traced."

"It's all circumstantial evidence."

"I agree. Another thing that was mentioned while you were out for the count is the matter of a Volvo car that was used to knock down Giles Ashley. Luigi Ricardo confirms that you were at the club that day. Nothing like getting someone who's threatening you off your back by using his car to try to kill a man, is there?"

"I deny it. Utterly."

"And it's possible that you hired Colin Morgan to put a bullet in Piers Ashley in order to frighten Mrs Ashley into parting with either more jewellery or money. You might even have told Morgan to *miss* as you didn't really want to hurt him. You only wanted money. Tell me, what did Ricardo threaten to do to you if you didn't pay up soon?"

Blake told him and Rawlings dropped his pencil.

"Picturesque," Rolt murmured dryly. "This could be brought out very strongly at your trial, you know. An eminent surgeon hounded by London thugs." Rolt did not add his other thought; that if half the jury were women, Blake would probably be found not guilty. Unless he, Rolt, had a much better case against him than he had at present. "You were desperate for money. You're very highly paid of course, but there is the matter of the young lady who seems to be on television every night and who doubtless has very expensive tastes. She's been the real cause of your trouble, hasn't she, Mr Blake?"

Blake's good-looking features suffused with red. "God, that young bastard Ashley's been telling a few tales. When I was his age I kept my trap shut about things people told me in confidence."

Rolt's eyebrows rose. "Did you tell him that in confidence? I thought you yarned with him in a pub in Arundel where you were having lunch. But you mustn't be too hard on him – I asked him to talk to you."

But Blake was looking appalled. "I didn't give him her *name* though."

"No, you can blame me for discovering that. I have a few well-placed friends of my own – in the medical world." Rolt's gaze rose to where Rawlings was sitting. "Do I perceive that you have a question of your own to ask?"

"Well, yes, sir," Rawlings said, trying to organise his thoughts as well as look into the hawk-like eyes. "I know nothing about this case, sir, but it was just mentioned that it was suspected that Mr Blake had hired a man called Colin Morgan to shoot at Mr Ashley. If Mr Blake was so badly off, what with one thing and another, how is he supposed to have done that?"

"It's complicated," Rolt said with a smile for the pro-bationer that helped to stop him drawing squiggles on his pad. "I think I can answer the question. Colin Morgan's father is estate manager for the Ashley's, and although the farms he's responsible for are doing badly, the Morgan family is very well off, thank you, with new cars and other such things. Mr Blake, how did you discover that Charles Morgan was defrauding his employer?"

"That's no secret in Ashleigh Coombe," Blake said after hesitating.

"But you don't live in the village."

"No, but I sometimes lunch at the pubs there. You do overhear gossip."

"Or, of course, the Colonel might have mentioned to you that the farms weren't doing very well and being a perceptive man you saw that the Morgan's had their nest well feathered. Was that the way it was, Mr Blake?"

Blake sighed loudly. "I would be lying if I said that Mycroft hadn't mentioned to me that the farms were going through a

156

bad patch. Agriculture is in the doldrums right now."

"Did you bring to Colonel Ashley's notice what was being said in the village?"

"No, of course not. That would have been a dreadful impertinence. Besides, I don't believe in repeating gossip."

"Do you like Charles Morgan?"

"I don't know the man well enough to like or dislike him."

"Please answer the question."

But before Blake could say anything there was a knock on the door and, in response to Rolt's bidding, Piers Ashley entered. Following orders that Rolt had given earlier he seated himself, took the balaclava helmet from his pocket, put it on for a few moments and then pulled it off and replaced it in his pocket.

There was a very long silence.

Then the Commander said, "So I think that explains most of the questions that must have been going through your mind, Mr Blake. That is the reason why a policeman, myself, who is not really supposed to be an ordinary detective, is investigating this case. My department isn't supposed to replace the CID in any way. We're undercover people. But all of us, every single man and woman, is keen to discover why you arranged to have this man – a very promising officer – shot."

"He's a *policeman*?" Blake said huskily and at the second attempt to speak.

"Yes, and it doesn't matter if you know now because he'll never be required to work so dangerously undercover again. One of the reasons for that is the injury he sustained. I'm sure that he'll attain a very high standard of fitness again eventually but I don't think it would be fair to ask the same of him as I did in the past. So I think it's safe to say that you've been responsible for not only hazarding his life but his career too. What do you have to say to that?"

Rawlings was trying not to look thunderstruck. Evidence had been the watchword at Hendon College. But the thing that struck him most – and up until now he had not believed the grapevine's insistence that Rolt was utterly ruthless – was the obvious shock with which these remarks had been heard by Ashley. One could only assume that nothing had been said in private to him concerning his future. Rawlings discovered that he was extremely angry, an emotion not at all mitigated by the knowledge that Blake was even more horrified and likely not only to confess but to burst into tears as well.

Rolt went on, "You didn't feel too badly about doing it, did you, Piers being a common crook? People who take the law into their own hands deserve it if others take pot-shots at them. They're used to it really. But when Morgan either chose to forget your instructions to shoot to miss or bodged it, then you had a crisis of conscience and did everything you could to save his life."

Blake sat quite motionless, ashen, biting his lip.

Rolt slammed his hand on the desk top. "Dammit, man, you're his *Godfather!*"

Then Blake's face did contort and he covered it with both hands, bent over, shoulders shaking. But for his sobs there was silence for at least two minutes.

"Tell the truth," Rolt said quite gently. "If you're straight-forward with me I'll make things as easy as I can for you."

After a few moments Blake sat up slowly. "I thought the police weren't supposed to make bargains."

"It's not a bargain," the Commander replied patiently. "But it seems to me that we have a large nest of vipers here. Ricardo obviously isn't running a clean shop for a start, and from what he said he's also subscribing to a protection racket. Then there's the business of Charles Morgan. Do you have any evidence that he's lining his own pockets?"

"He had too much to drink at one of the Ashley's Christmas parties," Blake said. "Bragged to me about it as we were collecting our coats to leave."

"Then you're the key to sorting out quite a few problems, aren't you?"

Furiously, Piers said, "But you must have had blackmail in mind then or you would have told my father."

"I'm really sorry," Blake whispered and wept afresh.

158

Chapter Fourteen

When Blake had himself under control and at a sign from Rolt, Piers took over the questioning.

"How did you know the shooting had actually taken place?"

Haggard, Blake said, "Colin Morgan rang me in a state of utter panic. He said he'd fired to miss as I'd asked, but you'd moved into the line of fire just as he'd pulled the trigger. Piers – "

He swept on. "My father said you'd given him hell because I had a sword cut on my arm. How did you know he'd had a go at me with a sword?"

Rawlings, a witness to all this with something approaching avarice now, observed that this was new to the Commander who stared at Ashley in surprise.

"Charles Morgan phoned me that same night – very late. He was trying to defuse the situation because he knew I was furious with Colin for making such a mess of it. Giles had said to him apparently that Mycroft had lost his temper and grabbed a sword. Morgan thought that proved the Colonel detested Piers and wouldn't make too many waves – throwing his weight and influence about – to find out who had done it. I didn't agree with this line of thinking and told him so. I slammed the phone down on him as a matter of fact."

"And you took my father to task over the cut in an effort to deflect any suspicion that might have come your way?"

"Yes," Blake said. "But look, I – "

"Did Colin Morgan get in touch with you after I'd asked him questions at the saw-mill?"

"No, I never heard from Colin Morgan again."

"Think," Piers snapped. "It's very important."

"I know what *you're* thinking," Blake said wearily. "I never spoke to him again or received any communication from him."

"No, as a matter of fact I don't think you killed Morgan," Rolt said. "But you drove the car that knocked down Giles Ashley. For no other reason than to try to incriminate Luigi Ricardo – it was you who tipped off the police – and therefore get him and his henchmen off your back. It was your big mistake. It gave us the connection between you and why you wanted to borrow money from the Colonel. Still, I suppose not many men would think clearly after the fate promised to you if you failed to pay up." Rolt smiled in a fashion that reminded Rawlings of the trailer for *Jaws*. "*That* would have curtailed your expensive activities with young ladies in show-biz."

But it was nice to know that Rolt was human after all, Rawlings thought.

From his briefcase Rolt took a sheet of paper and handed it to Blake. "This is a photocopy of the final letter received by Mrs Ashley. If you could just confirm that you sent it. It's for the record really, she destroyed all the others."

Blake glanced at it. "No. I didn't send this."

"You didn't send it," Rolt said very slowly.

"No. This isn't one of mine."

Rolt and Ashley exchanged glances.

Blake said, "I think you realize that I intend to co-operate. But I'm not going to say I did things that I didn't."

"No one came to collect on that occasion if you remember, sir," Ashley said.

Rolt addressed PC Rawlings. "Be so kind as to get us all some coffee and biscuits."

When Rawlings had gone out Blake undid his bow tie. "This'll finish me. You're looking at a ruined man."

Rolt nodded. "Yes, and to have a surgeon of your calibre behind bars is a terrible loss to the world. I'm all in favour of careful flogging for people like you. You're not the sort who would offend again anyway. You could spend a couple of days getting over it and then offer your services to a Third World country until folk over here had forgotten about you. It would save the British taxpayer a hell of a lot of money."

"I suppose you're in favour of hanging too," Blake said bitterly.

"No, as a matter of fact I'm not. Too many mistakes have been made in the past to justify its re-introduction." He stood up and stretched. "I'm giving you a rest, Blake. Make the most of it."

"You're not a conventional copper in any sense of the word," Blake declared.

"No," Rolt said with a bleak smile. "I learned all my interrogation techniques in the army. I was one of the army officers brought in to the police force by the Thatcher government. I wouldn't say that it was a particularly popular move as far as senior officers in the Met are concerned, but from my point of view it helps me in my new rôle as undercover policeman, having been an undercover soldier."

When Rawlings had brought in the refreshments, Blake said, "So who did compile that nasty little missive then? I'm quite offended that you thought I'd make up anything so crude." He seemed to have recovered most of his usual self-confidence.

"D'you want us to congratulate you?" Rolt asked mildly. Then he said, "What I'd like you to do now is give us a full account of everything. Right from the moment that you decided you badly needed money."

"Last autumn," Blake began slowly after draining his coffee mug. "That was when it started. When Ricardo really began to put the pressure on me. I didn't owe him that much then. But you know how it is – you think that if you chance a bit more money you'll win and be able to pay all your debts. When that idea went wrong I knew I'd have to think of something else – and pretty quickly."

"So you immediately thought of Elizabeth Ashley and the jewellery that her mother had just left her."

Blake nodded, looking at Piers warily. "I took it for granted that the stuff was insured. I thought that if Elizabeth had to part with it, she could say it had been stolen. I had no idea, of course, what it – "

Rolt halted Piers's headlong rush by succeeding in catching

161

him by one wrist and twisting smartly. He stopped as though poleaxed, unable to stifle the exclamation. The Commander held him there for a moment until he felt him yield.

"Go outside and cool off for ten minutes," Rolt ordered. After Piers had gone, slamming the door, he said, "I was waiting for that to happen. I think I would have done the same if someone had suggested that my mother was all ready to swindle an insurance company. I've changed my mind about you, Blake. I'm beginning to think you're not so much a desperate man as a rat. Carry on with what you were saying."

After gathering his thoughts Blake spoke in an undertone. "Of course I had no idea what the value of the jewellery was. Ricardo said he'd take it as long as it was worth more than what I owed him. And when I sent the first letter to Elizabeth, I didn't really think she'd go along with it. She'd always seemed – well, tough."

"A woman's immediate family do tend to be her weakest point," Rolt said in such chilling tones that Blake shuddered. "How many letters did you send?"

"Several. I'm not sure exactly how many."

"But after co-operating she then refused to go any further and failed to make the drop – as crime stories have it."

"Yes."

"So you made arrangements to have Piers Ashley shot at."

"That's right."

"Do keep talking. Otherwise I might just get Ashley back in here."

"It had been so easy up until then," Blake said, the words all coming out in a rush. Understandably, Rawlings thought. "It occurred to me that she might ask Mycroft for some money if I frightened her a bit. Piers has always been her favourite. I suddenly remembered that Colin Morgan hated Piers's guts. It was no secret – they'd practically had a stand-up fight in a pub one night. But the pressure had to be put on Charles Morgan, not his son. Colin wasn't very bright and probably wouldn't have cared a damn if his old man had gone to prison for embezzlement. But luckily for me, Charles had him right under his thumb."

"Are you saying that you didn't offer Colin any money and

that his father did all the persuading as far as that was concerned?"

"Charles gave Colin five hundred pounds to do the job."

"But he accidentally hit Piers. Then what happened?"

"Well, as I said just now, Colin rang me in a panic to say that Piers had walked into the bullet – or he thought he had. And then later that night Charles phoned me, hoping that I was going to keep my trap shut about the whole episode. Too right I was – did he think me a fool?"

"Someone found out about it. And that person must have got the entire story out of Colin. When Piers questioned Colin it was this person who Colin contacted afterwards. And we know what happened then."

"I didn't kill him," Blake said with another shiver. "I swear to you, I didn't."

"Has it occurred to you that whoever it is probably knows all about your part in this as well? Lucky for you, man, that you're in police custody."

"It must have been this other person who sent the letter you just showed me."

"Yes, but why didn't someone turn up to collect the fake money that Piers planted?"

"They got wind of his plan, perhaps."

"The arrangements were made in private and Ashley left for the usual place where the packages were dropped before anyone arrived at the Hall to see him depart. Did you tell either of the Morgans that you were blackmailing Mrs Ashley?"

Blake stared at him scornfully. "Of course I bloody well didn't."

"Then there's only one possible explanation," Rolt said calmly. "The Hall is bugged."

"Or a member of staff overheard and is in the pay of this person."

"What, overheard several conversations over days – weeks even? If that is so, it's just as dangerous." Rolt picked up the phone on the desk and requested to be put through to Inspector Leadbetter. Then he changed his mind and cancelled the order. "No, I think we'll keep this in-house. I'll send some of my people down to have a look over the place."

163

"Is that all you want from me?" Blake asked, slumped in his chair.

"No, not quite, was it you who suggested to Ricardo that if you brought the Colonel to the club he might be persuaded to pay up for you, or vice versa?"

"I suggested it. But I didn't know the little rat would hold a gun to his head."

"Really?" Rolt said, disbelief writ large.

"Really," Blake replied.

"It was just as well that Mrs Ashley had told Piers everything and also, eventually, her husband, isn't it? If she hadn't you might have got away with it." Rolt picked up the phone again. "I'm now going to have you taken into custody. You'll have to tell the story all over again, I'm afraid. Several times probably. But you'll be in the safest place until this affair's finally solved and we know who killed Colin Morgan. I'll keep my word to you though. I've a suspicion that they run crooked gaming tables at The Boneyard and there's a fairly strong case when it comes to the threats made against you. That will help. I suggest that in court you play the part of the top-of-the-tree surgeon who forgets the ghastly pressures of work by being a feckless playboy. But then again, that's not far from the truth, is it?"

"I'm glad you stayed away," the Commander said several minutes later.

"Sorry, sir," Piers muttered. "But I could have – "

Coldly, Rolt interrupted. "The next time I even have the *suspicion* that you're about to lay hands on a suspect, you'll be out of F.9 so fast that not even your backside'll touch the ground. Is that understood?"

"Yes, sir." His wrist still felt that it had come off worst in an argument with a gin trap.

"Right. Now, what was in the safe besides the jewellery?"

"Ten thousand, four hundred and fifty-one pounds and seventy-six pence, the deeds of a house in Potter's Bar, and a couple of letters promising payment of debts on certain dates."

"Does it look as though Ricardo's likely to talk?"

"Yes, but only after his two minders started to sing their heads off."

164

"Were they running a bent house?"

"It looks like it, sir. I don't know the full details but there was some trickery involved when customers had had too much to drink. And it looks as though there was some kind of fiddle going on in the restaurant with the wine. Labels changed on bottles when the clients didn't look as though they were wine experts."

"That old chestnut!" Rolt exclaimed. "I thought that went out in the days of Good Queen Bess. Oh well, Leadbetter and the Met can sort it out together now we've landed most of the fish for them. I understand that your father has made a statement and returned to where your parents are staying. Where *are* they staying, by the way?"

"At my flat in Shepherd's Bush. If they're not safe there, they're not safe anywhere."

"I intend to send a couple of people from the interior surveillance team to Ashleigh Hall. With your father's permission, of course."

"You think it's bugged, sir?" said Piers in amazement.

"How else were your plans overheard? Someone must have known you intended to set a trap. That's if Blake is to be believed."

"It's possible he did send that letter and then decided not to collect."

"Suffered a crisis of conscience?" Rolt said with a twist to his mouth. "Perhaps. But I don't think so somehow. Would he leave five hundred pounds in a litter bin?"

Unconsciously Piers was rubbing his wrist. "What are your orders for me, sir?"

"You can go with the bugging team. You know the house well enough to be of some help to them."

"Thank you, sir," Piers said, getting to his feet and not bothering to try to keep the bitterness from his voice.

"Doctor Miller was very annoyed with me," Rolt said, leaning back in his chair in order to look him right in the eye. "He accused me of squandering you and of ignoring the fact that you'd been very seriously injured. I assured him that I intend to withdraw you from active duty until I have his blessing on your return. So please don't imagine that you have to hurl yourself into acts of folly and questionable heroism in order to make me change my mind. It's already made up."

"Yes, sir," Piers acknowledged, making for the door. "Will I meet the team at the house or collect them on the way?"

"I need another assistant, Piers. Inspector Ellis has to stand in for me when I'm off duty and things are getting so busy that I'll need to find someone to relieve *him* occasionally. But I need someone too. A man who can do a bit of the running about for me. Liaise with the teams at the coal-face if necessary – accompany me when I attend a scene-of-crime. And he'd be armed. Frankly someone to watch my back. It's a dogsbody job in a way."

Piers slowly came back into the centre of the room. "Are you offering *me* this job, sir?" he enquired, only a little breathlessly.

"Yes. Until you're fit enough to perform fifty pressups a minute or whatever the norm is these days. Then I thought I might put you in charge of Records."

Just as slowly Piers re-seated himself, not taking his eyes off Rolt's face for a second. For a long moment neither spoke. Records was the responsibility of a man by the name of Hall who had been severely crippled by a fall from a building during his days working for Special Branch and who was now in a wheelchair.

"I think I would prefer the dogsbody job, sir," Piers said.

"So you don't fancy tearing round in Records doing all the macho stuff?" the Commander asked, the merest twinkle in his eyes.

"No, I'd rather . . ." He broke off, bereft of words.

"It might mean you'd have to drive the car instead of me getting a driver," Rolt elaborated. "I try to catch up on all these confounded reports I'm supposed to read. But it always helps to share ideas with close colleagues, doesn't it? That's how things get done."

Piers nodded dumbly, actually feeling a little faint.

"The team can find their own way to Sussex," Rolt said, changing the subject without pausing for breath. "You go and get written permission from the Colonel to have them on the premises and then make your way there. I shall require an up to the minute report at mid-day. Meanwhile, I'll arrange to have Charles Morgan picked up."

Piers was a good hundred yards from the building before he realized that he hadn't actually voiced acknowledgement of the order, just dived out of the door.

"This is a very nice flat," said Elizabeth from the tiny kitchen when he had let himself in. "What can I get you for breakfast? We discovered the little corner shop was open."

"It never seems to close," he said, yawning. "I've only time for coffee – I've got to go out again."

"Oh, poor you. Where?"

"Home. Rolt wants the place looked over for bugs."

"Bugs!"

"Listening devices."

She laughed. "For a moment I thought you meant creepy-crawlies."

"Where's Dad?"

"Asleep. He's quite worn out with all the excitement." She took the kettle to the sink to fill it. "Is this dreadful business nearly over?"

"Almost. Blake's confessed to blackmailing you, getting Charles Morgan to persuade Colin to shoot at me, and knocking Giles down with the car. But it's almost certain he didn't kill Colin Morgan."

"Then who did?"

"That's the big question. But it looks as though the mystery person sent that last letter you had – Blake's denied being responsible for that one. That makes it look as though Colin told whoever it was what was going on, and suffered the ultimate penalty."

"Someone might have seen him take a shot at you."

Piers took from his wallet the form that his father had to sign in order to authorise F.9's presence on his property. "If this was a Sherlock Holmes story it would be simple. Or at least, relatively simple. There were several people in the vicinity of the lodge that night. Colin Morgan, who might or might not have been in the car on his own – we haven't established that yet, Sylvia Webb, who saw the car come from the lane after the shooting and nearly fell off her bike, and William Turner who had gone to the lodge to look for a saw and then turned back when he realized it was too dark to see. He saw the car parked under the trees. He also saw someone

167

else who at first he thought was Tom Jackson. But then he changed his mind and said he wasn't sure. But William can't be regarded as a very reliable witness as he had a stroke not all that long ago and is a little vague in remembering things. Tom said that his eyesight's not all that good either."

"No, that's not right," Elizabeth said. "He might be a bit hard of hearing of late but there's nothing wrong with his eyesight. I wouldn't say he struck me as being vague either when I last spoke to him. He was telling me all about his holiday in Scotland and all the places he and his wife had been. He seemed to remember it all perfectly."

"Sylvia says she has to leave him notes about what she wants doing in the garden."

"Sylvia has a quiet voice and, as I said, he's getting hard of hearing. But William won't admit it – he can be a stubborn man sometimes. I was talking to his wife in the bakers, that's how I know these things."

"But supposing he's right – what would Tom have been doing at the lodge?"

"Have you asked Tom where he was that evening?"

"Yes. He said he was at home and didn't go out until much later."

"How odd."

"Why should he lie?"

"Goodness knows, Piers. I don't really know why you're asking me these questions – you're the policeman."

"But Tom Jackson's part of the family – it's never occurred to me to think of him as a *suspect*. What motives would he have for getting involved with blackmail and murder?"

Elizabeth frowned. "Yes, I find it rather difficult to consider it too. He's always served us very well and Mycroft was always very appreciative of him in his army days. You ought to speak to your father really. There is something at the back of my mind, now I come to think of it – some trouble or other that took place years ago. It's probably nothing, of course, but do go and ask him about it."

The Colonel wasn't too pleased at being roused from sleep. "Tom?" he queried crossly. "Why do you suddenly want to know about Tom?"

"He was interviewed by the local police," Piers agreed.

"But it's just occurred to me that no one's thought seriously about his possible involvement. Mother said something about some trouble years ago. What was it?"

"I'm damned if I can remember anything about trouble," Mycroft said after a pause.

"Please try. Did you ever have cause to reprimand him?"

"No. At least . . . But that was a *hell* of a long time ago."

"What happened?"

"It can't possibly have any bearing on this case."

"What *happened*?" Piers said again.

"There's not a lot to tell. Jackson came to me when I was promoted lieutenant-colonel and given my first command. He had been batman to my predecessor and I sort of inherited him when the poor chap had to resign his commission due to ill-health. I was immediately impressed by Jackson's efficient and quiet manner and we got on very well. So well in fact that when I retired when my own health got a bit dodgy I suggested that when he'd done his stint he and his wife came to work for me on the estate. The only condition I placed upon him was that he sorted out his drinking problem. This he did and there's never been any trouble since."

"But at one time . . ."

"Yes. It was odd really. Only happened about twice a year. Then he'd go out and drink himself absolutely blind. Not with anyone else either. Just on his own. That's what I found rather strange about it."

"And the trouble happened during one of his drinking bouts." '

Mycroft nodded soberly. "A woman was raped in the town."

"Aldershot?"

"Yes. For some reason I was working late that night. I bumped into Jackson. He was staggering drunk and there was blood on his face. I told him to disappear to his quarters and I'd think about putting him on a charge. I didn't know that the woman had been attacked then, of course. The next day, a Sunday, the Military Police were going through the place like Hercules did the Augean Stables. The woman had said that she was fairly sure the man who raped her was a soldier. I remembered how I'd seen Jackson and sent for him. He felt

169

pretty rough and said he'd got into a fight after an argument about football. I told him I knew the difference between scratches from a woman's fingernails and the result of a belt on the chin. He just stared stonily at me and refused to give me any more details. So I reported him."

"What happened?"

"There was no evidence. The woman said she hadn't seen the man's face in the dark. And you know what it was like for women some years ago. The view was that if they stood on street corners after dark, then they asked for it. And she *was* one of the town's prostitutes. The affair all blew over. I seem to remember it was Aldershot Display week and the place was stiff with brass hats. Everyone was only too keen to shove local difficulties under the mat."

"Do you think he was guilty?"

A few seconds elapsed before Mycroft replied. "Yes, I do actually. And so did the woman's brother who was a serving soldier. He got Jackson's name somehow over the grapevine and he and a bunch of his friends exacted revenge. They put Tom in hospital for a week. Some of the things they did to him you couldn't mention in polite company."

"Bad enough to have left a lasting injury?"

"It's possible, I suppose."

"Would you say that he might have harboured a grudge?"

"Well, he was a little distant for a while afterwards but he never mentioned the incident again."

"Did you?"

"What, mention it? Of course not. You have to get on with life – you can't let things like that stand between you and other people."

With a feeling of deepening apprehension Piers was remembering a conversation deep in the cellars of the Hall. He reached for the phone and dialled. There was no reply.

"Don't you want your coffee?" Elizabeth called after him.

There was no sign of Thea's two minders so Piers called Rolt over his car radio. There was then a ten-minute wait while Rolt asked for a report from Special Branch.

"She's gone home," Rolt said finally. "She said she'd had an urgent request to go to Sussex so she's driven herself there. I had asked her to stay put."

"Who was the request from, sir?"

"She told them the call was from Tom speaking on behalf of your father. But he's still with you, isn't he? By 'Tom' I presume she meant Tom Jackson."

"Do you know what time she left?"

"According to the Special Branch pair she left her flat to speak to them at ten thirty-five last night. Have you contacted home?"

"Not yet, sir."

"Call me back in five minutes and I'll see if I can get in touch with her."

Piers was never sure afterwards how he managed to stay sitting quietly in his car outside Thea's flat while the interminable minutes ticked by. And when Rolt's voice came over the radio again with the news that there was no one answering the phone at Ashleigh Hall he had to wait for a few moments before he trusted himself to reply without shouting.

"There might not be anything sinister in this," Rolt said carefully.

Piers told him about Tom.

"I'll ask Leadbetter to take a few men over there," the Commander said when he had finished. "We'll stick to the original plan. So get down there yourself. And drive *carefully*."

Piers didn't.

Chapter Fifteen

The sense of foreboding increased. Piers parked his car next to a police van, got out and ran through a torrential downpour towards the front door. He paused fractionally as he passed Thea's car but then carried on. The door was locked. He found the key his father had given him some days previously in a pocket and plunged in, surprising a constable who was standing in the entrance hall.

"Well?" Piers barked at him.

"Did you want the Inspector, sir?" the man asked, obviously at a loss as to whom he was speaking.

"Is Miss Ashley *here*?" Piers demanded to know.

"They're looking now, sir. Ah, here's Inspector Leadbetter."

"We had to force our way in around the back," Leadbetter said. "Luckily, the dogs were all shut into a utility room."

Sure enough, faintly in the distance could be heard a frenzied canine clamour.

"I'll let them out," Piers said. "Don't worry, they're all harmless and if anyone can find her they can. Are the Jacksons at home?"

"No," Leadbetter said.

Their gaze met.

"Have you forced your way in there too?" Ashley enquired.

Leadbetter shook his head. "Not yet." After a second or two he added, "The Commander said something about Jackson being a possible suspect now."

Piers kept his temper with great difficulty. "My sister was

172

asked to come home by Tom who said he was speaking on behalf of my father. Her car is outside. Where is she? I take it she hasn't left a note. The weather's hardly conducive to going for a walk."

Leadbetter hesitated and then said, "Perhaps we'd better try the Jacksons' lodge again."

A car drew up as they prepared to make a dash into the rain. It was the team from F.9. Piers told Leadbetter the reason for their presence and the two men went into the house.

"If it is Jackson . . ." Leadbetter began.

"There won't be any listening devices," Piers finished for him. "Just a pair of large ears."

"Plus those of his wife perhaps."

Piers did not respond to this but ran into the rain. He was quite surprised when he reached the Jacksons' home – the water trickling down his neck – to find that the Inspector was still with him. He rang the doorbell twice. Not a sound came from within.

"Still in bed do you think?" Leadbetter ventured.

"It's nine-thirty," Piers said. "They're both supposed to be at work."

"Do you think . . ." Leadbetter started to say and once again he did not finish, Piers having gone round the back.

The back door yielded after two determined shoulder charges from Piers. He was still suffering the consequences when Leadbetter pushed past him and went ahead. Piers heard him say something, sounding surprised, but did not catch the exact words for by this time the Inspector was in the living room.

Mrs Jackson sat in one of the two arm chairs staring straight ahead. Such was the intensity of the stare, her eyes utterly fixed on a point somewhere on the opposite wall that, for a moment, Ashley thought she was dead. Then, her gaze snapped on to him. The action was so horribly mechanical that the hair stood up on the back of his neck.

"She's stoned out of her skull," Leadbetter whispered.

Piers picked up the almost empty gin bottle from the small table by her elbow and placed it on the sideboard. It was a pointless thing to do but he needed a few moments to fight down the inexplicable nausea. He had always known this woman as an efficient, if slightly distant, housekeeper. Now she resembled a hideous dummy in a waxworks.

"Mrs Jackson, can you hear me?" Leadbetter was saying in a loud voice.

"I hear you," she answered, still looking at Piers.

"Where is your husband?"

Her head rolled but she still succeeded in keeping her eyes fixed on Piers. "He's gone away," she said.

"Where?" Piers snapped.

"Only the good God above knows," she intoned sleepily. "As for me . . ."

Piers shook one of her shoulders, forcing himself to be gentle.

"I don't care a damn," she concluded as if nothing had happened.

Leadbetter said, "When did he go?"

"I don't know. Last night perhaps." Her eyes closed.

"This isn't getting us anywhere," Piers said impatiently. He left the room and started to search the house. There was not a lot to search; two rooms plus a kitchen and bathroom on the ground floor, two bedrooms and a boxroom above. Everywhere was very untidy and in the master bedroom clothing was strewn over the floor, a chest of drawers open, the contents in disarray. It was difficult to decide whether someone had been looking for something or merely packing in a desperate hurry.

There was no sign, not a hint, that Thea had ever been in the house.

"Can you give me a hand for a moment?" he called down to Leadbetter. When the Inspector had come up the stairs, he said, "My shoulders are a mite too broad to go through there. Perhaps you'd take a dekko if I give you a leg up."

"There" was the small trap-door into the loft.

"I'll get Hodges," Leadbetter decided. "He's thin."

"That'll take time," Ashley told him.

"But – "

"You only have to pop your head through."

"All right," Leadbetter agreed reluctantly. "If you're sure you're strong enough."

"No problem," he was assured.

174

If Leadbetter hadn't been so fed up with the entire Ashley affair, not to mention being thoroughly put out by the peremptory order to go skywards from a man he knew to be his junior in every way, he might have permitted himself a smile. Thus, as a boy, he had stood on his father's shoulders in order to see over a wall and thereby witness the last steam train to use the branch line to Bramber. Now the line had gone as well, terminating at the hideous cement works at Beeding. One small sop to his present wounded pride was that Ashley did not seem to be the sort of man who would chalk this up as any sort of victory to be remembered with relish. Piers, if he was absolutely honest, hadn't even noticed.

And there was, Leadbetter recollected unhappily as he was hurtled upwards, that very embarrassing matter of his having used highly questionable methods when he had "arrested" Piers in connection with Colin Morgan's death. One small outcome he was never to know; the affronted member of the T.S.G., still a little groggy and carefully feeling his jaw, had perceived his attacker in a cell that was not only unlocked but with the door open. He had shaken the sleeping one and not particularly gently. The sleeper had stirred and spoken. An economy of words but nevertheless pithy and the truth. After a short but meaningful silence the two had shaken hands.

"I'll have to go right up there," Leadbetter said when he was aloft and had pushed open the trap door. "There's too much junk to see clearly." He placed his hands on the frame of the trap door and hoisted himself up.

"D'you need a torch?" Piers asked.

"No, there's a light switch," Leadbetter replied, and clicked it down.

There was one bad moment when he perceived what turned out to be a tailor's dummy, horizontal, wrapped in an old sheet, but otherwise there was no sign of Thea Ashley. Not that he had really expected to find her up here. But her brother's anxiety – no, that was not the right word for the man was of a mood that could be described as frantic and having ever more difficulty in controlling it – was catching.

He had to drop down from the opening unaided – Piers had gone back downstairs. When he caught up with him it was to see him holding the almost empty gin bottle, regarding it

175

thoughtfully. In the armchair Mrs Jackson snored.

"I'm going to sober this bloody woman up," Piers announced all at once.

"That's not really wise," Leadbetter said, slightly alarmed by the look on the other's face.

"To hell with it! Thea's somewhere and so's Tom Jackson. I don't think either of them are far away. I also think the mess upstairs was made to *look* as though someone packed a bag."

"Where are you going?" the Inspector asked, really alarmed now as Piers headed purposefully into the kitchen.

"To get a bucket of water to throw over that sozzled old cow."

"No!" shrieked the woman, sitting bolt upright.

Piers came back into the room. "Ah. You don't seem to be drunk at all. I was sure someone said you used to be in rep. Where's your husband?"

"I told you the truth just now. He's gone away."

"That's what he ordered you to say. When did you last see him?"

She hesitated and then said, "This morning at about nine. I know because the radio news was on."

"Shouldn't you both have been at the Hall at work by then?"

Her thin face flushed. "Well, yes, but – "

"No one was at home so you decided not to bother. But my sister should have been at home. Tom rang her last night with an urgent request to return here. We know what time she left London – she would have got here probably not long after midnight. Her car is outside the Hall but there's no sign of her. Where is she?"

"I haven't caught even a glimpse of the girl," Mrs Jackson said defiantly. "And I'm sure Tom hasn't either."

"He's been brooding a lot lately, hasn't he?"

"No, I wouldn't say so," she replied immediately.

"Since I was shot, I should think," Piers continued. "On the night – or late afternoon rather – when he saw Colin Morgan at the lodge with a gun. And afterwards – a couple of days later perhaps – when he cornered Morgan somewhere and forced him to tell the truth. That was when he started to brood on an old grievance and decided that he could get his own back at last."

"That's rubbish!" Mrs Jackson shouted.

"You deny he has a grievance against my father?"

"No, but – "

"Oh, you do know about it then? Most men wouldn't brag to their wives that they'd raped a woman before they were married."

"We *were* married," she said tautly. "But I don't believe the accusation that was made against him."

"The woman's brother did."

"You don't have to remind me about that. It ruined my Tom's life in a way."

"How?"

"After the kicking they gave him he couldn't father any more children. We've only got our Eileen. She was a baby when it happened."

"But why blame the Colonel?" Leadbetter said.

"Because he pointed the finger," the woman answered, her eyes slitted with spite. "There was no evidence and yet he accused him. After all the good service my Tom had given him too."

Piers said, "Do you think a Commanding Officer can ignore it when one of his men returns to barracks roaring drunk and with his face covered in scratches?"

This silenced her.

Piers was thinking back to the conversation he had had with Jackson when the man had shown him round the cellars. Referring to Thea and after Piers had commented that she might get married soon and there would be children who would have to be kept out of the dangerous underground places, Tom had said, "That's if she ain't number three." Piers had only just recollected the remark.

That's if she ain't number three.

"Oh, God," he whispered.

He knew where she was.

It was still pouring with rain but he didn't notice. The constable who had been on duty at the door was still there and started violently again when Piers once again burst in.

"Has anyone searched the cellars?" he asked.

"They've been in the wine cellar," the constable said. "At least, I think so."

"But not the cellars that are reached from the door under the stairs?"

"I'm not sure," the man admitted.

It didn't occur to Piers that he ought not to go alone. Just after he had opened the door beneath the stairs and entered therein the constable was ordered to help his colleagues search the attics. It was a long time before he gave the quick question and answer further thought and by then any retrospection on his part was pointless.

No one had replaced the failed lightbulbs. Piers went fairly quickly but with great care along the passageway, pausing only when he rounded the slight curve and came to where a light was still functioning. This was where the passage effectively split. His mind open to all possibilities he took the right hand turn, running lightly on his toes. After twenty yards or so he was in that part of the building he remembered from childhood; the butler's pantry just off the vast kitchen with its roasting jack and rows of copper pots and pans. This area had obviously been searched for several police uniform jackets and two hats were thrown over chairs where their owners had presumably changed into overalls.

He went back to the fork and, moving slowly now, took the left hand passage. Cold air smelling faintly of earth fanned into his face as he descended the flight of steps. All sound was deadened, even the soft scuff of his shoes on the steps muffled. By now he was cursing his stupidity for not pausing to find a torch. But he had no intention of going back now.

The small square room at the bottom of the steps was in darkness. He had expected that. He now knew where the light switch was, however, and carefully felt around the rough stone wall until he came to the doorway where his fingers brushed against the rusting metal box that housed the switch. As he clicked down the switch he swiftly ducked but there was no one in the room, armed or otherwise.

He paused to examine the room closely this time, bearing in mind what Jackson had said about the possibility of other old passages that might or might not have been filled in after the fire and rebuilding of the Hall. There was one dark recess in a corner that looked as though it might have originally been

178

the entrance to another cellar. In the poor light Piers could make out the remains of a carved stone portal bearing a curling letter A. Now the doorway was sealed with what looked like coarse hand-made bricks.

He went into the long, low vault with the curving roof. On his first visit he had been too busy talking to Tom to notice that it too had a grimy light bulb. This was presumably controlled by the switch as well for it gave out a dim illumination, just enough to see his way by. Another thing he had not noticed previously was that besides the opening he had gone through with Tom to reach the well-room there was another in the wall to his left. It was quite small – about five foot high and four wide and that was all that could be said about it, it was as dark as a grave within. To explore it he would have to fetch the flash-lamp that was on the shelf in the well-room.

The well.

Piers endeavoured to quell his worst fears and stooped to go through the opening into the well-room. There was the same feeble glimmer of light in here, high in the roof; it was most extraordinary the way in which these cellars varied. Once inside he stopped to listen. Such was the silence it was as if he had been suddenly struck deaf. But for his own heart pounding, that is.

When he saw that the grating had been removed from the top of the well his self-control broke. He ran to it shouting, "Thea! Thea! Are you there?"

The echo of his own voice seemed to mock him.

He shouted again and once more the words died away without an answer.

"She ain't down there," said Jackson from behind him.

Piers had been in the act of pounding one fist on the stone parapet of the well. The pain from that and the shock of hearing the man speak brought him to his senses. He turned round, slowly.

"I always thought there was something a bit unhealthy about the way you regarded your sister," Tom said in conversational tones. He was sitting on one of the benches that lined the walls.

"*Unhealthy*!"

179

"It seemed to me you might be having some kind of unnatural relationship with her." He raised the gun he was holding.

Fortunately Piers's training had now asserted its influence. Otherwise he might have taken his chance with the gun and wrung Jackson's neck. "For pity's sake forget all your old grudges and tell me where she is," he pleaded.

"Forget?" This with a grim laugh. "I don't think so. But I didn't expect you though – I thought the old man would come."

"What made you think anyone would come?"

"The Colonel ferrets everything out. He's that sort. Ferrets things out – sticks his nose into other folks' business."

Piers leaned on the wall by the doorway. "Are you saying that you've worked for him all these years, waiting for an opportunity to get even?" It had occurred to him that Tom wasn't merely bitter but that his sanity was in question.

Jackson lowered the gun slightly. "No, I wouldn't say that. I suppose the chance came and I took it."

"When you caught Colin Morgan with a gun at the lodge after he shot me."

Tom looked surprised. "You've worked it out then? Yes, this gun. It was his old man's. He didn't know that I'd seen him. But he knew all right when I collared the little beggar the next day and got the full story out of him."

"So you decided to get in on the act."

"Why not?" Jackson said with a shrug. "At the beginning I didn't think that anyone would shed any tears over your demise – and everyone did seem to think you were going to die just after it happened. Not after what they'd all been saying. It came as a real surprise when they had you at home. But when you think about it, blood's thicker than water."

"Surely you've nothing against Thea. She's never done anything to hurt you."

A thoughtful expression on his face, Jackson said, "No, I suppose not. But when you've started something you can't just stop. That's not what they teach you in the army. You get on with a job and finish it. No halfway measures."

Piers savagely fought down the desire to hurl himself at the man. "So you killed her. You threw her down the well."

"No, I've just said so, haven't I? The well's where you're going."

"To get even with my father? That's crazy. You'll go to prison for life."

"Who'll find you? Who will guess it was me?"

Piers knew that he had to be very careful. "I'm not here alone, Tom. The whole place is full of police looking for Thea."

"Looking for her? Why should the police be looking for her?"

"Because since I was shot there's been a police guard on her. When she left London to come here after you rang last night, she left a message with the men who had been watching her flat. We knew my father hadn't called her home because he was in London. Crispin Blake's been arrested, Tom."

"Blake doesn't know about me," Jackson said smugly.

"No, but we're fairly sure he didn't kill Colin. And he didn't send the final blackmail note it seems. That was you. Only you heard my mother and me talking about it and didn't collect the money."

"There's nothing to connect me with any of this. No evidence at all. Nothing that would stand up in a court. Not now . . ."

"Not now you've killed Charles Morgan?" Piers said when Jackson stopped speaking.

"He was a swindling bastard," Tom spat out. "Been fiddling the books for nigh-on two years."

"Didn't that suit your purpose though – anything that hurt my father?"

"I couldn't stand Morgan. He looked down his nose at the wife and me. We were just servants – peasants – as far as he was concerned. And that bitch of a wife of his with her furs and shiny trinkets. Real snobs. People like that shouldn't get away with crime. You didn't. You paid the price."

Piers played for time. At any moment the search team might appear. "I thought you prided yourself on being a good judge of character, Tom."

"So what?"

In the last few moments a change seemed to have come over the man. Up until now Piers had been talking to the Tom he remembered; the perfect butler when required, the trusted

181

family retainer at all times, a steeple-jack if necessary, prepared to excel in any rôle asked of him. Tom Jackson, in fact, was a chameleon, able to fit into any situation. No doubt, but for his drinking bouts, he had been an excellent soldier.

Piers's skin crawled. Now he was looking at a perfect murderer. He said, "Have you ever really thought about it? Do I look like a criminal?"

Jackson cocked his head, listening. Then he got down off the bench. "It doesn't matter, now, does it?"

"Yes, it does. As far as you're concerned it's very important indeed."

"I can't see how."

"I'm not the only one who suspects you. I told my boss too."

"And who might that be?" Jackson mocked. "Old Nick?"

"Commander Rolt. He came to the house. Don't you remember?"

"Of course I remember. I opened the front door to him."

"In a way it's a pity you didn't listen at a few more keyholes recently. Then you'd have learned the truth." Piers was wondering if he could make a grab for his own gun.

"You're lying," Jackson said after a short silence. "You can't expect me to swallow *that*."

"What have you done with Thea?"

But Jackson was shaking his head in disbelief and ignored the question.

"Put the gun down and tell me where she is. Killing me achieves nothing."

"But it does. It'll be the end of it. All three kids. Blake took care of the youngest for me. He'll be crippled for life with a bit of luck. So the Colonel will remember. For always he'll remember me and how I got even. It'll be worth doing time for. And when I get out I'll probably do for him too."

Piers had expected to be shot. He was not expecting the lightning kick that took him in the chest. The agony was instant and quite insupportable. He was aware only of a swift manhandling and then he was falling and falling.

That he had ceased to fall and was now choking to death caused him to flounder wildly. Surely this *was* death and he was in some kind of purgatory; a kind of endless floating in soft, choking . . .

Feathers?

There was a loud clang above him as the grating was slammed into place. He distinctly heard the click as the padlock slotted home.

It was feathers; eiderdown, goosedown, hen feathers, in his hair, up his nose, down his throat, seemingly into every part of his being. Retching on feathers he struggled upwards, almost swam in the overwhelming darkness until he reached air, trod in feathers as they threatened to drown him until one of his flailing hands latched on to a metal rung on the wall. He clung, sobbing with shock.

After a while there was the strength to draw himself up and grope above the rung to feel for others. Yes, there was another, a couple of feet up the shaft of the well. He felt with his feet but could discover no more beneath him so hauled himself up painfully to grasp the higher rung. It was loose in the stone but held.

Panting with effort he drew himself higher and found yet a third. Yes, there was a fourth and a fifth. The sixth came away in his hand and he plunged back again but he had the presence of mind to hold his breath and did not ingest any more feathers. Then it had to start all over again, a blind groping in a darkness so intense that he completely lost his bearings.

It took him a very long time to find the first rung again. When he did he held on to it for a while, resting.

This time he reached the twelfth rung or so when it was wrenched from the wall by his weight but by now he had his feet on them so it did not hinder him unduly. His greatest fear was that the rungs would not continue all the way to the top. At least if he reached the top of the shaft he could shout, hoping that someone would hear him. Perhaps that constable who had been on duty at the front door would remember where he had gone and raise the alarm when he failed to return.

Most of his strength came from the knowledge that Thea hadn't been at the bottom of the shaft.

The climb was endless. He probably hallucinated a little for he heard voices that seemed all around him, jeering voices.

Perhaps they were the ghosts of people who had lived, fought and died at Ashleigh. Once, he thought he saw a light above him and shouted his relief but no one came and his only company was a thick cobweb that stuck to his face as he thrust it eagerly upwards.

One could go mad, was the surprisingly calm thought, if one so chose.

He did not so choose and struggled on. It came as an enormous surprise actually to strike his head on the grating. Kissing it fervently was the one nod to madness that he permitted himself and then he rested as well as he was able.

How long could he remain holding on?

He shouted several times, to no avail, and after a period of time that he judged to be ten minutes shifted his position slightly on the rungs to try to rest aching muscles. His chest was still dull agony. Another eternity went by – probably only a further ten minutes. At last, in extremis, he detached a hand and, in a kind of final defiant gesture, grasped the grating and furiously shook it. It moved, banging up and down on the stonework.

Piers didn't stop to ask questions, just heaved upwards. The grating squeaked up on its hinges and fell back and away with a crash. Using the last of his energy he climbed out and collapsed face down on the floor. It didn't matter that the sound he had thought was the padlock slotting into place had merely been the steel catch that it was normally fastened to knocking against the hoop that it fitted over. The whys and wherefores were now of no importance. He was free and for a few moments, he paused to thank God.

To minimise the risk of losing his way in the dark and falling down the hole again he crawled to the doorway, finding it without trouble. It was then a simple matter to pull himself up and reach over to where he knew the shelf was with the torch. But the shelf was empty, Jackson had obviously taken the flash lamp with him. He had also turned all the lights off. So be it.

Chapter Sixteen

Inspector Leadbetter now knew that he had another murder enquiry on his hands. He had not been long at the Hall with his team when he had realized that if he did not order up reinforcements the search would take all day. These soon arrived and were put to work in the many extensive outbuildings. Almost immediately, in a locked garage, they came upon a car with a body lying on the back seat.

"The girl?" Leadbetter demanded to know when this was reported to him.

No, it was Charles Morgan.

He had been killed with a single shot to the left temple and had been dead, Leadbetter guessed, no more than three hours. With heavy tread the Inspector went back to his radio. He was returning from his car when Sergeant Pettifer, his assistant, came hurrying towards him. Leadbetter braced himself for more bad news.

"We've found Mr Ashley," Pettifer said breathlessly.

"I didn't know the man was missing," Leadbetter said in amazement. "I only saw him about an hour and a half ago."

"No – well, sir . . ." Pettifer swallowed. "He'd gone to look in the cellars on his own and came upon Jackson down there. Jackson shoved him down the well."

"But Ashley's *armed*," Leadbetter roared. "I was told by Commander Rolt himself that he's armed. Oh, for God's sake. Is he seriously injured?"

Pettifer had taken a couple of steps backwards. "No, I wouldn't say he was hurt at all really. Just shaken up, of course."

"Take me to him," Leadbetter ordered, striding off. And to think he had imagined that West Sussex CID would be tame and boring after being stationed in Brighton . . .

Piers was in what Leadbetter knew to be the family kitchen drinking a cup of tea someone had just handed to him. "I made a complete cock-up of that," he said when he saw the Inspector.

Leadbetter had been about to make several remarks concerning the efficiency of certain experimental and supposedly crack police departments and had, in fact, been rehearsing them on the way. But he didn't utter them, not when he saw Piers. Afterwards he put this down to the fact that he now quite liked the man.

"He had the gun," Piers continued. "The same one that Morgan shot me with. I hadn't expected that. I hadn't expected that Jackson would be down there either. I just had this idea in my head that he'd dumped Thea down the well."

The Inspector grabbed Pettifer's arm. "Go and talk to everyone.Find out if Jackson was spotted leaving the house. And be *quick*."

"There's another cellar that I'd like to take a look at,"Piers said. "I came back for a torch."

"My lot can do that," Leadbetter said. "I'd like you, if you don't mind, to come and positively identify Charles Morgan's body. It'll save his wife an unpleasant job." He eyed Piers up and down. "How deep's this well?"

"About a hundred feet."

"But – "

"There's a load of feathers at the bottom. God knows how they got there."

"Feathers!"

"Yeah. Probably old feather beds and eiderdowns that someone wanted to get rid of."

Outside, the scenes-of-crime team were arriving. In the garage Piers looked into the car and was able to confirm that the dead man was Charles Morgan. Fairly inured as he was to such things the body was not pleasant to behold for the close shot had done dreadful damage to Morgan's skull.

"It's Morgan's car too," he said, straightening up.

They made way for a police photographer. Nothing much

could be done until the pathologist arrived. Leadbetter had to content himself with putting out a description of Tom Jackson together with a warning that he was armed.

"I still can't think straight," Piers admitted quietly. "It knocks you for six when it's people you know."

Leadbetter said, "I'm afraid there's not a trace of your sister."

"And her bed wasn't slept in last night?"

"No. It doesn't look as though she even went indoors – there's a packed overnight case in her car. Didn't Jackson even hint where she was?"

Piers shook his head.

"Is there anyone else who might be at risk? Anyone connected with this whom Jackson might want to take out as well?"

"I don't think . . ." he started to say. "No, wait a moment. There's William Turner. I actually mentioned to Tom that William thought he had seen him near the lodge that night."

"Did Turner make a statement?"

"Not at the time. He spoke to me afterwards and I suggested that he reported what he thought he had seen. But he was doubtful himself – it was nearly dark when it happened."

"But if Jackson knows about it . . . What's his state of mind?"

"Difficult to say. Not particularly rational. He thinks he's killed me, of course. It was all to get even with my father for something that happened during their army days. I'll go and check on William though."

"You do that," Leadbetter urged. It would give Ashley something to do, he thought, get him away from the house for a bit. Then he might not be around when the body of his sister was found. Leadbetter was convinced that it was only a matter of time.

Piers had no idea at which house in Maple Drive William lived so knocked at the first he came to, Number 3, to ask. After quite a long wait during which he could hear dragging footsteps within, the front door opened. An old man peered at him suspiciously.

"I'm looking for William Turner," he said.

187

"Speak up, young fella," bellowed the ancient, cupping an ear. "I can't hear as well as I used to."

Piers repeated his quest, a lot louder.

The old man shook his head. "He don't live here no more."

"He must do," Piers protested.

"What?"

"HE MUST DO. I ONLY SPOKE TO HIM RECENTLY."

"No. He doesn't. He moved."

"BUT HE DIDN'T SAY ANYTHING ABOUT MOVING."

"About five year ago he moved from here. It must have been."

Piers prepared to give up. Then he yelled, "WHERE DID HE GO?"

"Number 16. That's on the other side of the road down at the bottom."

Piers gratefully wrung one frail hand and departed.

As was to be expected, the garden in front of the bungalow with "16" in plastic figures over the door was immaculately tidy. Praying that William was in and that all was well, Piers pressed the bell-push. A small dog of some kind yapped. It was still yapping when the door opened and a woman smiled at him.

"Yes?"

"Is William in? I'm Piers Ashley."

"Mr Ashley! Oh, how nice. I'm so pleased to meet you after what happened. William will be so sorry he missed you."

"Can you tell me where he is? It's rather important."

"Yes, he's doing Sylvia Webb's garden. He always does her garden on Thursday mornings. Would you like to come in and ring him there?"

Piers thought about it. "No, it's all right. I've got my car – I'll go round there." He half turned away and then said, "Please don't think I'm rude, rushing off like this. You must both come to the Hall for tea one afternoon."

"Oh, that would be *lovely*," William's wife breathed. "Thank you so much."

Piers felt a fool and a boor. He knew that what he had said was inane in the present circumstances but she had looked so pleasant and homely, like a brown mother hen in her tweed dress, that he hated the thought of offending her.

There seemed to be nothing amiss at Sylvia's cottage; two cats in the front garden sunning themselves in the purple, pink and mauve cushions of aubretia, a blackbird scolding them, flicking its tail, from the lilac. Piers had already decided that he would openly drive up to the cottage. To burst in, waving a gun on the presumption that Jackson was there, seemed a trifle over the top.

"What the hell," he said to himself, slamming the car door. "I've already made a mess of everything. And who needs to impress Leadbetter?"

"Talking to yourself is the first sign of desperation," Sylvia called from the doorway.

"Is William here?"

She looked taken aback. "Yes, well, he was until a while ago." When he got closer she said, "Piers, is something wrong? You look ghastly."

"Everything's wrong. Where is he now?"

"I asked him to mend the fence where the branch fell off the tree and damaged it. He said he had to go and get some tools."

"Yes, but *where* has he gone?"

"How should I know? And you're the second person who's asked for him this morning. What on earth's going on?"

"Was it Tom? Tom Jackson?"

"Yes."

"How long ago was Tom here?"

"Only about a quarter of an hour ago. I couldn't help him either."

Piers took a deep breath. He hadn't seen William on the way to Sylvia's and from what he knew of the topography of the village he was sure that William would have to walk home the same route that he, Piers, had driven. So William hadn't gone home.

"Think carefully," he said. "What exactly did William say?"

Some of his own urgency seemed to have transferred to her. "He said it would need a new end post. I told him there was a spare post in the garage but when he looked at it he said it must have come from the fence I had put up at the end of the garden so it wasn't suitable somehow. Oh, dear, I wasn't

189

really listening. I suppose he's gone to find a tool to make it more suitable. I'm sorry, but I'm an awful duffer at things like that."

"Show me," he asked.

"You mean show you how the broken fence is different from the other one? But as far as I can see it's exactly the same – you know, larch lap sort of thing."

Piers ran round the side of the house and into the back garden. Up near the house on the left hand side there was a large elm tree. This had indeed shed one of its lower branches, William having cleared most of it away but for the main stem. The weight of it when it had come down had snapped off the post at ground level, the fence itself now leaning inwards and only slightly damaged.

Piers's gaze went to the far end of the garden. "But that fence is *higher*," he said. "Therefore if the new post you've already got was left over from it, it's too long to be used here."

"Yes, I suppose it is," Sylvia said brightly.

"Which means he needs a saw."

"I'm sure you're right."

"And his saw is at the old lodge."

Sylvia beamed at him and was about to say that she could see why he was such a good policeman when he turned and raced off again.

"I'll paint you as Mercury," she whispered.

Piers parked his car well out of earshot of the lodge and went the rest of the way on foot. He did not run: the time for running was past. It was doubtful now whether he had the energy to run and he was ignoring, or trying to, an alarming weakness. This manifested itself, infuriating him, in an ever-increasing tendency to trip on the rough ground.

He did not meet anyone on that quiet, careful walk towards the old lodge. He had thought that he might catch up with Jackson and rounded each curve of the track circumspectly. When he first glimpsed the chimneys of the lodge through the trees he halted and then climbed a bank at the side of the road. That Jackson, an ex-soldier, was as likely as not trained in what was commonly known as jungle warfare was not a comforting thought. Fuddle-headed from sheer exhaustion it

190

took a moment or two for him to remember that the same could be said of himself.

One thing he was sure of, however – it was contrary to all his training to go in alone like this. The trouble was that the entire affair had been a dreadful *private* thing; old friends, trusted employees, proved to be false. But all the world now knew. The world was free to think that the Ashleys deserved such perfidy. He was not a proud man but he was a very angry one.

As silently as possible he edged his way through the thicket of hawthorn that crowned the bank on this side of the lane. At the spot he had chosen the hawthorn merged into a copse of birch, scrub oak and yet more hawthorn. This, he remembered from his days at the lodge, covered an area of about an acre and extended around one side of it.

For a full two minutes he lay flat, listening and watching. It seemed strange to notice that it was now a fine sunny day, the sun past its zenith but warm and pleasant on his shoulders as it shone through the partly opened leaves above him. Other than the twittering of birds it was very quiet with only the distant sound of an occasional lorry or motorbike on the main road to disturb the peacefulness of the scene.

On his stomach Piers moved closer. At any moment he expected to hear a gun fire. But what would Jackson gain by killing William? He *had* been asking about his whereabouts however. In his present state of mind perhaps he intended to do away with everyone he regarded as being involved. And afterwards – what then?

"He'll turn the gun on himself," Piers said under his breath. "They usually do."

It seemed inconceivable that Jackson wouldn't expect the police to be on to him by now. Sooner or later he must realize that Charles Morgan's body would be discovered. Perhaps on the other hand he was living in some kind of cloud cuckoo land and, assuming Piers to be dead, saw no reason why he himself should be a suspect.

And, of course, there was Thea. Or rather there was the almost overwhelming thought that she no longer . . .

The idea that she might be dead was almost enough to overturn his own mind.

191

The shot, when it came, was remarkably loud and close by. It sent up a couple of dozen rooks from a nearby tree with a great flapping of wings and cawing. A few broken-off dead twigs rattled down.

Silence.

Piers breathed out slowly and wriggled forwards a few feet. The shot had not been aimed at him, of that he was certain, it had come nowhere near him at all. And he wouldn't have thought that whoever had fired was inside the lodge, the sound had been very much in the open air. Then Tom Jackson shouted, seemingly only feet away.

"You stupid old fool! Always shoving your nose in where it ain't wanted."

Other things were said by Jackson, or rather muttered, Piers did not catch the words. He guessed that Jackson was standing in the front garden of the lodge. In order to approach the building directly from the rear Piers changed course, moving through the tall grasses that grew beneath the trees in a fashion – only he did not know it – that one of his instructors had described as reptilian.

Then, all at once, there was only a large clump of cow parsley between himself and Jackson. Piers froze. He had already drawn his gun. Jackson was prowling around the lodge, and having stopped for a few moments, continued until he went from sight around the gable end wall. Piers waited for a couple more seconds and then broke cover and followed. Pressing himself to the wall of the house he looked round the corner and was in time to see Jackson go through the front door. There was no sign of William.

Almost immediately Jackson came out again. This time he was carrying a small suitcase and Piers recognised it as one belonging to his father. Intent on securing the padlock on the door of the boarded-up building he did not notice Piers until he had picked up the case again and was preparing to walk away.

The element of surprise was quite perfect and, as far as Jackson was concerned, utterly crushing.

"You're under arrest," Piers told him quietly, walking forward. "I want you to put down that suitcase, throw down the gun that's in your pocket, and then I want you to lie face down on the ground."

"I've never been anyone's prisoner," Jackson said sullenly.

"You're mine," Piers said through his teeth. "And if you don't do as I say, I'll bloody put a bullet in you. Is that the kind of language you understand?"

Slowly, muttering, the man complied.

A sudden movement, glimpsed only out of the corner of an eye, distracted Piers for a moment but he was careful not to risk giving Jackson any opportunity to escape. He kicked Morgan's gun out of his reach and then stepped back and gazed around.

"It's me," William called. "I'll be all right though. Don't you worry."

He was hobbling up the track, one hand clutched to his thigh. Blood was soaking through his trousers.

"Good man," Piers called back. "Can you make it here so I can see how badly you're hurt? I can't leave this one."

"Haven't moved so fast since a Jerry took a shot at me in Normandy," William puffed when he got closer. "Got a coupla tree-ties in my pocket. Do fine for handcuffs for that little toad and a tourni— whatever they're called for my leg."

The tree-ties – strong plastic straps with buckles with special "stops" on to prevent them coming loose – were absolutely ideal for both purposes. Piers attended to both of these things and then fired his revolver three times into the air. It was taking Leadbetter a long time to send someone to investigate the first single shot. Medical attention for William was his first priority, the flesh wound just above his knee was not very serious but one had to remember that he was not a young man.

Piers found the key to the padlock on the front door in Tom's jacket pocket and opened up the lodge. He wanted to rush from room to room searching for Thea but did not dare leave Jackson unguarded and William was in no fit state to watch over him.

"I saw your sister last night," William said all at once.

Piers ran over to where he sat with Piers's sweater draped around him. "Where?"

"She was in a car with a fella who I hadn't seen before. Nice sort of car too."

"Where did you see them?"

"In the village. But they were heading out. In the direction of Arundel."

"Are you sure it was Thea?"

"Sure as sure. The car was parked when I first saw it and she'd put the interior light on to do her face the way young women do. She was looking at herself in the mirror that's on the back of those things you pull down when the sun's in your eyes."

Piers was looking at Jackson. "You said you were going to kill her. All three kids, you said."

"I haven't," Tom growled. "But I would have done if I'd had the chance."

Piers sat down on the ground, weak and with strange ringing noises in his ears. When he was able he leaned over to loosen the strap around William's leg for a few moments.

"Now it's bleeding again," William complained.

"Yes, but we don't want your leg to fall off because the circulation's stopped, do we?"

William chuckled. "I'm proud to have known you, Mr Ashley. Despite the fact that you're sitting there with a gun in your hand."

Piers said, "Then you'll be terribly disappointed when I tell you I'm allowed to carry it."

At that moment people came running through from the orchard.

Commander Rolt arrived some time during the late afternoon, bringing with him in the police helicopter – to Elizabeth's everlasting joy – Colonel and Mrs Ashley. But the joy was a thing that she promised herself would come later. She would revel in the memories of her home seen from the air only when she knew that her daughter was safe and well. At the moment no one could promise either of these things.

Rolt made a point of not taking charge. There was no need. Crimes had been committed and an arrest had been made by the local CID. Inspector Leadbetter was grateful for this, of course, but had not really expected himself to be forced to abdicate. If he had witnessed Rolt's straffing of West End Central he might have anticipated otherwise.

"Jackson simply refuses to say if he knows where she is,"

Leadbetter said to Rolt, the two of them standing just outside the massive gatehouse. "He seems to be enjoying keeping mum – the only clue we have is when he told Piers Ashley that he hadn't killed her. But he might have left her somewhere. That's why Piers was so convinced he'd thrown her down the well."

"What's the significance of this well?" Rolt asked. "Why was Piers so worried about it?"

"Apparently he and Jackson went on a tour of the cellars some time ago and while they were down there Jackson made a remark that Thea Ashley might be the third victim. Just an association of ideas really. At least we know that worry's unfounded now."

"It's been searched then?"

Leadbetter gazed at his superior for a moment before he replied. "Perhaps you ought to speak to Piers, sir."

"Inspector, I'm asking *you*."

"Jackson got the better of Ashley and heaved him down it. I'm still not sure how he either survived or got out again."

"Do I understand that you somehow doubt his word?" Rolt enquired, reading Leadbetter's expression exactly.

"I can believe a lot of things," Leadbetter continued stolidly. "But I have to think carefully when someone tells me that the bottom of a well is full of feathers."

"Feathers!" Rolt exclaimed.

"Feathers."

"Feathers?" asked Elizabeth, coming upon them both. "Do come in. I've asked cook to turn to here for a few hours. I think everyone ought to have something to eat. What's this about feathers?"

This was the last lady on Earth to whom Rolt wanted to expose Piers Ashley as a liar. Smoothly he said, "It's nothing at all important. Just that when the Inspector's men searched the well for clues they found a lot of feathers."

She was clearly embarrassed. "Oh dear. How your sins and silliness find you out. That was me, I'm afraid."

"You?" Leadbetter said.

"Women sometimes do things that men can't understand," she told him slightly severely as she noted the incredulity in his voice. "It was when I'd just had Giles. I suffered from a

195

severe bout of Post-Natal Depression. Baby Blues it's sometimes called now. You men might be interested to know that it wasn't really recognised in those days. Men told you to pull yourself together. I was having dreadful nightmares. I kept dreaming that Piers had fallen down the well."

Rolt decided that he wasn't cold but had merely shivered.

"I knew there was a door on the passageway so at least that part of the underground places could be kept locked. But Piers was running about by this time with Thea, and really he was exactly the sort of child who could pick locks and get up to all sorts of mischief. I went on to Mycroft about the danger and he promised to have a grating placed over the well. But you know how it is – nothing was done. One day I was turning out the attics and I came upon piles of old feather-beds and eiderdowns, all full of the moth. So I lugged them all to the cellars and dropped them down the well. I did it quite on my own. I was terrified people would think me raving mad. Then, shortly afterwards, Mycroft had the grating fixed." She smiled at them. "I rang the hospital before we left Town and they assured me that Giles is well on the mend. His kidneys are functioning normally."

"But how did you know the well was dry?" Rolt persevered.

She shrugged. "I didn't. I never gave it a thought. No, I suppose in the back of my mind . . . Yes, I know now. In the dreams I had there were just stones at the bottom and he . . ." Momentarily she placed a hand on Rolt's shoulder. "Do come in. I'm sure there's some beer somewhere."

"Bloody hell," Leadbetter whispered when she had gone. "I sometimes get the feeling that people like this – people from families that go back to the year dot and live in castles – aren't quite like you and me."

"Everything's on a larger scale and they've learned to cope with it in a grand matter," Rolt said. "The likes of you and me don't have things like feather beds knocking about and wells in the basement. One of the reasons I took on Piers is that he thinks big. It gets him into trouble sometimes but – admit it – how many of your men would fall a hundred feet down a hole in the ground, climb out and then still have the bottle to go and arrest the man responsible?"

"It's just as well for William Turner that he did."

Rolt nodded. "Are you sure you've looked *everywhere* for the girl?"

"Short of digging up the gardens."

"Who d'you think this man might be who Turner reckons she was with?"

"I've absolutely no idea. Any one of several boyfriends. Let's hope the old man's right. But I'm damned if I can see the sense of it. She left London to drive here. Her car's here. No one's seen her – I've had people asking in the village. So where is she? I'm afraid Turner might have seen someone else."

"And if she'd stayed with a local friend, she'd be here by now. Someone would have told her that the place is full of police."

They went indoors. The search of the house having been accomplished some time previously, all police personnel had either been recalled or were still on duty in the area where Charles Morgan's body had been found. This had now been removed and so had his car, taken away plastic-sheeted on a lorry for forensic testing.

The two men strolled into the Great Hall. Hands in their pockets they wandered slowly around the room gazing at the portraits. Suddenly, Leadbetter exclaimed softly.

"There. See that ring – the one with the seal?" He looked more closely. "Joseph Ashley, 1817–1888. That ring he's wearing was in the suitcase that Jackson was carrying when he was arrested. There were other things as well he was hoping to make off with. Several pairs of the Colonel's gold cuff-links, silver boxes and silver-backed hairbrushes. And fifty-three pounds in cash."

Rolt came to look. Leadbetter had briefed him on the way from the helicopter but not with exact details. He said, "It makes you feel a bit strange, doesn't it? History rolls on and a ring is returned to where it ought to be."

Both turned as they heard footsteps. It was the Colonel.

He said, "I made Piers rest for a bit. He looked frightful. Perhaps I should get a doctor to him."

"May I see him?" Rolt asked. "Then we can both make the decision."

The three started up the stairs. Their mission was proved to be unnecessary, however, as Piers Ashley was seen to be coming down.

"There's a red Porsche just arriving," he reported. "There was a red Porsche parked outside Lee Haasden's London apartment." And with these two brief statements he brushed through them and resumed his descent.

"Will he do the fella any harm?" Mycroft said in a loud stage whisper to Rolt.

"Well, I *hope* not," the Commander replied. "Because with a bit of luck . . . Shall we go outside?"

The tinted windscreen gave away no clues as to the occupants of the vehicle, not with the late afternoon sun shining down the drive and directly into Piers's eyes. The thought crossed his mind as he stood, hardly breathing, that the scene could be from one of those films that he really despised and which had even normally strong-minded women reaching for their handkerchiefs.

It did not mean though that he stood back when Thea got out of the car and did not hurry forward and hug her tightly.

"We were coming back *much* earlier," she was saying, speaking quickly into his ear, his head resting on her shoulder. "But something electrical in the car went wrong and Lee couldn't drive it at all. And I did ring last night and no one answered. Piers, do tell me what's happened."

She had, it transpired, started for home the previous night. But after only a short while she had begun to have misgivings and had stopped at a phone box. She had phoned the Hall, hoping to speak to her father. (Unbeknown to her Jackson had rung from his own house.) There was no reply which seemed very strange in the circumstances. Assuming Piers still to be in Sussex and possibly in his own flat where there was no phone, she did not try to reach him in Shepherd's Bush. Thea had then recalled that Lee Haasden had been very good in emergencies, and to ask a man's advice was a good way to break the deadlock that pouring soup all over him had created. There was good reason to believe that the news of the affair that had given such strength to the hand holding the soup plate was no more than a malicious rumour.

Haasden's advice – and he had not really minded being

hauled out of bed where he had repaired with a heavy cold – was indeed practical. They would both drive to Ashleigh Coombe, taking a car each in order to give them travel independence for any return journeys. When they had arrived the entire place was in darkness, for Tom Jackson, watching from the lodge, had stayed put when he had observed two cars. Thea had been confused as to what she should do, and even more confused because after she had apologised *en route* Lee had told her he loved her and had never touched, even with the longest barge pole, the young lady in dispute. Face to face under a midnight sky they had conversed earnestly.

"I don't think we ought to stay here," she had said. "If it was a hoax to get me here there might be some danger or other. And I don't want to wake Piers if he's here. Let's come back in the morning."

In the total confusion of being in love she had left her overnight bag in the car. As it happened this did not prove too awkward. She borrowed Lee's toothbrush and the rest did not really matter.

"When did you first decide you were in love with me?" she had asked dreamily.

"After that big brother of yours had been to see me."

"How was that?"

"Oh, it's corny – you'll only laugh."

"I never laugh at things like that," Thea had protested.

After a pause Haasden had said, "Well, I could see that the guy *hurt* – it was only after he explained that he'd been shot that I understood. And when he'd gone I realized that you were like that. From what I knew of you I recognised the same kindred spirit. You stuck by him, didn't you, when he was in trouble?"

"We'd have been here *hours* ago if it hadn't been for the car," Thea said now, embracing her mother.

But they hadn't been in any real hurry, Rolt decided, eyeing the couple. Oh well, never mind. He who hesitated was definitely lost when it came to a girl like Thea Ashley.

"I've just remembered something," Elizabeth said over dinner, and all eyes swivelled in her direction. Commander

Rolt had been persuaded to stay but Leadbetter had declined, pleading a previous engagement.

"Such a funny little man came to your flat, Piers," she continued. "I'd forgotten all about him what with everything else. He asked me to give you a message."

"Who was it?" Piers asked.

"He didn't give his name. But he said you'd know who it was. He said to tell you that it was all arranged and he'd meet you in the usual place to discuss details."

"Is that all?" Piers asked.

"Yes. He seemed to think you knew all about it."

"What did he look like?" Rolt wanted to know.

"Like a little old monkey. But he was very polite. Especially after I'd said I was your mother, Piers."

"Dorney!" Piers gasped. "Len Dorney. The diamonds job. It must have been."

Rolt shot to his feet. "That body that was found after the fire has never been properly identified."

They both ran to the Commander's car.